Thunderstruck . . .

Lord Ashdon was quite cognizant of the inadvisability of his remaining upstairs alone with a young, unmarried lady while the rest of the party was belowstairs. It would not do his or Miss Weatherstone's reputation a bit of good. He wished that he had been able to stop the inn's mistress from leaving and had been able to leave Miss Weatherstone in her care.

Reluctantly he stepped forward to take one of her trembling hands in his in a reassuring gesture. "Miss Weatherstone, I must go."

Belle's eyes flew to meet his. Her fingers tightened on his for the briefest moment, then abruptly relaxed. "Of course. I completely understand."

"I shall send one of the other ladies up to you," said Lord Ashdon, in an attempt to comfort her.

"Thank you. You have been very good to me," said Belle in a low voice.

A resounding crack of thunder boomed overhead. With a cry of distress, Belle flew out of the chair and flung herself into Lord Ashdon's arms. She was shaking like a leaf. Her face was pressed tightly against his shoulder, and her hands gripped the front of his coat. "Don't leave me! Pray, don't leave me!"

BELLE'S BEAU

Gayle Buck

A SIGNET BOOK

SIGNET
Published by New American Library, a division of
Penguin Putnam Inc., 375 Hudson Street,
New York, New York 10014, U.S.A.
Penguin Books Ltd, 27 Wrights Lane,
London W8 5TZ, England
Penguin Books Australia Ltd, Ringwood,
Victoria, Australia
Penguin Books Canada Ltd, 10 Alcorn Avenue,
Toronto, Ontario, Canada M4V 3B2
Penguin Books (N.Z.) Ltd, 182–190 Wairau Road,
Auckland 10, New Zealand

Penguin Books Ltd, Registered Offices:
Harmondsworth, Middlesex, England

First published by Signet, an imprint of New American Library,
a division of Penguin Putnam Inc.

First Printing, December 2000
10 9 8 7 6 5 4 3 2 1

Copyright © Gayle Buck, 2000

Chapter 1

One fine morning in early April, a nondescript hackney cab pulled up to the curb before an elegant town house on Park Lane next to Hyde Park. A gentleman of medium height and considerable breadth of shoulder, attired in a brushed beaver hat and a long military greatcoat, leaped down out of the cab. The cab's jarvey carried the gentleman's bags up the stone steps to the front door of the imposing house. The gentleman himself carried his own kit, which he set down on the porch next to the decorative iron railing in order to withdraw his purse and pay the driver.

Clutching the coins, the driver touched his forelock. "M'thanks, m'lord."

Lord Adam Alan Ashdon, Viscount, nodded with a friendly smile. He did not watch the jarvey's departure, but turned around to give the polished brass door knocker a good banging.

The door opened slowly to reveal an elderly attendant somberly attired in black livery. This individual looked out with a superior expression, eyeing the visitor down the length of a long, thin nose. "Yes, sir?"

Lord Ashdon grinned confidently at the servant, certain that he would be recognized even though it had been some years since he had last been in England. "Have I changed all that much?"

The dignified old man's expression underwent sudden transformation. "My lord!" The door was thrown wide. The servant bowed. "Welcome home, my lord!"

"Hello, Regis. You look just the same, you old rascal. What are you doing getting the door? Is her ladyship at home?" asked Lord Ashdon as he stepped inside across the wide threshold. He took off his beaver hat and handed it to the attentive butler, then started stripping off his pale kid gloves.

"The porter has taken ill, my lord. A great inconvenience it has been, as you can imagine, as many visitors as we have. Her ladyship is resting, my lord, but I shall send word up to Lady Ashdon at once, sir!"

The butler snapped his fingers to summon the footman who had emerged from the nether regions. He spoke a few words in a low voice. The footman sent a startled glance at the viscount, then, with a nod, strode away. The butler turned to the viscount. "I will see that your baggage is taken upstairs, my lord. I assume that you will be staying with us?"

Lord Ashdon glanced around him once more. There was the portrait of his grandfather on the front wall and the massive vase of his mother's favorite white blooms arranged on the hall table. That much at least had remained the same.

Memories crowded his mind, most particularly of his late father. How well he recalled past years. Lord Ashdon smiled at the waiting butler. "Yes, if my mother shall have me."

"Have you, sir! Why, her ladyship will be beside herself," said the butler. He ushered the long-awaited scion of the house into the sitting room. "I will bring refreshment in at once, my lord."

"Thank you, Regis. You are too good to me," said Lord Ashdon with a swift smile.

The butler made the slightest bow, then looked across at the viscount. "If you don't mind my saying so, my lord, it is good to have you back."

"Thank you, Regis. It is good to be back," said Lord Ashdon. He surveyed his surroundings. The sitting room did not look the same as he remembered it. He should not have expected it to, of course. It had always been his mother's habit to refurbish her surroundings whenever the latest fad dictated a change.

This time the sitting room had been decorated in black and gold and a florid style that he found quite distasteful. Carved, gilded dolphins acted as arm supports for the armchairs, while seashells formed the legs. Those fanciful touches would have been done in honor of Nelson's great naval victory, naturally. There was also a delicately curved stool that looked as though it would have been better acquainted with an Egyptian tomb than an English sitting room. The striped silk sofa had lion's claws for feet. Around the room, three-legged stands that looked like graceful columned Grecian temples had been placed here and there, the flat tops supporting overflowing green plants in marble bowls.

"I see that fashions have changed," remarked Lord Ashdon.

"Indeed they have, my lord," agreed the butler impassively.

"It looks a bit like a museum of antiquities, don't you think, Regis?" asked Lord Ashdon, glancing ruefully at the servant.

The butler gave a slight cough, hiding the twitch of his lips. He asked respectfully, "Have you sold out of the army, my lord?"

The viscount's easy smile flashed. "No, I have not, Regis. And let that be our little secret."

"Very well, my lord," said the butler with a dignified smile.

When the butler exited and closed the doors, Lord Ashdon crossed to the draperied windows overlooking the busy boulevard. A frown pulled his well-marked brows into an unbroken line above his straight, well-molded nose. There was an abstracted expression in his eyes as he stared out at the sunlit scene.

Lord Ashdon had lately returned to England from the long war. The abdication of Napoleon Bonaparte had meant a huge exodus of officers and rank-and-file from the British army, but he had not been one of their number. He thought privately, and had publicly voiced his opinion on several occasions (to the derision of his fellow officers), that he did not believe that Bonaparte was done. So he had not sold out of the army but instead had taken a lengthy leave of absence from his official duties. The leave was willingly granted to him, with the explanation proffered to his commanding officer that it was time to see to the duty due to his family name.

That was, to wed and beget an heir.

Behind him, the door opened and Lord Ashdon turned quickly.

"My dear Adam!"

An elegantly attired lady bustled swiftly toward him, and Lord Ashdon stepped forward to meet her. He caught her soft hands, which she held out to him in welcome. "Hello, Mother."

He kissed the powdered cheek that her ladyship held up to him and as he did so, he caught the wafting scent of a familiar perfume. He straightened and grinned at his parent. "You are looking extremely well, ma'am."

"Thank you, my dear," said Lady Ashdon. She took a step backward and surveyed him from head to toe, then smiled and squeezed his strong fingers once more before releasing them. "It is good to have you home, dearest. You can have no notion how my heart gave a leap to be told the good news. We must celebrate your return! I am going to a small soiree this evening, and you must escort me. It will create quite a stir, believe me!"

Lord Ashdon shook his head, his smile fading but still intact. "I have but just arrived, Mother. I prefer a quiet evening tonight, if you don't mind."

"Of course! You are fatigued after such a long journey. Look at you! Why, you are still in your greatcoat. What was Regis thinking? And you should have refreshment, too!" said Lady Ashdon. "I shall ring for Regis immediately."

The doors opened before her ladyship had finished speaking. Lady Ashdon turned her head and watched as her butler entered, followed by a footman. Both carried laden trays. With a frown, Lady Ashdon said, "Regis—"

Lord Ashdon stepped forward quickly, forestalling the scold that he saw forming on his parent's lips. "Ah, just as you promised, Regis! Thank you! I am famished."

The butler had set down his burden and now came forward. "Allow me to relieve you of your greatcoat, my lord, so that you will be more comfortable." He performed the service with alacrity and smoothed the dense folds of the heavy garment over his bent forearm. "Will there be anything else, my lord? My lady?"

"That will be all, Regis," said Lady Ashdon with a regal nod. The butler bowed and ushered his underling out of the sitting room, quietly closing the doors after them.

Lady Ashdon swished over to the striped silk sofa and gracefully lowered herself to the cushions. She had once been a great beauty, and her figure was still elegant and her carriage upright. Her blond locks had faded to a subtle silvery gold, while her face retained the same proud expression that it had always had. She gestured to her son. "Come, Adam. I will serve you a plate. You are naturally hungry after your journey."

Lord Ashdon followed his mother, seating himself across from her in one of the dolphin-and-shell armchairs. He crossed his legs at the knee, allowing one booted toe to swing gently to and fro. "You are kindness itself, ma'am."

Lady Ashdon smiled as she placed several pieces of cold meat, a couple of tartlets, and some cheese on a plate. "Here you are, Adam. You see, I remember," she said, handing the plate to her son. "You will want a brandy, of course." She reached for a well-filled cut-glass decanter and unstopped it.

Lord Ashdon murmured his agreement, rather touched and amused by his mother's willingness to serve him. He leaned forward to take the glass that Lady Ashdon filled for him. "Do you not join me, Mother?"

"I never partake of such a heavy meal in the afternoon, Adam. Surely you recall that," said Lady Ashdon, raising her arched brows.

"Of course," agreed Lord Ashdon with a smile. He had forgotten that idiosyncrasy of Lady Ashdon's, actually, but it would not do to say so.

"You are staying here with me while you are in London, naturally. I will not have you going to one of those horrid hotels," said Lady Ashdon decisively.

Lord Ashdon gently swirled the brandy in his glass, inhaling the bouquet, as he glanced at her ladyship. "The hotels are scarcely horrid, Mother. In fact, travelers to our shore are amazed at the clean linens and abundant washing water to be found in our hotels," he said in a teasing tone.

Lady Ashdon shook her head. A small smile just barely touched her face as she watched him begin to eat. "I see what it is. You are funning me in your inimitable way. You are staying with me, are you not?"

"If you will have me, ma'am," said Lord Ashdon. "I do not wish to put you or your household out in any way."

"Pray do not be ridiculous! This is your home, Adam. You may do just as you wish," said Lady Ashdon.

"You relieve my mind, Mother. You see, I have already had the temerity to see that my bags were carried upstairs," said Lord Ashdon, flashing his smile again.

Lady Ashdon also smiled. Her eyes were not lake-blue like her son's, but rather a cool gray. There was rarely any real warmth in her expression. "I am glad that you are in such good humor, Adam. Now that you have sold out of the army, you must tell me all about your plans. You will be here for the Season, of course?"

Lord Ashdon set aside the becrumbed plate and the empty wineglass, thus giving himself a second or two to best formulate his reply. He had no intention of informing his mother just at that moment that he had not sold out of the army. There would be time enough later, when his leave was up, to go through the inevitable explosion that such news was certain to trigger. It was best simply to allow Lady Ashdon to continue in her assumption that he was back in England for good. As for how much he should say about what he had been contemplating for several months, he did not believe that it would be wise to reveal all of his thoughts. Therefore, he settled on the simplest, most straightforward answer that he could possibly give to his parent at that moment.

The viscount looked directly at her ladyship and said, "Mother, I am planning to wed this Season."

Lady Ashdon's mouth dropped open. She quickly shut it and a brilliant smile lit her face. It was the most animated expression she had worn since the viscount had arrived. Her ladyship surged to her feet, holding out her hands. "Dearest!"

Lord Ashdon quickly rose, too. In her enthusiasm Lady Ashdon grasped her son's coat sleeves. "Adam! How wonderful! I had almost despaired of getting through to you how urgently your duty stood."

Lord Ashdon removed one of his mother's hands and lifted it to his lips to brush a light kiss across her smooth knuckles. He smiled down at her, not at all surprised by her fervent reaction. "I am glad that you are pleased, ma'am."

"Pleased!" Lady Ashdon gave a light laugh, and her gray eyes positively sparkled. "I am more than pleased, my dear! You need an heir to carry on the family name, as I have been writing to you for ages."

"Yes, each of your letters did refer to that fact," said Lord Ashdon dryly, but with an easy smile.

Lady Ashdon laughed again. "You make game of me, but I shall not take offense. Why, Adam, I am positively thrilled that you are finally going to heed my advice."

"It was very good advice, ma'am," said Lord Ashdon. He

let go of his mother's hand and took a turn about the sitting room, his hands clasped behind his back. "I have come to realize it very well." Even though he was preoccupied with his thoughts, he nevertheless took note again of the black-and-gold decor and unconsciously grimaced. Fortunately, his back was to her ladyship and so she did not see his disapprobation of her furnishings.

Behind the viscount, Lady Ashdon was already making plans, ticking them off on her beringed fingers. "We must throw a ball in your honor as soon as possible so that everyone will be made aware that you are returned. I shall invite several families with whom I am acquainted that have marriageable daughters. We shall naturally receive invitations from them also, of course, and you will have ample opportunity to become better acquainted with the most eligible young misses."

Lord Ashdon turned back to his parent, regarding her with a mixture of amusement and mild irritation. Her ladyship had always been a dominating personality in his life, but he was not a small boy any longer. Years under his father's influence had also shaped his character, as had the years at war. He said firmly, "You go too fast, my lady. I have no intention of plunging into a round of entertainments. In fact, I am not staying in London for long—a fortnight at most."

Lady Ashdon stared at him in great astonishment. "Why, whatever can you mean? Did you not say that you were here for the Season?"

Lord Ashdon shook his head. "No, Mother, I did not. I said that I meant to wed this Season. That does not necessarily mean that I shall remain in London."

"But what do you intend to do, then? You can scarcely expect to discover a suitable bride if it is your estates where you mean to ensconce yourself," said Lady Ashdon briskly.

"I am not going to my ancestral house, ma'am," said Lord Ashdon.

"Then where?" demanded Lady Ashdon.

Lord Ashdon gave a wide grin, his blue eyes dancing as he anticipated his mother's certain reaction. "I am going to Bath."

"Bath!" Lady Ashdon sat down abruptly on the sofa, not once taking her eyes from her son's face. "Of all the harebrained, idiotic notions! Adam! What do you possibly hope to find in Bath?"

"Not what, Mother, but whom," corrected Lord Ashdon cheerfully. "I hope to find my future wife in Bath."

"Adam, I realize that you have a fondness for the place since your recuperation there, but pray listen to reason," begged Lady Ashdon. "There is no one of any consequence in Bath during the Season, only tradespeople and old maids! You must remain here, in London, for the Season. You'll be able to meet all of the misses making their come-out in the upcoming weeks. You may have your pick of them, I assure you, dearest."

"Vastly flattering, ma'am," said Lord Ashdon lightly. "I could scarce ask for better inducement, could I?"

"I am perfectly serious, Adam. Pray do not dare to make a jest of it," said Lady Ashdon, frowning at her son.

Lord Ashdon at once sobered. "I apologize, Mother. I recognize that acquiring a suitable bride is no jesting matter. Indeed, I have given much thought to it."

"Then you'll stay," said Lady Ashdon, satisfied that she had carried her argument. Getting up, she moved toward the door. "Now I must run, dearest. I have so little time left to have my hair done and dress before the soiree. You will be all right this evening without me?"

"I think that I can manage," said Lord Ashdon with the slightest of grins. "And I am staying for a fortnight."

Lady Ashdon glanced back at the viscount as she opened the door. "We will talk of this again, Adam," she promised.

Lord Ashdon bowed, a hint of irony in his expression. "No doubt we shall," he murmured.

"Do you know, at this moment you remind me very much

of your father," observed Lady Ashdon, her voice leaving little doubt that she was making an unflattering comparison.

Lord Ashdon's defense was impenetrable. He bowed again. "Thank you, ma'am. I shall treasure the compliment."

Lady Ashdon sent a speaking glance in his direction before she stepped out and closed the door.

The viscount grimaced. "I wish I were already in Bath."

Chapter 2

~~~~~

Miss Anabelle Weatherstone left her bedroom and the attentions of her maid and ran swiftly downstairs. She entered the well-appointed drawing room, where she knew that her aunt would be waiting for her.

"Will I do, Aunt Margaret?" asked Belle gaily, twirling around and smiling over her shoulder at the elegant lady seated on the satin-covered settee. Her olive-green velvet bonnet was set at a rakish angle above her sparkling hazel eyes and lively countenance, the pale-brown satin ribbons tied close under one delicate ear. The merino pelisse she wore was also olive green, corded in the popular military style, and was vastly becoming to her slender figure. Small kid half boots peeked out from beneath the hem of her swirling skirt.

Mrs. Weatherstone smiled tolerantly at her niece. The white egret feathers in her own handsome bonnet bowed gently as she nodded her approval. "You will do very well, dear Belle. I am glad that we chose the olive. It complements your complexion and hair." She paused a moment, her considering gaze rising to her niece's headgear. "However, I believe that we might adjust your bonnet just a trifle."

"Oh, is there something wrong with it?" asked Belle, going at once to stand before the fireplace, where a huge gilded mirror hung above the mantel. She peered anxiously into the glass at her lovely reflection.

"Stand still a moment, Belle." Mrs. Weatherstone rose, her

skirt whispering across the Persian carpet as she approached her niece, who was obediently waiting for her ministrations.

Unfastening the olive satin ribbons, Mrs. Weatherstone shifted the bonnet so that it was centered on Belle's head. "That is much better," she said, retying the ribbons in a competent bow under her niece's chin. "Don't you think so?"

Belle eyed her demure reflection dubiously. She did not think that it looked half as good now, but she felt that something positive was expected of her, so she replied, "I am certain that you know best, Aunt."

Mrs. Weatherstone smiled and picked up her silver-knotted reticule. "Now, let us be off. The park will be quite nice this afternoon, I am persuaded."

"Oh, yes! The weather is just perfect for an outing," said Belle, turning eagerly. "I shall be so glad to get out-of-doors for a bit."

"The air has seemed rather close in the house since the rain that we have had," agreed Mrs. Weatherstone. She ushered her niece out of the drawing room and toward the front door, their kid boots making dainty sounds on the marble tiles. The porter opened the door for them, bowing as they passed.

The ladies emerged from the open door of the town house, and Belle at once exclaimed, tilting her face upward to catch the warmth, "Isn't the sunshine lovely?"

"Yes, dear, but so debilitating to a lady's delicate complexion," said Mrs. Weatherstone in mild reproof.

"Yes, Aunt." Chastened, Belle docilely descended the stone steps to the sidewalk alongside her aunt.

A footman handed them up into Mrs. Weatherstone's carriage and shut the door, then stepped back up on the curb and signaled the driver.

Belle settled back against the comfortable leather seat squabs. Though she would have preferred a good gallop on her gelding, Rolly, rather than this sedate outing, she was not entirely unhappy about going for a drive in the park. First and foremost, it was as she had told her aunt. She was very glad to be able to step outside and breathe the clean spring air.

She had always adored being out-of-doors, and she longed for days past when she would get up at dawn, her breath showing white on the cold air, to set off on her hunter for a full morning's ride. Since coming to London she had had very little exercise of the sort that she was used to. She reminded herself, though, that she should not allow regret to cloud her mood, because she was in London for the Season, which had always been her heart's desire.

The other reason Belle was willing to oblige her aunt and accompany her for a drive was that Mrs. Weatherstone had explained that the fashionable always made an appearance in the park around five o'clock, and quite frankly, Belle was curious to see whom they might meet.

Mrs. Weatherstone had gone on to say that it would be wise for them to do likewise, making an appearance at the accepted hour, since Belle had only just begun to be introduced around. Belle accepted her aunt's explanation, for she was relying on Mrs. Weatherstone's social expertise to launch her into polite society.

Belle and her aunt conversed lightly on a number of topics as the carriage carried them safely through the bustling thoroughfares. Whenever Mrs. Weatherstone let drop some hint of what was expected of a young miss who was making her entrance into society, Belle listened attentively, for she was well aware that her aunt had only her best interests at heart. If that were not so, Mr. and Mrs. Weatherstone would never have taken on the obligation of bringing her out.

"I do so hope that you will attract an eligible *parti* this Season. It will be quite a feather in my cap if I am able to see both you and your sister Cassandra wed this summer," said Mrs. Weatherstone.

"Quite," agreed Belle mildly, covering up a degree of indifference with civility.

Catching what she no doubt interpreted as the polite doubt in her niece's voice, Mrs. Weatherstone laughed. She reached out to pat her niece's arm reassuringly. "You mustn't be too anxious about it, Belle. If you do not receive an acceptable offer this Season, we shall simply return next year."

Belle shot a laughing glance at her companion. "I assure you, Aunt, I am not in the least anxious on that count! Why, my sole ambition is to attend as many functions as I possibly can. I intend to leave the fretting over finding a suitable *parti* to you and Uncle Phineas!"

Mrs. Weatherstone chuckled, but shook her head at her niece's frivolous words. "I can well understand your thirst for gaiety, Belle. You have lived a very secluded life, after all. However, I believe that we must keep an eye to the future as well."

"Yes, Aunt Margaret," murmured Belle agreeably, though she mentally shrugged. Marriage was a remote concern to her, one that she did not dwell on very often or for very long. She was living for the moment and eagerly looking forward to the evening when she would actually be formally presented to London society.

Belle was unreservedly anticipating her first Season. She had never been farther afield from the country home that she shared with her grandfather than an afternoon's horse ride, so everything was novel and of interest to her. Before coming to London, she had attended only one house party in all her life, and that only because for a few months she had traded places with her twin sister, Cassandra, who had lived with their aunt and uncle. This Season was particularly piquant to Belle because until a few months previous, her grandfather and legal guardian had adamantly refused to consider a come-out for her.

"I am so glad to be here, in London, with you and Uncle Phineas," remarked Belle suddenly, following her train of thought.

"Do you not miss Sir Marcus and the Hall just a little?" asked Mrs. Weatherstone curiously.

"Of course I do. I love Grandpapa dearly and I even miss him on occasion. After all, he raised me and I have lived all my life at the Hall. However, I doubt that a more obstinate, hardheaded old tyrant ever existed," said Belle.

"Yes . . . well."

Belle slid a glance toward her aunt. Mrs. Weatherstone obviously wanted to agree with her assessment of the old gentleman, but was torn about the wisdom of doing so. Her niece understood the older woman's dilemma perfectly. Giving a merry laugh, Belle said, "You would not set a very good example if you agreed with me, would you, Aunt Margaret?"

"No, I would not," agreed Mrs. Weatherstone with a smile.

"I am so glad that Cassandra prevailed upon Grandpapa to let me have this Season," said Belle.

"Yes, so am I. We—your uncle and I—had always wanted to have a better relationship with Sir Marcus, especially since our coolness kept you and Cassandra apart. We had always felt that you needed to be with one another occasionally," said Mrs. Weatherstone. She smiled warmly at her niece. "Now it has worked out very well for everyone."

"But you miss Cassandra and wish she was here, too," suggested Belle shrewdly.

Mrs. Weatherstone laughed and nodded. "Oh, I shan't deny it. I had planned every nuance of Cassandra's come-out. It quite took me aback for a moment or two when she and Philip announced that they had become engaged." She sighed at her reflections, a smile still trembling on her lips, before turning once more to her niece. "But I don't repine, Belle, for I know that Cassandra is happy with her choice, and now I have you to lavish all my attention on."

Her aunt's smiling expression warmed Belle. "Do you know, I would not have missed this opportunity for anything," said Belle earnestly. "And not only because it was my dearest wish to see something of the world." She reached out to squeeze her aunt's gloved fingers. "I gained more than I can possibly say when I came to know you and Uncle Phineas."

"Thank you, Belle. You have no notion how glad it makes me that I can mother you a trifle, even after all these years," said Mrs. Weatherstone, returning the pressure of her niece's hand. "Cassandra was like our own daughter, and you have become just as dear to us in the short time that we have known you."

"Thank you, Aunt," said Belle, even as she smiled a trifle wistfully. "I do miss her, though." Dear Cassandra had bearded their grandfather in his own den and had unflinchingly braved his wrath to secure this wonderful opportunity for her to see something of the world. She owed much to her sister, more than she could possibly ever repay.

"Never mind. We shall see Cassandra before the wedding."

"What do you mean?" asked Belle quickly.

At her niece's look of surprise, Mrs. Weatherstone asked with a smile, "You don't think that I have allowed her to order all of her own trousseau, do you? She will have to come up for a few fittings."

"Oh, how lovely! Cassandra is coming up to London, after all," said Belle, instantly excited by the prospect. "When will she arrive?"

"Not for a few months."

"I do wish that she was here now. It would be such fun to be brought out together. I am certain that we would take polite society by storm," said Belle confidently.

Mrs. Weatherstone laughed. "Indeed! Certainly it would cause a mild sensation for two identical and beautiful misses to grace the same functions. But Cassandra has chosen to set aside her own formal introduction to polite society for the much more interesting activity of getting up the trousseau."

"I am happy for my sister. But I must confess, Aunt Margaret, that I still do not understand how Cassandra could have fallen in love with Philip," said Belle with a slight shrug.

"Of course you don't, Belle. You and Philip were childhood friends. Despite every hope that Sir Marcus had harbored otherwise, there was not even the spark of attraction between you," said Mrs. Weatherstone, nodding.

"Not the least," agreed Belle cheerfully. "Philip is a dear, but a bit dull, I am afraid. He was always one for books and quiet pursuits, and he hasn't changed. I can scarcely conceive that he was ever a soldier. One always thinks of a soldier as being dashing and devastatingly handsome and ruthless, if need be."

Mrs. Weatherstone eyed her niece somewhat askance. With amusement, she asked, "Is that your ideal, then, Belle? A gentleman who is handsome and dashing and ruthless?"

"Well, Aunt, can you conceive of me settling happily with someone like Philip?" asked Belle, her eyes dancing as she smiled at the older woman.

Mrs. Weatherstone regarded her for a moment, then shook her head. "You have a point, Belle. No, now that you have made me reflect on it, I do not believe that you would be happy unless you were wed to someone as energetic as yourself."

"Good! Than I may rest easy that you shan't urge me to accept any dodderers or slowtops," said Belle, sliding another laughing look at her aunt.

"Belle!" Mrs. Weatherstone was mildly shocked, but she started chuckling nevertheless. "You are outrageous, my dear. However, I do assure you that you may rest easy on that head!"

Belle noticed the occupants of an oncoming carriage. "Aunt Margaret, someone in that carriage is waving at us," she said, nodding at the vehicle as it rolled toward them. "Is it someone with whom you are acquainted?"

Mrs. Weatherstone looked around. As she recognized the occupants of the approaching carriage, a smile lit her face.

"Why, that is Miriam Carruthers and her daughter, Millicent. They are close acquaintances of mine from Bath. Driver, pull up, please."

The carriages drew abreast, and Mrs. Weatherstone exchanged greetings with her friend. The ladies spoke for a few moments, catching up on what had been happening since they had last seen one another, several months past.

Belle listened with interest to their conversation and studied her aunt's acquaintances. Mrs. Carruthers was obviously a good-humored lady. It showed in her relaxed expression and her friendly manner. She wore a mauve pelisse, cut in a style that complemented her matronly figure. Miss Carruthers had inherited her mother's dark brown hair and expressive brown eyes, but her figure was still girlish. The younger lady's manners were good, not forward in any way, as she greeted Mrs. Weatherstone and Belle with quiet friendliness.

Mrs. Carruthers nodded in a civil fashion to Belle. "It is good to see you again, Cassandra, and in such fine form. I have brought Millicent with me to town, as you see. It will be good for you girls to know at least one person among the tangle."

"Oh, but I'm not—" began Belle, at once realizing the mistake that the lady had made.

Appearing somewhat embarrassed, Mrs. Weatherstone laughed. "Forgive me, Millicent. I had forgotten that I must make things clear to you. This is Anabelle Weatherstone, Cassandra's twin sister. Belle was raised by my father-in-law, Sir Marcus, and we have just lately gotten to know her better. She is staying with us at the town house we have leased for the Season."

Mrs. Carruthers stared hard at Belle, as did her daughter. Belle waited for their verdict, an amused smile touching her lips.

"But, Mama, it must be Cassandra," blurted Miss Carruthers.

Belle laughed merrily. "Cassandra and I look just alike. I

don't think that anyone could really tell us apart, unless they saw us on horseback," she offered with a swift smile. "I am much the better rider, as my sister would readily admit."

"My word! No, you are not Cassandra, for she doesn't care overmuch for riding. We don't do much riding in Bath, you see. The resemblance is remarkable, however. I am very glad to meet you, Anabelle," said Mrs. Carruthers, extending her gloved hand.

Belle leaned far over and shook the lady's hand. "Pray call me Belle," she begged. "Everyone does."

"Very well! I shall do so, of course. I trust that you and Millicent will become good friends," said Mrs. Carruthers.

"I hope so, too," said Belle, smiling. She glanced at Miss Carruthers and caught the girl's shy smile and still-wondering expression. She nodded to the girl, which caused Miss Carruthers's smile to deepen, bestowing deep dimples in the girl's rounded cheeks.

"But where is Cassandra? I quite thought that you meant to bring her out this Season," said Mrs. Carruthers, turning once more to Mrs. Weatherstone.

"Cassandra did not come up to London with me, after all. She is engaged to be married and is spending a few months with her grandfather while she is preparing for the wedding," said Mrs. Weatherstone. She gave a small chuckle. "So much has happened over the last several weeks that I wonder at times if I am on my head or my heels."

"I know that my own head is spinning," said Mrs. Carruthers, shaking her head. "I can scarce take everything in. Cassandra's twin sister here in London and Cassandra already engaged! May I ask to whom?"

"Mr. Philip Raven, my father-in-law's godson. He is lately out of the army and a very respectable gentleman," said Mrs. Weatherstone proudly. "I like him very well, as does Phineas. Sir Marcus also thinks very highly of him. In fact, my father-in-law is exerting himself on Mr. Raven's behalf to secure him a diplomatic post. We are very hopeful of the outcome."

"Well! This is good news, indeed! I am very happy for you, Margaret. And so you are bringing Belle out instead, is that it?" asked Mrs. Carruthers, her frank gaze returning to Belle's animated face.

"Oh, yes. I have the best of both worlds now! A dear daughter who is to be wed and a new daughter upon whom I may lavish all of my attention for the duration of the Season," said Mrs. Weatherstone, glancing at her niece with a fond smile.

Belle felt her eyes misting. Her heart was full of joy. She said quietly, "Thank you, Aunt. That was very prettily said."

"You are fortunate, indeed, Margaret," said Mrs. Carruthers, nodding and smiling at Belle in approval. "She is every inch the lady, just like Cassandra."

"You must come to our opening ball, Miriam. I will send an invitation," said Mrs. Weatherstone warmly.

"Thank you! We shall be glad to receive it, won't we, Millicent? And you must be sure to come to our little gatherings this Season, too," said Mrs. Carruthers. The ladies exchanged addresses, then Mrs. Carruthers remarked, "Mr. Carruthers and I hope to send Millicent off in style, of course."

"Mama!" exclaimed Miss Carruthers, coloring prettily.

The two older women laughed, exchanging mutual glances of amusement.

"Millicent, you know very well that I shall speak so openly only to Mrs. Weatherstone," said Mrs. Carruthers indulgently. "I shan't embarrass you, I promise."

"You—and Belle, too!—must allow us some forthright speaking. We do have hopes and dreams for you, and we feel compelled to share them with at least one sympathetic ear," said Mrs. Weatherstone.

"Exactly so," nodded Mrs. Carruthers.

"At least you do not dream of a dodderer or a slowtop for me," murmured Belle mischievously.

Miss Carruthers overheard her and started to laugh. Guiltily, she put a gloved hand to her lips, murmuring an apology. "Oh, but that was too funny!"

"I see that you and Belle have had some plain speaking between you, too," observed Mrs. Carruthers with a raised eyebrow.

Mrs. Weatherstone smiled, glancing tolerantly at her niece. "Yes, Belle and I are very comfortable with each other."

"It is not to be wondered at, is it? I am certain that she is as like Cassandra as a pea in a pod," said Mrs. Carruthers.

Belle scarcely dared to glance at her aunt, memories running through her mind of how often she had puzzled both her aunt and her uncle when she was masquerading as her twin. She did not always do or say precisely what her sister might in the same circumstances. With the faintest hint of mischief in her voice, she said, "Oh, indeed. We are very much alike."

"I cannot explain to you how very like, and yet unalike, they are," said Mrs. Weatherstone, with the slightest shake of her head, as though in puzzlement.

Mrs. Carruthers nodded thoughtfully. "Now that you have mentioned it, I imagine that is so. Being a twin must be an odd thing. Well, we must be off. It was very good talking to you, Margaret, and of course meeting you, Belle. We shall look for you again."

Belle exchanged good-byes with Mrs. Carruthers and her daughter. The other carriage pulled away and their own continued on. She turned her head and burst out laughing at her aunt's still-puzzled expression. "I know! Cassandra is by far the quieter and more ladylike of us. I do feel for you, Aunt! You shall have your work cut out for you, for I am not in the least accomplished."

Mrs. Weatherstone's knitted brows smoothed. She met her niece's gaze, saying, "Pray do not speak so disparagingly of yourself, Belle. I like you very well as you are. As for accomplishments, you play the harp beautifully. And you are very graceful on the dance floor, too."

"Those are my sole assets, however," said Belle. On a regretful sigh, she added, "I wish now that I had been more interested in ladylike pursuits. My governess Miss Bidwell quietly despaired of me, of course. I had little inclination toward my studies, so that I am not in the least a bluestocking."

"Thank God for that!" interposed Mrs. Weatherstone with a smile.

Belle smiled, but shook her head. "Nor am I very good at embroidery or watercoloring or playing the pianoforte."

"I am certain that Miss Bidwell made many earnest attempts to awaken some spark in you, but I scarcely find it surprising that you were not an apt pupil," said Mrs. Weatherstone with a smile and the slightest shrug.

"Why, Aunt, should I take offense at that?" asked Belle lightly.

Mrs. Weatherstone shook her head. "Not in the least, Belle, for it was not your fault. You were brought up in a rather slap-dash fashion, after all. You rode unchaperoned all over the countryside, and your grandfather was indifferent to the finer accomplishments, caring only that you knew how to ride and hunt at an early age. I place the blame altogether squarely on Sir Marcus's shoulders." Mrs. Weatherstone ended with unexpected vehemence.

Belle was astonished by her aunt's sweeping assessment. Even though she recognized that her aunt was speaking from the standpoint of an uneasy history with her grandfather, nevertheless she was hurt, too. It seemed to her that Mrs. Weatherstone harbored doubts about her upbringing that would surely affect a successful come-out. Yet although her background was found to be lacking, Belle felt compelled to defend it.

"You mustn't criticize my grandfather to me," she said with a direct look at her aunt. "However much I chafed at times because of his intolerance, I still loved him. He gave me a home when I had no other, and he is exceedingly fond of me."

"Yes, you are right. Forgive me, Belle! I spoke out of turn," said Mrs. Weatherstone in a contrite voice, reaching out to take her niece's slender fingers in a brief squeeze.

"Do you really feel that I am backward?" asked Belle slowly.

"Belle! No, of course not! Not in that way!" Mrs. Weatherstone shot a swift glance at her niece's face. Seeing Belle's pensive expression, she sighed suddenly. "I know that it is no excuse, but I was only expressing my own frustration and anxiety. I want only the best for you this Season. I do not wish you to feel any sense of inadequacy, and yet I must be honest with you. You have been brought up differently from other girls. There might be some who will not be kind because of it."

"Much I care for that," exclaimed Belle, relieved that her aunt's fondness for her was not measured by her accomplishments or lack of them. "I am not insensitive to my inadequacies, but I know my own worth, too. Do not be overly anxious on my account, Aunt Margaret, for I don't doubt that I shall make my own way very well, I assure you."

Mrs. Weatherstone regarded her almost with a sense of wonder. "When you speak like that, I have no difficulty at all in believing that you are not Cassandra."

"Oh, dear, have I done it again?" exclaimed Belle, dismayed. "I had determined to use Cassandra as my pattern-card, and I had promised myself to behave just as properly as my sister would if she were coming out."

Mrs. Weatherstone laughed and reached over to hug her. Very earnestly, she said, "Never mind, my dear! You must be yourself, and not try to be Cassandra."

"I'm glad to hear you say so, Aunt, for I don't think that I can do otherwise," said Belle, only half in fun.

Chapter 3

After their return to the town house, Belle went upstairs to change from her walking pelisse into a simple day gown. While the maid tended her, she thought over the drive in the park, most particularly reviewing what her aunt had imparted to her at the last.

As Belle had informed her aunt, she had no illusions regarding herself. She was practically unschooled in social graces except for what little Miss Bidwell had been successful in instilling in her. Her personal charms, however, were considerable. She had heard enough compliments at the house party she had attended to be assured of that much, at least.

Belle studied herself in the cheval glass as the maid put the final touches to her toilette. Her reflection revealed a young miss of average height, with fiery highlights in her dark hair and a set of fine hazel eyes. She was slim and lithe, having been used to riding practically every day of her life. Though the cheval glass did not show her inner character, she knew that she had a zest for living and a confidence of manner that inspired others to warm to her.

Belle also had a respectable dowry and inheritance, which she had already realized stood her in good stead. Her uncle had been very approving when he learned what Sir Marcus had settled on her. Belle had gathered that many faux pas could be forgiven a young lady of beauty, intelligence, and grace, especially when it was all connected to a considerable inheritance. It was a very interesting sidelight to the new world that she was now entering.

In addition, Belle had learned over the course of the last several weeks that Mrs. Weatherstone had very precise notions of how a lady should look and act. Her aunt had taken her to the best shops and had had her hair cut in the most fashionable crop. She also spent considerable time in instructing her on social protocol and gave lectures on conduct. It was not only Belle's appearance that had changed, but in some ways her mannerisms as well.

Belle looked in the mirror and frowned. It was sometimes difficult to live up to her aunt's high standards. Belle honestly did not know how Cassandra had borne it, being raised with such strict notions of propriety.

Her sister was different from her, of course. Cassandra was the bravest individual imaginable, given a difficult set of circumstances, but otherwise she was a quiet, submissive miss.

A traitorous reflection flashed through Belle's mind. Undoubtedly Cassandra would have greeted the suggestion of a sedate drive in the park as a high treat. For the most part, Belle had thought it a dead bore. She would far rather have gotten up on her powerful gelding, Rolly, and gone for a proper ride.

Belle made a face at her reflection. "Proper" was exactly the wrong term for the sort of exercise she was envisioning, she knew. In London, a neck-for-nothing ride was not viewed as at all proper behavior for a young lady.

Belle considered herself with bald honesty. She knew that she could ride and hunt with the best. She could play the harp so well that it moved others to tears. These were her only true accomplishments. As her aunt had so gratifyingly mentioned, she also possessed a natural grace on the dance floor. But that was all that she could boast. With a deep frown, she wondered what someone, perhaps someone like Miss Carruthers, could list as her accomplishments.

"Is anything wrong, miss?" asked the maid, pausing in the

act of smoothing Belle's hair with a brush. "Haven't I done it right? Your aunt did say I was to put your hair up."

"Oh! Oh, no, it is perfect," said Belle hastily. "I was just thinking, Sommers."

The maid nodded, satisfied, and returned to her task. Belle's thoughts continued to revolve around her present situation and how she had arrived in it.

Mr. and Mrs. Weatherstone had told her that they would provide everything for her just as they would have done for Cassandra, including ordering a new wardrobe to replace her own outmoded one. Her grandfather had insisted that the bills for that be sent to him, however. "You may do everything else befitting the girl, but I shall continue to have the clothing of her," Sir Marcus had said in his obstinate fashion. Mr. and Mrs. Weatherstone had agreed to it and had promised Sir Marcus that they would bring Belle out and present her at court and accompany her to every social affair that was de rigueur.

Belle had been dazzled by the plans laid out on her behalf and had agreed to everything with alacrity, even her grandfather's order that she was to obey every stricture given her by her aunt.

She still had nothing but enthusiasm for the original plan. After leading such a rigidly secluded life, she had been starved for some taste of the world. She was infinitely grateful to her uncle and aunt, and she was doing her best to make them proud of her.

She had never known them, except through her sister's letters, and she had often wished to be able to visit them at their home in Bath.

However, there had been bad blood for many years between Sir Marcus and his son and daughter-in-law. After the tragic accident that had orphaned the little girls, each household had pledged itself responsible for the raising of one twin, and the sisters had never met again until they had been able to change places and lives for a few awkward and rewarding months.

The masquerade had led to a long overdue reconciliation of the family and had opened up the world to Belle.

When Belle accepted her uncle and aunt's invitation to go up to London with them for the Season, she had promised to be guided by their wisdom and worldly experience. And so here she was, going for sedate drives in the park rather than for proper rides.

Belle sighed a little regretfully. No matter how difficult it might seem at times, she was determined to be a proper lady. She would make a successful come-out, of that she was fully convinced. What would happen after that was not quite as clear in her mind.

Her aunt had expressed concern that afternoon that she was not quite up to the task of making a success of the Season. Belle felt an almost physical stumble in her natural self-confidence. But she had never in her life turned away from any jump, no matter how wide, and she decided that she would not do so now.

"Miss, your handkerchief," said the maid, holding it out.

Belle took the tiny scrap of linen and lace and looked at it. "I can't imagine that this will do me much good if I should ever need one," she remarked with a quick smile.

The maid folded her hands in front of her, responding with a small twitch of her lips. "No, miss. Howsomever, you must have it."

"Yes, of course." Belle thanked the maid for her services and marched out of the bedroom, tucking the useless handkerchief into her buttoned cuff. She started downstairs, certain that she would find her aunt again in the drawing room.

As she left the last carpeted stair and started across the entry hall toward the drawing room door, which stood slightly ajar, she heard the rumble of her uncle's voice coming from within and realized that Mr. Weatherstone must have returned from his club. Without hesitation, she pushed open the paneled door and entered. "Uncle Phineas! How good it is to see you."

Mr. Weatherstone stood up and took the hands that she held out to him. "Belle, you move me. I did not anticipate such a fine welcome."

"You are quite one of my favorite people," said Belle truthfully. She reached up to give his cheek an affectionate peck, before turning away to join her aunt, who was seated on the settee.

"I am well able to understand why we find ourselves the recipients of a flow of invitations," said Mr. Weatherstone in some amusement.

"Indeed! We have been in residence in London for little over a month, but already each morning's post brings several invitations, as well as the occasional billet or posy directed to Belle," said Mrs. Weatherstone in obvious satisfaction.

"Yes, and Belle is obviously thrilled with the tokens from her admirers," said Mr. Weatherstone teasingly.

Belle felt a blush stealing into her cheeks. "It has been very pleasant, in truth."

"She has never been the object of such attention in her life, and she is reveling in it, Phineas," said Mrs. Weatherstone with a chuckle. "As for the invitations, Belle eagerly agrees to my every suggestion on which ones are proper for her to attend."

"You are very accommodating, Belle," said Mr. Weatherstone.

"It doesn't matter to me what sort of entertainment is being offered. Everything is still so novel to me that it never enters my head to be bored," said Belle with a slight shrug.

"A sterling quality in anyone," observed Mr. Weatherstone.

"Quite. Nor do you complain of the heat in the closed houses. And you haven't picked up silly affectations like some of the other young misses," said Mrs. Weatherstone.

Belle looked from her uncle to her aunt and gave a spurt of unaffected laughter. "This is high praise, indeed!"

"I particularly like that about you, Belle. You're friendly and open. It is little wonder that you are swiftly becoming a very popular young lady," said Mr. Weatherstone. He raised a heavy brow. "I trust, however, that all of this adulation does not go to your head."

"I wondered if it might not, since Belle has been very sheltered and is just up from the country," said Mrs. Weatherstone, nodding. She smiled at her niece. "After our conversation this afternoon, however, I do not believe that we need worry overmuch, Phineas."

"Tell me why you have drawn that conclusion, my dear," said Mr. Weatherstone with interest, as he glanced again at his niece.

"While it is true that Belle is somewhat dazzled by all the attention and admiration she has already received, she is at the core a very sensible young woman," said Mrs. Weatherstone. "She can be devastatingly honest with herself. She has informed me that self-deception is not one of her faults, and I believe her."

Belle felt that her face must be fiery red. She was not used to being discussed and complimented in such a fashion. "I scarcely know what to say, Aunt Margaret!"

"You have embarrassed the poor girl," said Mr. Weatherstone with a chuckle.

"So I have. True humility is rare, my dear. I am glad to see that you possess it." Mrs. Weatherstone gave a rueful laugh as she shook her head. "If anything, Belle, I dread your inexhaustible energy, but I have no anxiety that you will lose your head."

Mr. Weatherstone laughed. "I admit that I, too, feel more my years when I am around you, Belle. I hope that you will not wear your aunt to a bone, my dear."

"I shan't. I promise that I shall not be a drag upon you, dear Aunt Margaret," said Belle swiftly, a new anxiety rising in her. It was very, very difficult to be so perfect.

"I know that you shall not," said Mrs. Weatherstone, smiling at her niece. "By the by, that is a very becoming gown on you, Belle. I am glad that we purchased it before coming up to London."

"Thank you, Aunt," said Belle, smoothing the fine material beneath her fingers. She had never had such clothes in her life, nor had she been brought up to rely upon a maid to dress her. Gone were her comfortable gowns that she could button for herself and the simple way that she had tied back her hair. Now whenever she glanced at a mirror, she had to look again to be sure who it was that was looking back at her. It was a different world, indeed.

"Speaking of gowns, a package was delivered before you ladies came downstairs," said Mr. Weatherstone. He gestured toward the occasional table. "I had Monroe set it down over there."

"Phineas! Why ever didn't you tell me? That must be Belle's gown for our first ball," said Mrs. Weatherstone, rising at once and going over to claim the package.

Belle followed her aunt. As Mrs. Weatherstone began untying the string, she exclaimed, "I know that it must be beautiful!"

"The ball is a fortnight away, isn't it? Well, I must be certain to be here for the grand occasion," said Mr. Weatherstone. From across the room he smiled at his niece. "You have already garnered a handful of admirers, Belle. I, too, have seen their posies and other tokens of admiration in the morning post. Hasn't there even been a poem or two?"

Belle's eyes twinkled at her uncle. "Yes, sir, I have received two very pretty odes. One was to my eyes, which were likened to sherry drops, and the other to my hair, which is said to be like a waterfall at dusk and tipped by the dying sun's rays."

"Preserve me from fledgling poets," he said with a groan.

"As I recall, you were a fair poet, Phineas," said Mrs. Weatherstone over her shoulder as she ripped away the layers of paper that were wrapped around the box.

Mr. Weatherstone took up the poker from its stand and prodded the burning log in the grate until a shower of crackling sparks flew. "I suspect that your tender sentiments at the time exalted my poor efforts beyond their actual worth, Margaret."

"Perhaps," agreed Mrs. Weatherstone with a smile. She had opened the box and pushed aside the delicate tissue paper inside until the folded gown was revealed. "Look, Belle! The beads and lace on the bodice are just as we requested. You must try it on tomorrow."

"I will, Aunt Margaret. Oh, it is so very lovely!" exclaimed Belle, smoothing the tips of her fingers over the tiny pearl beads that had been sewn onto the fragile lace. "How very costly it looks."

"Quite! I am certain that your grandfather dreads the post these days, since all it brings him is the bills for these expensive creations," said Mr. Weatherstone, replacing the poker on the hearth.

"Grandpapa may grumble, but I am persuaded that he doesn't regard the cost. Not really," said Belle, not paying close attention to what her uncle had said.

"Undoubtedly you know my father better than I do," said Mr. Weatherstone dryly.

Belle shot a glance over her shoulder at her uncle, uncertain of his meaning, but there was nothing in his pleasant expression to indicate that he was harboring any undercurrent of feeling. For the first time, it occurred to Belle to wonder whether her uncle, as well as her aunt, did not still resent the abrasive treatment that they had once received at Sir Marcus's hands. If so, it was all the more wonderful that they had agreed to sponsor her for the Season, since she had been brought up by Sir Marcus and could conceivably be sided with him in the event of a family row.

"Ring for Sommers to come down for the gown, Belle," said Mrs. Weatherstone, refolding the delicate rustling tissue over the exquisite gown and fitting the top back onto the box.

"Yes, Aunt," said Belle, going over to pull the tapestry bellpull that hung beside the painted mantel.

"It is such a pity that we do not have time to look at the gown properly just now," said Mrs. Weatherstone regretfully. "I know that you will look extremely well in it, Belle. I am certain it is precisely what I had hoped it would be. Phineas, will you be escorting me and Belle this evening to Almack's?"

"I believe that I shall. I have not been for some little time, and it is probably wise to make an appearance now and again," said Mr. Weatherstone with a sigh. "I shall say this, however. I do not care for the refreshments to be had, nor for the very respectable, very boring company."

"Lady Moorehead mentioned that she and his lordship would be attending this evening," offered Mrs. Weatherstone. "Lady Moorehead wanted it known that Clarice was once more in circulation."

Mr. Weatherstone's countenance lightened. "Then at least Lord Moorehead and I may commiserate with one another over the dry cake and orgeat. A man might well starve if he was solely dependent upon Almack's offerings."

Mrs. Weatherstone shook her head, looking fondly at her husband. "Do not be anxious, dear sir. I have requested an adequate repast for this evening before we go."

"Then I am entirely reconciled to the evening's program," said Mr. Weatherstone, rubbing his hands together in obvious anticipation.

"I like to go to Almack's, of course, but I think more than anything this evening I shall be glad to see Clarice Moorehead again. We haven't seen one another in a week, since she caught that horrid cold. She is my dearest friend in the world, outside Cassandra, of course," said Belle.

"I have always liked little Clarice Moorehead," remarked Mr. Weatherstone.

"I understand that Lady Moorehead has high hopes for Clarice's chances this Season," said Mrs. Weatherstone conversationally. "She has already excited the interest of two or three gentlemen. All totally ineligible, of course. But the Season has just begun, so Lady Moorehead is confident of there being other offers."

"Clarice is a pretty chit," agreed Mr. Weatherstone. He glanced at his niece. "However, I tend to think that Belle outshines her."

"Careful, Uncle," warned Belle with a laughing glance. "After what has already been said, you may completely turn my head."

"Pray do take a care for your head and heart, Belle. I shouldn't wish you to be carried away by the first gentleman that makes up to you," said Mrs. Weatherstone.

"Yes, Aunt," said Belle, her natural exuberance deflated a notch or two.

Mrs. Weatherstone smiled at her. "Lady Moorehead confided to me, and I am certain that I may relate it in perfect confidence to you, for you shall not repeat it, that Clarice's short indisposition was actually quite fortuitous. They were thus able to discourage one of the more persistent of the ineligible parties, for whom Clarice had shown signs of partiality."

"Fortunate, indeed!" murmured Mr. Weatherstone thoughtfully. He glanced in his niece's direction.

Belle was aware of her uncle's scrutiny, but she directed her reply to her aunt. "You need not be anxious on that head, Aunt Margaret. I am too levelheaded to be taken in by some counter-coxcomb. And I rely completely upon you and my uncle to advise me, of course."

"Bravo! You are right to place your trust in us, Belle. We shall not steer you wrong, I promise you," said Mr. Weatherstone.

"We shall make certain of your future happiness," agreed Mrs. Weatherstone.

"I know that," said Belle with a smile. "And in the meantime, I am persuaded that I shall have a most delightful Season."

Chapter 4

In the company of her aunt and uncle, Belle stepped through the portals of Almack's Assembly and felt vaguely awed. It was not the first time that she had been to Almack's, of course, but she had never gotten over her first impression that the famous and exclusive society club was very grand and that she was very fortunate to have been admitted. After all, she was a country miss and could not claim acquaintance with anyone of importance. She would always feel grateful to her aunt and uncle for bringing her to London and presenting her to society.

The Weatherstone party chanced to meet Mrs. Drummond, that august and proud grande dame who had been good enough to extend vouchers for Belle's entry into the club. Mrs. Drummond greeted Mr. and Mrs. Weatherstone with the scarcest nod and a clipped greeting before she sailed off, her nose still elevated in the air.

Belle stared after the haughty lady. It never failed to astonish her that Mrs. Drummond had sponsored her. Behind her fan, she said in a low voice, "Aunt Margaret, however did you dare to ask Mrs. Drummond for vouchers for me? I do not know whether I would have had the fortitude."

Mrs. Weatherstone smiled, a twinkle in her blue eyes. "My dear Belle, I've known Mrs. Drummond these several years. Why should I not approach her? She may be a trifle high in the instep, but she doesn't bite."

"That is debatable," murmured Mr. Weatherstone. He gave an exaggerated shiver. "I thought I felt the nip of a winter's morn when the dear lady deigned to acknowledge me."

Belle chuckled, while Mrs. Weatherstone reprimanded her husband with a tap of her ivory fan on his arm. "Phineas, you set no good example," she said reprovingly.

"Quite right, my dear. Belle, pray do not heed me tonight. I suspect that I already suffer from that dreaded ennui that often afflicts us poor gentlemen whenever we enter Almack's," confided Mr. Weatherstone sotto voce.

"I shan't regard a single thing that you may utter," promised Belle gaily.

"Come, my dear. That is quite enough nonsense," said Mrs. Weatherstone, glancing at her husband, a slight smile on her face. "I perceive that the Mooreheads have already arrived. Let us go over and greet them. You will wish to speak to Clarice, Belle."

"Yes, indeed," agreed Belle, following in her aunt and uncle's wake as they made their way over to the Mooreheads. Lord and Lady Moorehead greeted Mr. and Mrs. Weatherstone with civility. Belle said all that was polite, then turned to their daughter.

Belle had formed a particular friendship with Miss Clarice Moorehead, who was also coming out that Season. She was the younger daughter (the elder of the Mooreheads' two daughters having made a splendid match the year before), and so her parents were very indulgent of her.

Miss Moorehead greeted Belle's appearance with a squeal of delight. "Belle! You have no notion how happy I am to see you!"

"Clarice, pray exercise a little decorum," said Lady Moorehead tolerantly.

"Yes, Mama," said Miss Moorehead submissively, though her green eyes still shone with excitement. She caught her friend's wrist and urged her to sit in the gilded chair beside her.

"I am glad to have found you, too," said Belle with a laughing glance at her friend's pretty face as she sat down. She liked Clarice Moorehead because they shared many of the same interests. They adored parties and could talk for hours about clothes. Clarice was also a bruising rider, which perfectly suited Belle's own neck-or-nothing style.

"My poor Rolly is getting so fat and lazy from lack of exercise. I wished to know if you could go riding with me tomorrow morning," said Belle.

Clarice shook her head regretfully, and her burnished curls bounced. The shadow of a frown dimmed the exuberance in her expression. "I cannot tomorrow, for I am promised to a breakfast party hosted by some of Mama's oldest friends. Such a bore, when I would far rather go riding!"

"Never mind. We shall make it another time," said Belle with a tiny shrug. She felt a twinge of disappointment. It would have been so wonderful to go riding with a friend. It was odd— at home, she had thought nothing of going riding by herself, but since coming to London she found that she much preferred having company.

"I have a new admirer," confided Clarice, leaning over in a conspiratorial manner so that she could speak softly into her friend's ear. She glanced over her shoulder as though wary of being overheard by her parents, but they and the Weatherstones were immersed in their own animated conversation.

Belle was at once diverted. "Do you? Who is it?" she asked, throwing a quick smile at Clarice.

Clarice shook her head and drew away, looking mischievous. "I shan't tell you just now. But I do so like him, very much!"

Belle laughed at her. "You like all of the gentlemen who make up to you, Clarice! Isn't there anyone that you prefer above all the rest?"

Clarice cocked her head, seriously considering the question. Finally, she shook her head. "Oh, no! I cannot choose, for one may be the most divine dancer and another might write the most elegant verse and yet another is proficient in providing me with a lemon ice just when I am thirsty. It is the most worrisome thing, as you may imagine!"

"Quite," agreed Belle on a chuckle. She surveyed the ballroom for faces that she recognized. There were several young ladies as well as gentlemen whom she had previously met. "It is a very nice company this evening."

"Yes," agreed Clarice eagerly. "We shall have our dance cards full in a trice, Belle. It will be such a merry romp."

"I suspect that Mrs. Drummond would frown on a romp," said Belle with a quick smile.

Clarice shuddered. "Oh! Isn't Mrs. Drummond simply too frightening? I am all tongue-tied in her presence. I much prefer Lady Jersey or dear Lady Sefton."

Belle agreed. She looked around. "Is Angus here with you tonight? Oh, Clarice, pray do not tell him that I said so, but his ode was so utterly ridiculous," she confided.

"Of course Angus is here. Papa made him come. He told Angus that if he had to dress up like a stiff rump, then Angus could very well keep him company," said Clarice mendaciously.

Belle gave a peal of laughter, but Clarice did not heed her. Instead her eyes suddenly widened. She clutched her friend's arm. "Belle! I have just remembered. You will never believe what I heard today from Angus."

"What has your brother done now?" asked Belle with amiable curiosity. She liked Angus Moorehead, and his antics never failed to astonish and amuse her. She had never had a brother; but if she had, she would have wanted him to be much like Angus Moorehead.

"Oh, not anything. That is to say— But that isn't what I wished to tell you at all! Belle, Angus told me the most amazing thing, and it concerns you!" exclaimed Clarice.

Belle looked at her friend in surprise. "Me! Why, what did he say?"

"Oh, there is Lord Hawthorne." Clarice bowed politely toward the gentleman. Through her friendly smile, she said, "His lordship has known me since the cradle, and he always sends me a very nice present for my birthday. I mustn't cut him or Mama will have my head."

"Clarice, what about Angus?" asked Belle.

"Oh! I almost forgot. Belle, it is the most amazing thing!"

"Yes, you said that," said Belle patiently.

"Then you've heard already? I wished to be the first to tell you," said Clarice, disappointed.

"Clarice, sometimes I could simply shake you. What did Angus say about me?" said Belle.

"Oh, that! Well, Angus told me this afternoon that he heard that you have earned a sobriquet. Everyone is calling you the 'Belle of London.' Now isn't that simply too amazing?" said Clarice.

Belle was taken aback for a moment before the humor of it hit her. "A pun! How extraordinary!"

"Yes, isn't it?"

The deep, merry voice came from one side.

Belle and Clarice both turned in their chairs. "Angus! You startled me!" exclaimed Clarice, fluttering her fan.

"Caught you gossiping, didn't I?" The tall, gangling young gentleman came to stand beside them, the flash of his attractive smile lighting his freckled face. His flaming red hair was several shades brighter than his sister's deep copper locks. His attire was correct but rather careless. He bowed with an easy grace. "How are you, Miss Weatherstone?"

Belle put out her gloved hand. "Very well indeed, Mr. Moorehead."

Angus held on to her hand for a moment while his blue eyes laughed at her. "Did you receive my last billet, Belle?"

"Indeed, I did. It—it was a very pretty poem, Angus," said

Belle handsomely. She felt badly for the falsehood, but she didn't wish to hurt her friend's feelings.

"It was pure drivel and well you know it, Belle," said Angus cheerfully.

Belle was taken aback by his frank admission, and she laughed. "Well! That is a fine admission, I must say."

"If it was so bad, whyever did you send it to Belle?" demanded Clarice with a quick frown.

"It's become fashionable to admire Belle," said Angus matter-of-factly. "Ask anyone. Ask Roland. He'll tell you it's true."

"I suppose I must thank you, Angus. So you admire me simply because it is 'fashionable'?" asked Belle teasingly.

Angus looked 'round at her quickly. Dismay colored his expression. "Oh, I say! Belle, I meant nothing by it. I like you rather a lot. For a female, you're a right 'un, a good fellow."

"You've dealt a severe blow to my ego, sir, but I think that I shall survive it," said Belle, laughing up at him.

"Go away, Angus," said Clarice in disgust, having no compunction in being uncivil to her brother.

"Has Angus disgraced himself again? I hardly need to ask, however."

Another young gentleman sauntered up in time to hear Clarice's command. He was attired in the latest fashion for an aspiring dandy. His coat was of ridiculous cut, the shoulders padded with buckram, the waist nipped in tight. His waistcoat was a stunning pink and yellow stripe. Several fobs and seals hung from ribbons at his waist. His breeches and hose showed to advantage a pair of shapely legs. He made an elegant bow to each of the ladies. "I am enchanted to see you both this evening, Miss Moorehead, Miss Weatherstone."

"Hullo, Roland," said Angus amiably, leaning over the top of his sister's chair, his arms folded.

"Roland, Angus has just insulted Belle," said Clarice. "He called her 'a good fellow'!"

"Shall I call him out for you, Miss Weatherstone?"

"Oh, not tonight, if you please, Mr. White. It would be far more excitement than is ever supposed to be found at Almack's," said Belle with a smile.

"I'd just as soon you didn't, Roland," said Angus candidly, straightening up from his negligent pose. He twitched one of his cuffs. "I am at outs with m'father just now. He knows about the donkey, you see."

"Ah," said Roland comprehensively.

"Donkey?" Belle looked from one to the other of the youthful gentlemen. Angus turned his eyes skyward, while Roland lifted a fob to wipe it carefully with his monogrammed handkerchief. She gave a warm laugh. "I perceive that it is too good a story for a mere female."

"I know what Angus and Roland did," said Clarice, tossing her head. "It had to do with a race. But I promised not to tell. Papa found out anyway, of course. He always does."

"I don't know how the devil he does it, either," muttered Angus with a rueful expression.

"It is my experience that one's parents are generally omniscient," observed Roland with a shake of his head and a resigned sigh. He waved his hand in a dismissive gesture. "But I have not come over to discuss past glories, Angus. No! I have come over in hopes of adding my name to the dance cards of these two lovely ladies."

"You may do so, and with my goodwill," said Belle, proffering the card with its attached pencil.

Roland took it from her with an elegant bow and signed on one of the lines with a flourish. "Here you are, 'Belle of London.' "

Belle looked up at him swiftly. "It is true, then? I am really being called that?" she asked.

"I informed Belle just a moment ago what you had heard, Angus," said Clarice helpfully.

"Why are you so surprised, Miss Weatherstone? There is

not a lady in all of London who can hold a candle to you," said Roland gallantly.

"Well, I like that!" exclaimed Clarice with a pretty pout, flipping open her painted fan and plying it rapidly.

Roland pretended not to notice Clarice's exaggerated displeasure. "Everywhere one hears of your beauty, your refreshing frankness, your friendliness—shall I go on, Miss Weatherstone?" he asked with a wide grin.

"Pray spare my blushes, Mr. White," said Belle, laughing.

Roland bowed in grinning acknowledgment. "As you wish, of course."

"Well, I think it fits you, Belle," said Clarice loyally, laying aside her fan. "You truly are an original."

"Do you know, Clarice, I have yet to discover a mean bone in your body," said Roland, finally glancing at her, with approval in his expression.

"You haven't had her for a sister," said Angus, flashing a quick grin.

Clarice had blushed prettily at Roland's compliment. At her brother's declaration, red flags suddenly flew into her cheeks. She looked up over her shoulder at her sibling with flashing eyes. "Angus Moorehead, if it weren't for Roland's being here, I would do something drastic to you."

"Which is why I'm glad that Roland *is* here," said Angus.

Clarice drew a deep breath, her color still high. Roland stepped swiftly into the breach. "Have I told you, Clarice? My cousin Ashdon is back in town. He set foot in England scarcely a week past."

Belle smiled as Clarice was instantly diverted from skirmishing with her brother. She knew that there was great affection between the Mooreheads. It showed in their easy manners with one another and even in their mild disagreements. Belle wondered what it would have been like to have been raised in a large family, and she almost envied her friend.

"Oh, is that the one that you have always liked, Roland? The one that went to war?" asked Clarice.

Roland nodded. His expression mirrored the enthusiasm that was suddenly present in his voice as he said, "Exactly so. What tales my cousin could tell us if only he would! He was mentioned in the dispatches more than once, you know."

"Who is your cousin?" asked Belle curiously.

Roland glanced at her in surprise, as though she should have known. "Why, my cousin Adam, of course! Viscount Ashdon, you know."

Belle recalled a certain imperious lady of that name to whom she had recently been introduced. She had not wished to further her acquaintance. "I have met a Lady Ashdon," she said cautiously, not wishing to give offense.

Roland grimaced. "My aunt. I daresay you didn't care for her."

"Oh, no! I—I thought her very polite," said Belle hastily.

With a crooked grin, Roland nodded his understanding. "Yes, she can be freezingly polite. I don't like her much. I don't know anyone who does, really."

"His lordship must. After all, his own mother," said Angus.

Roland considered it, then shook his head. "I don't care to wager on it, Angus."

"A pity. Not liking your own mother, you know," said Angus.

Roland shrugged. "Ashdon doesn't take after her ladyship. My cousin is a right'un, true to the bone. You always know where you stand with him, for he'll tell you."

"I should like to meet the viscount," said Clarice musingly. "I do not know very many eligible gentlemen with titles yet."

"Don't think Lord Ashdon will come dangling after you, Clarice," warned Angus. "He's not like a lot of these other fellows that cluster around you. The man has been to war. He's likely a hero, to boot. He probably thinks about more important things than making up to chits like you."

Clarice was not interested in her brother's observation. Ig-

noring him, she cocked her head and asked the question most
important to her. "Does his lordship have a wife?"

"Clarice!" exclaimed Belle. "My aunt is forever scolding
me for my forwardness, and here you are setting such a bad
example for me!"

Clarice smiled, her eyes dancing. "Oh, I know one shouldn't
display undue curiosity, Belle. But it is only Roland that I am
asking, after all."

Roland's eyebrows rose. "No, he does not possess a wife."
Still looking thoughtfully at Clarice, he added, "He's a handsome devil, though."

"Then I should like very much to meet him, I think," murmured Clarice.

Belle glanced quickly at Roland's face and thought she saw
some hurt reflected in his eyes. "Well, and so should I, naturally. You have made your cousin out to be something of a
paragon, Mr. White."

Roland's expression cleared and he smiled slightly. "I don't
know about that. What I do know is that my aunt has wished
him to wed for years. But my uncle bought his colors for him,
and he went to war instead. There was quite a family row over
that, my father says." Light suddenly flashed in his gray eyes.
"How I envy Ashdon. He saw every campaign of the war. He
was even wounded. Twice." Roland seemed particularly affected by this fact, and Angus patted him on the shoulder in
commiseration.

Belle could not imagine anyone as sartorially splendid as
Roland ever going off to war, unless he wore a hussar's brilliant uniform, but she did not voice that observation. Her
thoughts were on the viscount. What little that Mr. White had
said, quite apart from his obvious hero worship of his cousin,
had certainly aroused her curiosity.

"I hope that we shall all have the pleasure of meeting Lord
Ashdon this Season, Mr. White," she said.

"Oh, there can be no doubt of that," said Roland confidently. "If I know my aunt, and I do, her ladyship will do her level best to puff Adam off. She dotes on him, you see. Why shouldn't she? He was the only issue, after all."

"Do you mean that the viscount is the only heir?" asked Clarice with an interested expression.

Angus rolled his eyes. "Dear sister, you positively embarrass me. Pay her no heed, Roland."

Roland smiled. "But that would be intolerably rude of me, Angus." He turned back to Clarice and nodded, adding ruefully, "I am the next in line, worse luck."

"Why, how is this? Why is that bad fortune?" asked Belle, highly amused by the gentleman's expression.

"Lady Ashdon dislikes Roland," said Angus helpfully.

"Oh, I see," said Belle politely. She and Clarice exchanged glances, then she shook her head. "No, I don't understand. Not really."

"It's this way. Lady Ashdon didn't want my cousin to become a soldier and go off to war. She wished him to take his place in society. Now, I wished to be a soldier, but m'mother begged me to reconsider on account of being next in line to the viscountcy. She said, and my father agreed, that there was a good chance of Adam's being killed. So I took my place in society," explained Roland with a shrug.

"Then Lady Ashdon dislikes you because she wanted the viscount to stay at home and she had only you instead?" asked Belle. "What an idiotic reason for dislike!"

"Lady Ashdon must be a veritable dragon," said Clarice in a low voice, her eyes wide.

"No one likes my aunt much," said Roland, nodding.

"I begin to pity the poor viscount," said Belle.

Chapter 5

A t that very moment, the gentleman in question entered the ballroom. He paused to survey the company. Lord Ashdon felt uncomfortable, but his feelings did not affect his amiable expression.

He had submitted to his mother's wish that he attend Almack's Assembly rooms that evening for one purpose and one purpose only. Lady Ashdon had begged her son to look over the newest crop of young misses, in order that he might choose a candidate or two who might make a suitable wife. Rather than enter into an argument that he knew from past experience would be lengthy and futile, for Lady Ashdon rarely could be moved from a position that she had taken, his lordship had attired himself in the required evening dress and presented himself at Almacks. He intended to stay no more than a quarter hour, considering that to be ample time in which to discharge his duty.

It was not that the viscount was particularly malleable. He could be quite obstinate in his own right. In this instance, however, he had been dealing from a position of weakness, which he had known would be his undoing. He had agreed with Lady Ashdon that it was past time that he get himself a wife so that the family line could be secured. Since he had not yet set out for Bath, he had no excuse to forgo the pleasure of a look-in at Almack's.

Surprisingly enough, the viscount was immediately hailed. "Ashdon!"

Lord Ashdon turned. Recognizing who was coming up to him, he grinned, his eyes crinkling at the corners. He met the gentleman with a firm handshake of his wide, square hand. "Peter Crocker! It is good to see you again, Peter."

Still shaking hands, Mr. Crocker grasped the viscount's arm with his other hand, too. He was a short, stocky gentleman, dressed respectably but unremarkably. There was nothing of the fop, either in his frank, open gaze or in his speech. "I had heard that you were back in England. Sold out, I suppose?"

Lord Ashdon shook his head. "No. I am on extended leave from my duties. I shall be going back to the Continent in a matter of months."

Crocker looked at him curiously. "What holds you to it, Ashdon? Too much the soldier to want any other life?"

Lord Ashdon threw back his head and laughed. "Scarcely that, Peter. No; it is Bonaparte. I don't think that we have seen the last of him. He gave in too easily, and I wish to be in on the kill when he comes plunging onto the stage again."

Crocker shook his head. "There aren't many that would share in your opinion, my lord. The Congress of Vienna is even now deciding the fate of Europe."

The viscount smiled again. "I truly hope that they may do it. But enough of politics, Peter. I haven't seen you since I was last in England, a year ago. How have you been keeping yourself?"

"Yes, you were on wounded leave then," said Crocker, his gaze tracing the scar that cut through the viscount's right brow and into his hairline. "That was a wicked cut, Ashdon. You should have been killed."

"It was divine intervention that preserved my life," said Lord Ashdon with an easy smile. "Now, satisfy my curiosity. What has brought you to Almacks this evening? Your lovely wife?"

Crocker grinned and shook his head. "No, not precisely. It is family duty. My wife is sponsoring her younger sister this Season, Miss Abigail Fairchilde. I never suspected that Melissa's chaperoning her sister would mean that I would be enlisted, too. Come, let me take you over. Melissa will be delighted to see you again."

Lord Ashdon threw up a broad palm. "A moment, Peter. Pray tell me that you are not leading me into a web of marital hopes."

Crocker laughed. His eyes full of mirth, he said, "I admit that it crossed my mind. My sister-in-law is a good girl, a quiet miss who can boast all of the ladylike accomplishments."

The viscount groaned. "It is just as I suspected. This is precisely why my mother insisted that I attend this evening." He gave an exaggerated sigh. "I am to be put on the strut, Peter."

Crocker cracked a laugh. "That is good, Ashdon! Put on the strut! You don't care for it by half, I know!"

Lord Ashdon shook his blond head. "No, I do not, but I could not deny the core of my mother's argument. I have been away at war for years. It is only God's providence that has kept me whole, when all around me others were falling mortally wounded. Believe me, it has weighed ever heavier on my mind that I am the last of my line." He chuckled, his easy smile flashing again. "I could scarcely forget, for each of my mother's letters made reference to it! And so, friend Peter, I am dutifully, though somewhat reluctantly, in search of a wife."

Crocker eyed the viscount thoughtfully for a moment. "Yet you believe that Bonaparte will return."

Lord Ashdon's expression at once sobered, the smile fading from his firm, thin-lipped mouth. "I do, Peter. And I suspect that it will be the gravest, most desperate battle of all. That is why I must find a suitable wife. I am not at all reassured that I will return alive in the end."

Crocker whistled. His eyes widened as he stared at the viscount. "You are completely serious, aren't you, Ashdon?"

"Deadly serious," said Lord Ashdon somberly. "I need an heir to carry on my name, in the event of my demise."

Crocker shook his head. "Lord, what a depressing topic to bring into Almack's. War and death! I am glad now that I did not buy my colors. So many, so many that we went to school with are gone, Ashdon."

"Well I know it," said Lord Ashdon. He clapped a hand to his friend's shoulder. "But let us leave these morbid reflections, Peter. You are to deliver me into Mrs. Crocker's dainty hands, are you not? A title, no less! She will thank you a thousand times for bringing her sister to my notice. You see, Peter, I am fully cognizant of my worth on the market."

Crocker laughed as he led the way toward a small knot of people seated next to the dance floor. He slid a glance of amusement at the viscount, who paced beside him. "You haven't changed, my lord. You are as full of fun as ever."

"I hope I am as much as the next man," said Lord Ashdon, smiling.

A peal of feminine laughter rang out, and both gentlemen turned their heads. Two young ladies, seated beside the dance floor, were conversing animatedly with a couple of their admirers.

Lord Ashdon could not see the ladies entirely, his line of vision being partially blocked by the gentlemen who stood with the ladies, but Mr. Crocker apparently had little difficulty in recognizing them despite the limited view. He pointed with his chin. "The one seated on the left is Miss Clarice Moorehead, Lord Moorehead's daughter. Perhaps you know them?"

"I recall Lord and Lady Moorehead, yes. His lordship was a friend of my father's," said Lord Ashdon. "Who is Miss Moorehead's companion?"

Crocker smiled. "Ah! That is the 'Belle of London.' Like Miss Moorehead, she is just come out this season and is fast becoming all the rage. Perhaps you should solicit an introduction, Ashdon, for no doubt the lady would make a fine viscountess."

"For shame, Peter! What would Mrs. Crocker say if she were to hear such treason?" admonished Lord Ashdon.

Crocker laughed. "Yes, you are no doubt right. However, I am perfectly serious. From all that I have heard, the Belle of London would be a fitting bride for you, or for anyone else, for that matter. She is ravishingly beautiful, which poor Abigail is not, I fear, and she has a considerable portion to her name."

Lord Ashdon shook his head and said quietly, "I am not interested in a spoiled society miss, Peter. In fact, ever since I was recuperating in Bath last year, I have carried the image of a certain young lady emblazoned on my memory."

"Oh, I see!" Crocker regarded his companion thoughtfully, slowing his steps to deliberately delay their joining of his party. "Then you will not be staying long in London, I take it?"

Lord Ashdon's easy smile reappeared. His summer-blue eyes glinted with laughter. "Am I as transparent as all that? You have the right of it, Peter. I am but satisfying a promise that I made to Lady Ashdon before I am off to Bath."

"Poor Abigail," said Crocker with a sigh. He put a smile on his face as he came up to his wife. "Melissa, look whom I have found. You will recall Lord Ashdon, I am certain. He wasn't able to attend our wedding, but he called on us last year when he was on wounded leave."

"Of course I do!" Melissa Crocker held out her gloved hand in a friendly manner. Her shrewd brown eyes regarded the viscount with approval. "My lord, I am very glad to see you. I trust you are back in England for good. Allow me to introduce you to our party." She performed introductions to the two elderly ladies seated beside her, who turned out to be her mother and her aunt; to Mr. Crocker's younger brother, August, who flushed at being greeted by a hero of the war; and to Miss

Abigail Fairchilde, a demure miss who scarcely lifted her eyes to meet the viscount's gaze.

Lord Ashdon said all that was civil. Then he politely asked Mrs. Crocker to stand up with him. As he had expected, she gracefully turned down his invitation and suggested that perhaps her sister could stand up with him in her stead. Miss Fairchilde appeared alarmed and threw a wide-eyed glance at her sister.

The viscount bowed to the young lady, his ready smile coming to his face. "I hope that you will not disappoint me as well, Miss Fairchilde."

"Oh, no, my lord! At least—" Miss Fairchilde met his sympathetic gaze, and a shy smile crossed her face. "I will be most happy to stand up with you, my lord." She rose and placed her hand on his arm. With the most unaffected grace, she allowed his lordship to lead her into the set that was just forming.

The viscount was not the only one on the dance floor. Belle turned a corner with her partner, her eyes automatically surveying the others, and a fleeting glimpse of a handsome, browned face caught her gaze. She had only a second to absorb the impact of a rakish white scar and an easy smile before her partner reclaimed her attention. When she had the opportunity to glance around again, she was disappointed because she did not see the unknown gentleman.

Lord Ashdon finished the set with Miss Fairchilde and led her back to her chair. He began to make his excuses to part from the Crocker party. Melissa Crocker invited him to a small soiree that they were holding in a few nights, and the viscount expressed his delight at being able to attend. Peter Crocker shook hands with him, a gleam of sympathy in his eyes, and murmured, "I trust that we shall not be serving up roasted goose."

Lord Ashdon gave a quick smile, understanding his friend perfectly well. "So do I, sir, believe me."

Crocker chuckled. "We shall see you then, Ashdon."

Lord Ashdon left Almack's without a backward glance. He was relieved to have completed his duty for that evening. He could declare to his mother with good conscience that he had met one young lady of good family, and that news would pacify Lady Ashdon for at least a day or two. His rash promise of a fortnight's sojourn in London would soon be fulfilled, and he hoped he would be able to delay his mother's machinations on his behalf for that long. Then he could be off to Bath in search of the lady whose lovely face he had never forgotten.

As he started down the street, it occurred to him that he would be returning to the town house early. Lady Ashdon was probably not yet returned from fulfilling her own obligations. It was entirely possible, however, that she had cut short her own amusement to wait for him. Lord Ashdon grimaced. He did not wish to be pulled into a late-night discussion about his matrimonial prospects.

He decided that he was in just the right mood for a late dinner and perhaps a round or two of cards, so instead of returning to the town house, he hailed a hackney cab and gave the direction of his club. As he leaned back against the squabs, he grinned to himself. No doubt his appearance would occasion some surprise.

At the door of the club, Lord Ashdon paid off the hackney, then bounded up the steps, colliding with a gentleman who was just emerging. "Sir! My abject apologies. I did not see you coming out," said Lord Ashdon.

The shorter gentleman had almost instantly righted himself. "Quite all right, I assure you," he replied in a drawl.

Lord Ashdon looked more carefully at the gentleman in the uncertain light thrown by a nearby streetlamp. "By all that's wonderful! Sylvan Darlington!"

The smaller man, preparing to brush past, suddenly turned. "Wait a moment. I know your voice, do I not?"

Lord Ashdon laughed. "It is I, Ashdon. How have you been, Darlington?" The two gentlemen gripped hands.

"I am better than one might expect." The smaller gentleman hesitated. "You heard about my cousins, Richard and Phillip, I suppose?"

Lord Ashdon instantly sobered. "Yes, I am sorry. I did not see much of them while I was in Spain, since I was in a different division. But I understand that they acquitted themselves well."

"Thank you, Ashdon. That is kind of you. It came as a startling surprise to me, as you may well imagine. I never expected to inherit the title."

Lord Ashdon suddenly realized that his companion was now a marquis. "No, of course not. War changes many things. I was about to order supper. Will you join me, my lord?"

"I have already supped, but I will take a glass of wine," said Lord Darlington.

The two gentlemen went into the club and entered the dining room. Lord Ashdon made his order and poured the wine, then spent a comfortable hour in conversation with Lord Sylvan Darlington. The marquis was younger than himself, having been up to school with Ashdon's cousin, Roland White, but he felt no discomfort in their discourse. He had been fairly well acquainted with Darlington's cousins and had often had occasion to include the younger gentleman in their youthful exploits. They talked of several things, coming eventually to the duties that bound a gentleman's honor.

Ashdon leaned back in his chair, rolling his wineglass between his fingers. With a smile, he commented, "It seems strange to me to be back in England. It is all so very civilized."

"Yes, I wish that I had had the opportunity to escape it," said Darlington. He lounged back in his own chair, and a lazy smile lit his pale face as he met the viscount's surprised glance. "You see, I have always envied fellows such as yourself, Ashdon. My greatest ambition was to purchase a pair of colors and run off to war. But my familial duties bound me close to home, so that any dream of soldiering remained but a dream."

Ashdon frowned thoughtfully. "I had quite forgotten. Your father had died, had he not? And there were younger siblings, as I recall."

The marquis bowed from his sitting position. "My duty was plain, of course."

Ashdon nodded. "Yes; I understand that you were honorbound to support your family. I, too, find myself in the position of satisfying family duty."

Darlington's eyes lit with interest. "Indeed! How is this?"

Ashdon smiled ruefully. "I am the last of my line, Darlington. It behooves me to find a suitable wife."

"My condolences, my lord," said his companion, smiling a little. "Have you a fair damsel in mind, perhaps?"

"Yes. But whether she remembers me, or even remains unwed, I know not," said Ashdon.

"I scent a romance," murmured Darlington, his mobile lips twisting slightly.

Ashdon laughed. "Hardly that! The lady is simply someone whom I met when I was on wounded leave last year. I hope to discover her whereabouts, and perhaps wed, before I return to the Continent."

"Have you not sold out, then?" asked Darlington with extreme interest.

Ashdon shook his head, frowning slightly. "I have been called all sorts of fool, Darlington, but I continue to hold to my opinion. Bonaparte's abdication was not in his style. I believe that we shall see him again."

The marquis sat up straighter. His eyes glowed. "You interest me profoundly, Ashdon! Would that I could go with you."

"What of your siblings, my lord?" asked Ashdon. "Do you not still bear responsibilities?"

"Quite, but the situation is somewhat changed from what it

was when my father died," said Darlington. "Then, the estate was hopelessly encumbered. I have been able to retire the mortgages, so that my mother and sisters and brothers need not be in fear of losing the roof over their heads. Also, the sister closest in age to me has been married off, and another is betrothed, both having accepted offers from solid gentlemen of worth. One of my brothers is up at Oxford, and the other two are at Eton. The youngest sister is still with my mother."

"I have heard that good men are needed for the Congress of Vienna," suggested Ashdon.

"Politics?" Darlington grimaced. "Really, Ashdon. I hardly think that is quite in my style."

"Perhaps not. However, the experience would expose you to the notice of important personages, such as Wellington, who is always attaching another gentleman or two to his staff," said Lord Ashdon. He could see that the suggestion had made an impression on his companion. "If you need a sponsor, I can probably put you in the way of a good word. My commanding officer is a good sort and has the ear of a few people."

"Decent of you, Ashdon," said Darlington in a low voice. There was a controlled fervor in his voice.

Soon after, Ashdon took friendly leave of the marquis. He was glad to have been of some encouragement to him. He hoped that the marquis would take him up on his offer of introduction. He had had much experience at reading men, and unless he was very much mistaken, Lord Sylvan Darlington was ripe for trouble. In London, there were the seamy sides of life that could offer both the sort of thrills and challenge he felt the marquis yearned for and also very real dangers. He would spare the young marquis that, if he could.

Ashdon made his way on foot back to his father's town house. For a moment he stood looking up at the silent front of it from the sidewalk. Though strange to think of, his father was dead; it was his town house now.

As his gaze traveled further, he saw the reflection of light escaping from behind the curtains of his mother's sitting rooms.

He sighed. No, the town house was not his. It belonged to Lady Ashdon. It bore her mark and was ruled by her hand. He had been long away from his position, and he would soon be going away again.

Lord Ashdon climbed the stone steps and took out his key to let himself quietly in the door.

Chapter 6

‿

It was just before dawn, the hour where night began to fuse with day. The darkness had lightened just enough so that objects had taken on some form and shadow.

Lord Ashdon had not slept well, and he had risen with a feeling of restlessness, so he had set out on a ride with his favorite horse. He knew to what he could attribute his unsettled frame of mind.

His mother's gentle insistence that he remain in London for the Season was already wearing on him. Lady Ashdon had reiterated her wishes when he had returned to the town house the previous evening. Her ladyship had not only cut short her own outing in order to waylay him, as he had foreseen that she would, but had waited up for him until his return in the small hours of the morning. A man grown for some years and used to his independence, he had failed to see the humor in his mother's avowed anxiety for his safe return.

The viscount loved his parent, but since his return to England, he had found himself constantly forced into the position of steeling his emotions and his mind against her cajoling and arguments. For a man lately home from battle, it should not have been greatly wondered at if he did not feel inclined to plunge into a constant round of gaiety. At least, that was what he had told Lady Ashdon. Her ladyship had, however, responded with the opinion that that was precisely what the viscount needed to restore himself.

He urged the horse on faster, wanting to feel the resistance of the damp wind against him. More and more, thoughts of traveling to Bath were on his mind. He had found the slower pace of society in the popular watering spot appealing. Perhaps that had been because of his slow recovery from his head wound. He had suffered tremendous headaches, and for a time sunlight had hurt his eyes. Finally, however, the cure had been complete.

The tedium of those dreadful weeks had been pleasantly relieved by the polite friendship that he had developed with a certain young lady whom he had met in the Pump Room. Even now he smiled when he recalled their civil conversations. He had looked forward to those meetings.

There had been nothing the least bit clandestine in their blossoming relationship. She had always been accompanied by her maid, and he had behaved as a model gentleman, never by word or glance conveying anything warmer than what was conventional. They had remained, and parted, as mere acquaintances.

Now he wondered if he had not been a fool. He had never forgotten her face, nor the melodious sound of her voice. He should have pursued their relationship and asked permission of her guardians to court her. If he had, he would not now be in the straits that he was, former scruples set aside and compelled to wed before the war started again.

Despite any reasoning to the contrary, Lord Ashdon knew instinctively that it would not be long before the bugle call and the drums sounded again. Even as he questioned now his wisdom in not courting his lady, he understood why he had not taken the step to commitment. He had not wanted to wed and leave behind a young bride who might become a widow before the next packet of letters from the front had arrived in England.

The situation had not changed overmuch, but his thinking had. He might still wed and leave a widow, but he hoped he would also leave behind an heir. That had become more important to him in light of the weight he felt on his soul. He knew that the last battle was destined to be a monstrous one. Clear-eyed as he was, he had realized that the odds of his coming out alive might very well have swung against him. After all, he had already survived years of war and countless skirmishes.

The early-morning mists lifted, revealing another verdant green. A lone rider was cantering toward him. Lord Ashdon was astonished to discover another early riser such as himself, and even more astonished when he saw that the rider was a young female without an accompanying groom.

As he began to come abreast of the solitary rider, hearing the clip of the other horse's hoofbeats clearly, Ashdon suffered a shock. He recognized the lady's face as she passed him. "My God!"

Instantly he pulled up his horse, setting it almost on its haunches. Within seconds he had the animal turned, and he whipped it to speed. His mount stretched quickly into full gallop. It was a powerful beast, with good bottom, yet the viscount was anxious that he would not be able to catch the rider.

As though she had heard the thundering hoofbeats coming up from behind her, the rider glanced back. A merry look passed over her face, and she bent low in the saddle, encouraging her own horse to a gallop.

Lord Ashdon grimly chased his quarry. Bit by bit, his stallion gained ground, until he suddenly cut across the rider's path. The lady reined in her gelding, laughter bubbling from her lips.

"Well done, sir!" she called. Her hazel eyes, flecked with gold, gleamed with excitement. Her cheeks were rosy from the wind, and her generous mouth flashed a quick smile.

Lord Ashdon felt his heart thumping in his chest. He was almost as affected as he was on the eve before a battle. Adrenaline was pumping through his veins furiously, and he took a deep, steadying breath. "Forgive me for pursuing you in such a relentless fashion," he said diffidently. "I am Ashdon, you know."

Recognition lit the lady's eyes. "Lord Ashdon! I am an acquaintance of your cousin Mr. Roland White. He informed me that you had returned to London. I had hoped that we would meet at some function or other. I am Belle Weatherstone."

Miss Weatherstone extended her hand to the viscount. He hardly comprehended what she had said. It was enough that she had spoken. He took her fingers, slightly dazed. Perhaps he had a right to be, he thought incoherently, for certainly chance had played a huge part in this meeting.

Belle was quite surprised that the viscount had accosted her so boldly. She knew well enough now that good *ton* required a formal introduction. She was not one to cavil, however. The informality of their setting and the suddenness of their meeting must provide excuse enough to perform their own introductions. She would not allow the unorthodox to spoil the moment.

Belle studied Lord Ashdon's countenance, taking quick note of the scar that descended into his brow. It had been he whom she had seen at Almack's, then. She felt a thrill of satisfaction that was not lessened as she gazed at the laugh lines at the corners of his wide-set blue eyes, his straight, regular nose, the thin-lipped firm mouth and strong jaw. Belle liked very much what she saw. Lord Ashdon was quite the handsome fellow. Mr. White had not exaggerated.

"Miss Weatherstone." Lord Ashdon cleared his throat. A grin suddenly lit his tanned face. "It appears that I am struck dumb in your presence. Pray forgive my clumsy attempt to bring myself to your regard. I am usually much more polished upon making myself known to a young lady."

"Do you not always make a practice of running the ladies down on your horse, then?" asked Belle teasingly. She slid a laughing glance in the viscount's direction as she turned her stolid mount and set it walking toward the park entrance.

Lord Ashdon's keen eyes flared wide, as though in surprise. "You take me aback, ma'am."

At once, Belle was dismayed. She had put her foot in it again. Her aunt's gentle voice rang reprovingly in her thoughts. She shook her head ruefully. "It is the curse of my too-freely-spoken mind, my lord. I am constantly reminded that I am in London and must harbor such humor to myself, for it is considered to be too forward by some."

"No, do not apologize. I do not mind in the least being roasted," said Ashdon hastily.

Belle smiled at him, grateful for his forbearance. "I can see that we are destined to be good friends, my lord."

"So I hope," said Lord Ashdon with emphasis, dazzled by his good fortune. He turned his horse about also and rode beside her, admiring her excellent seat and handling of her mount. They had not had occasion to ride together in Bath, of course. He had been too unsteady even to think of straddling a horse. He was glad to see that Miss Weatherstone was an accomplished horsewoman, for he himself enjoyed riding. He nodded at the gelding. "Is he yours?"

Belle nodded and reached down to pat her chestnut's glistening neck. "This is my Rolly. I brought him with me when I came up to London with my aunt and uncle, for I could not bear to be parted from him."

"Are your aunt and uncle in residence, then? May I have their direction?" asked Lord Ashdon in a casual fashion, even though inside he was taut as wire. "I should like to call on Mr. and Mrs. Weatherstone one day, if you have no objection."

Belle looked at him, surprise in her eyes. His lordship was moving swiftly indeed. "Why, certainly, my lord. What possible objection could I have?" She relayed the address to him and then pulled up her mount so that she could offer her gloved hand. She nodded toward the entrance to the park and then smiled up at the viscount. "I must go now. I am already late for breakfast, I suspect."

Lord Ashdon held her fine-boned hand for an instant. There was warmth in his gaze. "I hope to further my acquaintance with you and your aunt and uncle very soon, Miss Weatherstone."

"Pray do so," said Belle cordially. "Good-bye, my lord."

Lord Ashdon watched her ride out of the park and merge into the early-morning traffic. The dispersing mists and rising sunlight created a strange effect, so that her silhouetted form appeared to be more phantasm than bone-and-blood woman. It was almost as though she was not real.

But, no, she existed. His chance meeting with Miss Weatherstone was not a figment of his imagination. He had spoken with her, and she had recalled him with cordiality.

Lord Ashdon felt much more like himself than when he had first come into the park. A smile curved his lips as he thought about their unexpected race across the green verge and their brief conversation.

He reflected that if he had to wed, he would far rather marry someone whom he liked. He had hoped that his memory would not play him false, and it had not. Miss Weatherstone was just as lovely as he had remembered. In fact, his recollections had not done her justice. He had forgotten the liveliness of her countenance, the vivaciousness in her expressive eyes. Her eyes had actually sparkled with the joy of the moment. Her high, healthy color, whipped up by the wind, had lent a rosy tint to her beautiful oval face.

Lord Ashdon turned out of the park and headed home to his own breakfast, his thoughts still lingering on his encounter with Miss Weatherstone. He was struck by the sudden realization that she had not been in the company of a groom. He recalled that at the Pump Room in Bath she had always been chaperoned either by her aunt or by a maid. But perhaps since coming to London, Mrs. Weatherstone had relaxed her vigilance slightly. London society was, after all, more permissive than the more insular society of Bath. In that popular watering place, one could scarcely nod to an acquaintance without the fact being observed and commented upon by a dozen people.

How odd. He had quite thought that Miss Weatherstone's name was something other than "Belle." Perhaps it was a diminutive or a pet name. Lord Ashdon shrugged. No doubt he had simply been mistaken. They had not been on a first-name basis, after all. One's memory could play tricks, and certainly he had had more excuse than many others for memory lapses during the recovery from his head wound.

Chapter 7

Lord Ashdon waited three days before he presented himself at the Weatherstone residence in Albemarle Street. He sent in his card, requesting to see Mrs. Weatherstone and her niece, Miss Weatherstone.

The butler returned to usher him into the drawing room, where he was cordially greeted by Mrs. Weatherstone. Lord Ashdon glanced quickly around, noting with disappointment that the lady of the house was alone. He bowed over Mrs. Weatherstone's hand, saying, "When I learned that you were in town, and recalling with pleasant memories our former acquaintance in Bath, I decided to call on you."

"I am very glad that you did, Lord Ashdon. Pray be seated, my lord," said Mrs. Weatherstone, graciously gesturing to a wingback. She seated herself on the settee opposite, as Lord Ashdon murmured his thanks and sat down.

"I was just about to take tea. Will you join me?" asked Mrs. Weatherstone.

"I would be delighted, ma'am," responded Lord Ashdon. He had deliberately chosen teatime for his visit, in hopes of catching the ladies at home. He wondered where Miss Weatherstone was, if she had been momentarily detained abovestairs, but civility barred him from inquiring at once.

Mrs. Weatherstone seemed to read his mind. "Unfortunately, my niece is not at home. She has gone to visit some young friends this afternoon," she said, beginning to pour the tea.

"I am disappointed to have missed her," said Lord Ashdon, feeling somewhat deflated. He had anticipated seeing Miss Weatherstone again, especially to test whether he would feel that same rush of adrenaline that had bespoken hope in his breast.

At Mrs. Weatherstone's inquiry, he indicated that he took his tea white and sweet. As he accepted the cup from her, he said with a smile, "I learned to like it this way while in Spain. When we had nothing else, strong, sweet tea meant the difference sometimes between life and death."

"It must have been a very difficult time," said Mrs. Weatherstone sympathetically. "I cannot fathom how you, or indeed, any of our young men, were able to survive. I must say that you appear to be in much better health than when we met in Bath."

"Yes," agreed Lord Ashdon. He touched the scar above his eye with a light hand. "This was very nearly the end of me. It made me an invalid, to my grave embarrassment. My stay in Bath proved to be entirely beneficial, however. I have suffered no ill effects since."

"That is very good to hear, my lord," said Mrs. Weatherstone with a smile, sipping her tea.

"Did Miss Weatherstone relate to you how we met the other morning in the park?" asked Lord Ashdon, as though it were a mere conversational gambit, but in fact he was keenly interested in the answer.

"Yes, she did." Mrs. Weatherstone shook her head, a small frown crossing her face. "I scolded her handsomely for going out without a groom, I assure you. I am only grateful that it was you, my lord, who accosted her and not some scoundrel."

Lord Ashdon made a short bow from his chair. "Thank you, ma'am. I am honored by the trust you have implied that you have in my character. I hope that I may be favored with your permission to call again in future."

"Of course, Lord Ashdon. You may call on us at any time.

We will be delighted to receive you," said Mrs. Weatherstone, giving a gracious nod.

"I hope that you did not scold Miss Weatherstone too stringently, Mrs. Weatherstone, for I thoroughly enjoyed being in her company. She is a delightful young lady," said Lord Ashdon.

"Thank you, my lord. Belle is such a vivacious, lovely girl, and she is extremely good-natured," said Mrs. Weatherstone.

"Quite. Your niece possesses a natural liveliness that is charming," said Lord Ashdon. He was once more struck by Miss Weatherstone's given name. Surely his memory could not be so faulty, not when he had recalled everything else about her. He was completely taken aback that he had forgotten such an important detail as that.

"Indeed." Mrs. Weatherstone looked at him over the rim of her cup and shook her head. "I shall not pretend to you, my lord, that I have not been concerned from time to time about her. Why, I am told that she is now called the 'Belle of London.' Such nonsense! Pray do not mistake me. I know that Belle would not deliberately put herself in an awkward position. Because of her sheltered upbringing, however, she is perhaps not aware of all the nuances of her actions. For instance, this business of riding off to the park without an escort."

"I am persuaded that your own example must hold sway, for Miss Weatherstone will surely not abandon all of the good sense that you have undoubtedly instilled into her," said Lord Ashdon politely. He was remembering how easily he had brushed aside Crocker's offer to introduce him to the Belle of London. What a fool he had been! It was pure chance that he had subsequently discovered Miss Weatherstone at the park. A few minutes one way or the other, he would have missed her altogether, and he would have left London for Bath without ever having met her. He smiled at his hostess without giving away his shaken thoughts. "As for society, London is certainly a far cry from Bath, or indeed, any other city that I know. I suspect Miss Weatherstone will discover tolerance for any small steps that she unwittingly takes beyond the most rigid boundaries."

Mrs. Weatherstone smiled at her visitor. "I am happy that Belle's unwitting flout of convention did not make you think ill of her, my lord."

"I could not think ill of someone whom I hold in utmost regard, ma'am," said Lord Ashdon.

Mrs. Weatherstone smiled again, and her manner became increasingly friendly. "My lord, I shall not stand on ceremony with you since we are already acquainted. I am also acquainted with your lady mother, Lady Ashdon, and your cousin Mr. White. Though I have already sent out the invitations, I should personally like to invite you to attend the ball that we are holding." She named a date. "It will be my niece's official coming-out, and I am certain that she would be delighted if you were able to come. Naturally, I will look for Lady Ashdon's presence as well, for I included her name on my list."

"I can think of little that would please me more," said Lord Ashdon quite truthfully. He gave an easy smile. "I shall certainly mark the date on my calendar."

He glanced casually toward the door. He had hoped that Miss Weatherstone would return to the house during his visit, but it did not seem likely that she would now make an appearance. He knew that the conventional fifteen minutes deemed proper for a social call had passed, and so he began to make his good-byes.

Mrs. Weatherstone walked with him as far as the drawing room door. She held out her hand to him. "Good-bye, my lord. I know that my niece will be most disappointed that she missed your visit this afternoon. I hope that the next time you call, she will be at home."

Lord Ashdon bowed over Mrs. Weatherstone's hand. "I appreciate your kind hospitality, Mrs. Weatherstone. Pray relay my compliments to Miss Weatherstone."

"I shall do so," said Mrs. Weatherstone with a nod and a smile.

Lord Ashdon left the Weatherstones' town house, well satisfied with the outcome of his first visit. As he had hoped, he had been able to reestablish his acquaintance with Miss Weatherstone's guardian. Mrs. Weatherstone had been all that was gracious and encouraging. She had expressed her willingness to pursue the acquaintance by extending the invitation to the Weatherstones' ball.

Lord Ashdon knew that his mother would not wish to attend such a function. Her ladyship generally confined her acceptances to only the most elite parties of the *ton*. He, however, meant to be at that ball, and he was determined that he would escort his mother. He knew just what would induce her to accompany him, too, and that was to casually mention that he had met a young lady of good family with whom he was interested in furthering his acquaintance. Lady Ashdon would leap at the opportunity to look over the Weatherstones.

Such a coup as drawing the haughty Lady Ashdon to her niece's come-out would certainly be a feather in Mrs. Weatherstone's cap. Lord Ashdon thought that his own credit with Mrs. Weatherstone would assuredly ascend with the delivery of his mother's person, and it was of some importance to him to be in good standing with Miss Weatherstone's guardian.

When Belle returned to the town house after her outing, she was at once commanded by her aunt to come into the drawing room. By this time Belle was well attuned to the nuances of her aunt's voice and mannerisms. She realized at once that some strong emotion was working on Mrs. Weatherstone.

Wondering what she could possibly have done to set her aunt's back up, Belle obediently followed her into the drawing room. She was even more concerned when her aunt closed the door against the possibility of their being overheard by the servants and requested that Belle sit down with her.

"Dear aunt, what is it? Oh, dear! What have I done now?"

asked Belle forthrightly as she sank down on the settee beside her aunt.

"Oh, nothing at all, dearest Belle. I simply wished to inform you about my visitor this afternoon at tea," said Mrs. Weatherstone. She was smiling suddenly. "Lord Ashdon paid a visit, Belle."

"Lord Ashdon! But I have only just met him," exclaimed Belle, much surprised. Her heart gave a bump and began racing a little. What had she done or said that the viscount should so honor her? Of course she had given her permission for his lordship to call, but that he should actually do so, and so soon, was astonishing.

"Yes, I am aware of that. He seemed to be so favorably impressed with you, however, that he decided to call," said Mrs. Weatherstone.

"How utterly extraordinary," marveled Belle. She shook her head. "It is very flattering, to be sure."

"Quite." Mrs. Weatherstone drew a breath and made her announcement. "I have invited him to your come-out ball."

Belle regarded her aunt in increasing surprise. She had been thoroughly instructed in the protocol surrounding the sending out of invitations. Written invitations were sent out a month or more ahead of the date, so that those who chose to respond could do so. She could think of only one thing to say. "I am persuaded that his lordship was not on your list, Aunt."

"A mere oversight, my dear. As you may know, I did send an invitation to Lady Ashdon. I did not know that the viscount had returned to London or I would naturally have included his name," said Mrs. Weatherstone, avoiding her niece's steady gaze.

Belle smiled at her good fortune. Everything was going exactly as she had hoped it would whenever she had dreamed about having a come-out in London. She was well liked and had several admirers. Though she was humble enough to realize that she could not include Lord Ashdon among her admirers, at least she could say that he was expressing an interest in her.

"I am not unhappy that you have invited Lord Ashdon," she said. "I liked him very well when I met him. He is very handsome and dashing, don't you think? That scar makes him appear a bit rakish, too."

"His lordship is not in the least rakish, Belle," said Mrs. Weatherstone quickly. "I do wish you would think before you speak, my dear. Cassandra would never have uttered such a thing."

Belle bent her head, making a pretense of smoothing a wrinkle in her skirt. "Forgive me, Aunt. Of course you are right. I spoke out of turn yet once again."

"Never mind, Belle. But I do so hope that you will be able to rid yourself of the habit," said Mrs. Weatherstone with a smile. "Now, what was I saying? Oh, yes! I met Lord Ashdon in Bath last year, when he was recovering from that terrible head wound that resulted in that very scar. His lordship and Cassandra struck up a bit of a friendship while promenading in the Pump Room. At that time I particularly took note of Lord Ashdon's behavior. He is quite thoroughly a gentleman, I can assure you."

"I don't recall that Cassandra mentioned him in any of her letters to me," said Belle, a tiny frown forming between her thin brows as she thought back to her sister's correspondence.

"Perhaps not. Cassandra was never one to make more of a thing than it was. When Lord Ashdon left to return to his duties, it was naturally the end of their friendship," said Mrs. Weatherstone with a dismissive shrug. "The important thing, Belle, is that he has taken you in regard. Yes, you may stare! Those were his exact words, or at least near enough as makes no difference." She reached over to take her niece's hands. "My dear Belle, you have attracted a very worthy and suitable admirer! I could not be more pleased for you."

"Nor I, Aunt," said Belle with a quick smile. "I have never

given much thought to it before, of course, but Lord Ashdon is just the sort of gentleman that I hoped to meet in coming to London. I already know that he is a good horseman and that he has seen something of the world. No doubt he can be a very pleasant companion, too."

"No doubt," agreed Mrs. Weatherstone dryly. She rose to her feet. "Well! That is enough excitement for one day. How was your shopping outing with Clarice Moorehead and Millicent Carruthers?"

"Oh! I completely forgot. I asked to have my packages taken upstairs. You must come up and see, Aunt. I found the most divine combs for my hair, and some ribbons and laces to refurbish that bonnet that we talked about, and a new pair of gloves to go with my gown for the ball," said Belle. She wound her arm through her aunt's as she was speaking and urged the other lady toward the drawing room door.

Mrs. Weatherstone laughed. "I see that I missed a very good opportunity to acquire what I might need. Perhaps I should have accompanied you."

Belle turned a dismayed countenance to her. "Oh! I am sorry, Aunt Margaret! You had only to commission me, and I would gladly have bought anything you wished to have."

Mrs. Weatherstone patted her niece's arm. "At this moment, I have everything that I could possibly want, dear Belle. Now let us go upstairs and inspect your wonderful purchases."

Chapter 8

As Lord Ashdon escorted his mother up the wide carpeted stairs to the receiving line, Lady Ashdon said acidly, "You needn't clutch my elbow so tightly, Adam. I agreed to accompany you tonight, after all. I have no intention of bolting."

"My pardon, Mother," said Lord Ashdon, at once relaxing his hold. "I did not realize that I was behaving uncivilly. I appreciate the effort you are making on my behalf."

"Yes. Well, it is quite true that I am putting myself forth for you in an extraordinary manner," said Lady Ashdon. She cut a glance around her. "I never attend these insipid affairs. How ever did I allow you to persuade me to do so this evening? I do not at all comprehend it."

"As I told you, Mother, Mrs. Weatherstone was kind enough to include me among her guests, and I did not wish to appear alone at such an event," said Lord Ashdon quietly. "Especially knowing that Mrs. Weatherstone had sent an invitation to you. It would be odd for me to do so."

"There would not be the least oddity attached to my absence, I assure you," snapped Lady Ashdon. "No doubt there will not be a single personage in attendance whom I shall wish to see."

With relief, Lord Ashdon saw that he and his mother were shortly to approach their host and hostess. At least he would be spared his parent's acid tongue for a moment or two.

Though she had been standing beside her aunt and uncle

already for half an hour, Belle was still nervous on the evening of her come-out ball. She had already been informally introduced to society, and so naturally there were many among the guests with whom she was already acquainted. This particular function was different, however, for she was to be the object of attention.

As she stood with her uncle and aunt at the head of the stairs, receiving the guests, she could at least reassure herself that she looked her best. Her coiffure had been carefully done, taking advantage of the natural wave in her chestnut hair so that wisps of curls softened her brow. The gown that her aunt had ordered for her was ravishing, all lace and seed pearls on pale blue, and showed off her slender figure admirably. Her grandfather had sent down the string of pearls that had once belonged to her grandmother, with a note urging her to wear the glowing, translucent necklace at her come-out ball, along with the expressed wish that he might see her on her grand night. Belle heartily wished that her grandfather had been in attendance, for she felt that she needed the support of Sir Marcus's bracing personality.

Belle smiled and replied graciously to all the greetings made to her, hardly recalling what it was that she said to anyone. She was all too aware of her aunt's occasional glance and considering expression throughout the interval, and she hoped that she was doing all that was considered proper. If she made any missteps, she was not aware of them.

Belle was relieved when she saw Lord and Lady Moorehead coming up the stairs with Miss Moorehead just behind them. Belle greeted the Mooreheads with all the reserved familiarity owed to those with whom she was well acquainted.

Lady Moorehead smiled and said, "Well! Your aunt must be very proud of you this evening, Belle. You show to great advantage."

"I truly hope so, my lady," said Belle in all sincerity.

"Indeed, Mr. Weatherstone and I are vastly pleased with

Belle," said Mrs. Weatherstone, smiling, extending her own hand to Lord and Lady Moorehead and drawing them forward.

As her aunt and uncle spoke a few moments with the Mooreheads, Belle was at last free to greet her friend. When she took Miss Moorehead's hand, she whispered, "I am so nervous, Clarice."

"You, Belle?" Clarice's glance was openly skeptical.

"Yes, I!" retorted Belle. At once she felt some of her tension ease. She said fervently, "Oh, thank you, Clarice! I feel ever so much better now."

Her friend giggled and passed on with her parents into the ballroom.

Hidden by the other guests in the receiving line until that moment, Lord Ashdon stepped forward. Meeting the viscount's gaze, Belle's heart bumped painfully. She felt warmth rise in her cheeks and wondered at herself for reacting at the sight of his lordship like little more than a schoolgirl. She had so many admirers, but only in Lord Ashdon's presence did she feel as though she became slightly light-headed. She could not imagine why the viscount should affect her so.

Lord Ashdon was escorting an elegant lady whom Belle had no difficulty in recognizing. Suddenly Belle felt her aunt's fingers grip her elbow and heard her astonished whisper, "Why, it is Lady Ashdon!"

Belle knew that she was highly honored by Lady Ashdon's presence, and if she hadn't known that she was, she would certainly have realized it by her ladyship's gracious yet distinctly condescending smile.

Lady Ashdon offered two fingers in greeting. "Miss Weatherstone."

"My lady," murmured Belle, meeting her ladyship's gaze.

Lady Ashdon nodded to her. Her gray eyes were cold and appraising. "Miss Weatherstone, I am glad to have the opportunity to further our acquaintance."

"And I, my lady," said Belle with a smile.

Lady Ashdon smiled again and moved forward, making her greeting to the Weatherstones. During the stilted exchanges between the Weatherstones and Lady Ashdon, it was revealed by Mrs. Weatherstone that they had been previously acquainted with the viscount.

"Oh?" Lady Ashdon cast a glance toward her son before bending a polite smile on her hostess. "I am quite in the dark, Mrs. Weatherstone. Pray do enlighten me."

"Why, did not Lord Ashdon mention it to you, my lady? We became quite well acquainted with his lordship during his convalescence last year in Bath," said Mrs. Weatherstone with a smile. "Lord Ashdon and my niece often spoke together in the Pump Room."

"Indeed," murmured Lady Ashdon. She said all that was proper, with a great deal more warmth than before, and paused a few steps away to await her son.

Lord Ashdon bowed over Belle's hand, and as he straightened, his eyes gleamed with amusement. He said quietly, "My mother is a veritable dragon, you know."

Belle started to laugh, but quickly changed it to a cough. "I scarcely know how to reply to that, my lord."

He grinned down at her and said, "Damned to perdition whatever you say, Miss Weatherstone?"

"Something of the sort," agreed Belle, with a lurking smile. "Though I do not think that I would phrase it just so."

Lord Ashdon chuckled. "Naturally not. Pray keep a dance open for me, Miss Weatherstone," he said.

"I shall certainly do so, my lord," said Belle. She watched as Lord Ashdon joined his mother and moved on to make way for other guests still arriving.

"Very well done, Belle," said Mrs. Weatherstone approvingly. "I do believe that you accredited yourself well in Lady Ashdon's eyes."

"I hope so, Aunt," said Belle, and turned to the next guest coming up the stairs.

As Lord Ashdon escorted his mother into the ballroom, Lady Ashdon said, "You first met the Weatherstones in Bath. How interesting, to be sure."

Instantly, Lord Ashdon realized what had happened. He pretended an indifference he did not actually feel. "Is it?" It was unfortunate that his previous acquaintance with Miss Weatherstone had come out so soon. He could see that his mother had made the obvious connection to his announced intention to see his bride in Bath. If there was one thing he did not need, it was Lady Ashdon making his tentative attempt at a courtship very much her business.

"I am completely reconciled to coming this evening. Suddenly I find myself very much interested in furthering my own acquaintance with Miss Weatherstone and her delightful guardians," said Lady Ashdon.

Lord Ashdon acknowledged an acquaintance who hailed him with a wave, but he did not pause in his leisurely escort of his mother around the periphery of the colonnaded ballroom. "Pray do not leap to conclusions, ma'am. Unsupported assumptions often fail to live up to expectation," he said quietly.

"Quite true, Adam. One must never pin one's hopes on imaginations. Miss Weatherstone is, however, obviously quite important to you," said Lady Ashdon.

They stopped in their progress to speak for a moment or two to others who were known to them both. Lord Ashdon accepted the welcoming words of those who recalled him from years past and who now pronounced themselves very well satisfied to see him once again in England.

"As am I," said Lady Ashdon to one of these. "I am confident that Ashdon will perform his duty at last and settle down with some worthy young lady."

"Oh, to be sure, to be sure," said their acquaintance, sliding a curious glance toward the viscount's amiable countenance. "Is the fortunate young lady someone with whom we might be acquainted?"

"As to that, I really could not say," said Lady Ashdon, bestowing her cool smile along with a significant nod.

Lord Ashdon could only smile over gritted teeth, as the obvious connection was made, based on his presence at a debutante's come-out ball. "The Weatherstones kindly included me in their invitation to my mother when they realized I was residing with her ladyship," he said hastily.

"Of course, dear boy. Nothing could be more natural," said their acquaintance. The conversation politely moved on to other topics, to Lord Ashdon's relief.

By the time Lord Ashdon resumed their promenade about the ballroom, he had had a few moments in which to formulate a strategy that might serve to throw a bit of dust into his parent's eyes, so that her ladyship would not be further tempted to imply a possible connection between himself and Miss Weatherstone. He had no desire to make of himself and Miss Weatherstone an object of public interest.

"Miss Weatherstone is not the only young lady whom I have honored with my attentions, my lady," he remarked.

As Lord Ashdon had hoped, Lady Ashdon's attention was firmly attached. Her gaze fixed upon his face. "What are you saying, Adam?"

"Only that I have done as you bade me, ma'am," he responded lightly. "I am widening my circle of acquaintances. For instance, earlier this week I attended a soiree hosted by Peter Crocker and his wife. Do you know them?"

"Crocker . . . no, I can't say that I do," said Lady Ashdon. She had stopped in her tracks and was plying her fan in a leisurely fashion that did not fool her son for a moment. Lord Ashdon knew that she was intensely curious. "Just what are you hinting at, Adam?"

"Why, you must certainly make their acquaintance, too, Mother," said Lord Ashdon. He paused a moment as he slanted a tantalizing smile at his astonished parent. "You see, I met Mrs. Crocker's younger sister at Almack's. Mrs. Crocker is sponsoring Miss Fairchilde this Season. Miss Fairchilde is not a great beauty, nor has she an immense portion, but she is gently bred."

Lady Ashdon was fairly gaping up at him. "Well! I must say that you have surprised me not a little, Adam. You have been industrious since our talk, have you not?"

"I am nothing if not a good soldier, ma'am," said Lord Ashdon. At his mother's questioning expression, he smiled. "I am reconnoitering the ground."

"Really, Adam!" Lady Ashdon snapped her fan shut. "What an absurd comparison. Reconnoitering, indeed!" She took his arm again. "But I shall not scold you, for I am very well satisfied with what you have imparted to me. I am glad that you have finally come to your senses and are taking your duty to heart at last."

"Then I am happy, ma'am," said Lord Ashdon, lifting his mother's hand to his lips and brushing a kiss across her gloved knuckles.

Lady Ashdon smiled, rather warmly by her standards. She was quiet for a moment, then her eyebrows rose as she inquired, "Are there any other young ladies, besides Miss Weatherstone and Miss Fairchilde, who have caught your eye?"

"Not at present," said Lord Ashdon quite truthfully. He was relieved, for it appeared that his little stratagem was serving him well, at least for the moment. Lady Ashdon's focus had been successfully deflected from its primary target, which had been Miss Weatherstone, to a broader spectrum, and that suited him perfectly.

"I believe you are correct, Adam. I must certainly make it my object to become acquainted with the Crockers," said Lady Ashdon decisively. "By the by, have you been introduced to the Moorehead girl, Miss Clarice Moorehead? She is the younger daughter and is very well favored, being an heiress as well as something of a beauty. It's a pity that she is a redhead, but one should not be too judgmental, should one?"

"No, I have not had that pleasure," said Lord Ashdon, his satisfaction dimming slightly as he realized that his little subterfuge had also strengthened Lady Ashdon's original determination to bring every respectable marriageable miss to his attention.

"Then I shall do the honors this very moment, for there are Lord Moorehead and his lady now, and that is Miss Moorehead sitting beside them," said Lady Ashdon with satisfaction. "They are not particular acquaintances of mine, of course, but that scarcely matters in this instance."

Lord Ashdon groaned inwardly, but nothing of his annoyance appeared in his face as he reluctantly accompanied his mother over to the Mooreheads.

It was thirty minutes after Lord Ashdon's arrival before Mrs. Weatherstone deemed there to have been sufficient time for receiving all those who intended to come. Belle was relieved to be done with her duty at last and readily acceded to her aunt's suggestion that it was time to leave the stairs. Mr. Weatherstone escorted his spouse and Belle into the ballroom to join their guests.

Belle was at once besieged by gentlemen who wished to sign her dance card. It was a heady feeling to be so sought after, but really there was just one gentleman that she hoped to dance with, and that was Lord Ashdon. She glanced casually about as she conversed with her admirers, at last locating his lordship across the ballroom. He was bowing to her friend Clarice, obviously soliciting her for the set.

Belle felt an unreasonable spurt of jealousy, for which she was instantly repentant. Of course Lord Ashdon would dance with others besides herself, and there was scarcely anyone whom she would consider more worthy of his lordship's attentions than her dear friend Clarice. Nevertheless, Belle, rather guiltily, felt that she would have been glad if Clarice had stumbled and torn the lace at her hem, necessitating a quick withdrawal to the sewing room.

She did not have long to think about it, however, as she was immediately whisked onto the dance floor and had no more than fleeting moments of opportunity to look for Lord Ashdon, since not one set went by that her hand was not bespoken. Then, all at once, it seemed, it was Lord Ashdon who was holding out his hand to her and requesting the honor of a dance. He looked down at her with his easy smile, his eyes crinkling at the corners as he gazed at her with an expression of admiration and good nature. Belle's heart gave a leap of happiness. "I would be most honored, my lord."

As she rose from her chair and took her place beside Lord Ashdon in the set, her whole being steadied, and nothing since her arrival in London seemed quite as gratifying as her come-out ball.

Chapter 9

Through the ensuing days, Belle became increasingly popular, and she was much admired and courted. There were invitations for every hour of each day, it seemed to her. She was actually somewhat dazed by the attention she was garnering, while her aunt appeared extremely gratified.

"It shan't be long, my dear Belle, before we are making plans for a wedding," said Mrs. Weatherstone with immense satisfaction. "I haven't been able to usher Cassandra through a successful Season, but certainly yours is making up for it in every respect."

"I hope so, Aunt," murmured Belle, not certain what she should think about her undoubted success. On the one hand, she was glad to have achieved what she had hoped to in coming to London. She had certainly expanded her circle of acquaintances and her worldly experience beyond what she could ever have thought or imagined. She had truly been blessed in that respect.

Increasingly, Belle heard herself referred to as the Belle of London. Everywhere she went, she received accolades from admirers. It seemed that she could do no wrong. Her uncle received two offers for her hand that month, but turned them both down on Belle's behalf. In Mr. Weatherstone's opinion, the gentlemen were not worthy of his niece.

Belle was relieved that she had her uncle to take care of her interests. Her ambitions had become strangely hazy. She had always known exactly what she wanted, but now she could not have told her friends or her aunt and uncle what hopes she harbored in her heart.

She had always aspired to be presented to Society, to see something more of the world than her own small corner, and her longing had been fulfilled beyond her wildest dreams. Now that that goal had been achieved, Belle questioned her own heart. Since she had no notion what else she could possibly desire, the future now seemed rather flat. In fact, a feeling that she was being squeezed and closed in was becoming increasingly familiar. Only when she was off for a ride on her gelding did the cobwebs seem to blow away from her mind so that she felt completely alive again. Belle was intelligent enough to realize that the rigidly structured life that her aunt had engineered for her was almost too confining for someone with her restless energy.

Once the Season was over, Belle supposed, she would return to her childhood home, the Hall, but that did not seem to be a particularly inviting outcome. She did not think that she could be content for the remainder of her life living quietly in the country with her grandfather after having tasted the broader society of London and its treats, but she did not know what else she wanted to do.

Her aunt obviously wished to find her a good match and establish her credibly. Perhaps that was as good an outcome as any, Belle thought. She certainly had enough admirers to choose from. Yet none of them had ignited the least bit of interest in her. She paused in her reflections, smiling a little as she acknowledged the truth. That is, she had had no interest in anyone until Lord Ashdon had appeared on the scene.

Upon their first meeting, Belle had felt her heart give a small bump. His handsome, scarred face, the warmth in his sunlit blue eyes, and his easy smile had all made an unforgettable impression. Later, when she had opportunity to observe the viscount on the social scene, she thought privately that there was not another gentleman in London who could compare to him. His lordship's wide shoulders and large, solid chest were set off admirably by his military-cut coats; his muscular legs were well defined, and there was no need of padding for his calves. His boot size was somewhat small for a man, and Belle had noticed how very quick he was on his feet. His stocky build gave an overall impression of manly vigor and strength.

Belle found that she was not the only lady who bestowed her approval on the viscount. One evening when she made some passing remark, Clarice Moorehead and Millicent Carruthers both agreed that his lordship was very handsome.

"Though I do wonder about his temper," said Clarice, cocking her head as she studied the gentleman in question. "He has a very firm mouth. One might say it even has an obstinate appearance."

"Oh, I don't know," said Belle, defending him. "I rather like the way that he smiles. It begins in his eyes and then springs forth."

"I do believe that you are smitten," said Millicent teasingly.

Belle gave her friend a speaking glance but did not answer. It would have been an untruth to say that she was indifferent to the viscount, but she was not prepared to announce that she had warmer feelings toward him, either. She actually did not know what she felt. She had never before felt anything near the turmoil of emotions that Lord Ashdon seemed to inspire in her.

While Clarice and Millicent conversed, Belle puzzled over her relationship with Lord Ashdon. She naturally saw him frequently at various social functions, and he had been particularly friendly with her since her come-out ball, which she was glad of. He always made a point of coming up to her to exchange a few polite words.

Belle regretted that there was rarely time at the crowded gatherings for her to converse at any great length with him.

In any event, she thought, even if there had been time, it wouldn't do. She was very aware that she could not show partiality to any of her admirers. Her aunt had drummed into her head the dangers of appearing fast or of gaining a coquettish reputation. Her social success could be extinguished with a single thoughtless act. She had to be a pattern-card of respectability, just like her twin sister, Cassandra, if she was to attain the pinnacle of success that Mrs. Weatherstone had mapped out for her.

Lord Ashdon and his cousin Mr. Roland White approached the trio of ladies. After the initial civilities, Roland said, "I say, Ashdon has had the most inspired thought. He has suggested a riding party at the park, to finish up at Gunther's for ices. How does that sound?"

"Why, it is a delightful notion," exclaimed Belle immediately, including the viscount in her smiling glance. His lordship's eyes met hers, and she felt a flutter in her breast.

"Indeed, I should like it above all things," said Clarice, smiling.

"I am not a very good rider, and I do not have a horse, but I should like very much to make one of the party," said Millicent shyly and rather wistfully.

"Do not worry, Miss Carruthers," said Angus Moorehead, who had come up in time to hear what was said. He smiled down at her, a gleam in his bright blue eyes. "If you do not have a suitable mount, I am certain that we shall be able to find you a gentle one from my father's stable."

"Of course we shall, Millicent," said Clarice at once. "We would not leave you behind."

"Good. Then it is in a fair way to being settled," said Lord Ashdon with his friendly smile. "Shall we say Wednesday at three o'clock in the park?"

All agreed to it, Belle with scarcely any attempt at hiding her enthusiasm. She knew that her aunt would have wished her to show some restraint, as a proper young lady would have done, but at that moment she did not care overmuch. She loved to ride, and the chance to ride with her friends—in particular the viscount—was too wonderful to pretend polite indifference.

Since their first unlikely meeting, she had chanced to meet Lord Ashdon a handful more times in the park during her morning rides. Those encounters had been some of the most enjoyable hours that she had experienced in London. Naturally, after her aunt's upset at discovering that she had dispensed with escort the first time, she had always been accompanied by a groom on her rides. The servant's presence had restrained the conversation between herself and Lord Ashdon to mostly the commonplace, for it would not have done to speak so openly or freely as she had wished they could have in the groom's hearing. Nevertheless, she had thoroughly enjoyed Lord Ashdon's company and his ready sense of humor. It would be very nice indeed to share his company again on an equestrian outing, even if it was in a full party.

While a lively conversation took place around them, Lord Ashdon asked quietly, "Does the outing truly meet with your approval, Miss Weatherstone?"

"Of course it does, my lord. You must know that I enjoy being horseback more than most," said Belle quickly.

"Yes, I have cause to know," said Lord Ashdon, even more quietly but with warmth in his eyes.

As Belle met Lord Ashdon's gaze, and realized that he was referring to their handful of rides together, she thought, as she had more than once, that he had deliberately limited the number of times that he met her in the park, in order to safeguard their reputations. She was grateful to him, of course, but, perversely, she wished that just once he would throw caution to the winds and seek her out with the dash and lack of convention that had attended their first meeting. How positively exciting that had been! She had never forgotten that race, pounding over the green with the thunder of his horse's hooves in her ears! And neither had she forgotten the manner in which her heart had hammered with excitement.

The conversation had turned and Belle began to listen, with increasing interest. There was to be a dinner party at Vauxhall Gardens, sponsored by Lady Moorehead.

"Everyone here is to be invited, of course, for it is to be only for Angus's and my own select group of friends," said Clarice. "Mama sent out the invitations just yesterday afternoon."

Belle was at once enthusiastic about the treat. "Oh, how very amusing it will be! I have heard of Vauxhall, and it sounds marvelously entertaining."

Sensing hesitation from one member of their circle, Clarice turned toward the viscount. "You will be able to make one of our party, will you not, my lord?"

Lord Ashdon demurred quietly. "I don't know, Miss Moorehead. It seems that you have included me very kindly out of civility, for I am of new acquaintance to you all. Perhaps it would be best if I should thank you graciously but decline."

"Nonsense, my lord. You have become a fast friend to us all since your return to England," said Angus.

"It would not be the same without you, Ashdon," said Roland White, slapping his cousin on a broad shoulder.

"Indeed, my lord, I would take it as a personal affront if you were to stay away," said Clarice with a persuasive smile.

Belle held her breath, for she was dismayed that Lord Ashdon would even consider withdrawing from the party. It would be as though he believed that there was a gulf of distance between himself and those whom she counted to be her best friends in the world. It had never occurred to her that he might think so, but she supposed that he might actually see it that way, since he was a few years older than any of them and had been a soldier who had escaped death, besides. She and the others must appear to be babies in his eyes, amusing but not terribly experienced in life. How boring they—she—must be to him at times, Belle thought with dismay. An unusual sense of insecurity touched her, making her wonder what Lord Ashdon really, truly thought about her.

When Lord Ashdon answered, his eyes were on Belle's face. "Then I would be delighted to be one of the party, Miss Moorehead."

"Very good, my lord!" exclaimed Angus.

Later, after the Weatherstones had returned home, Belle broached the subject of the outing to Vauxhall to her aunt and uncle. Mr. Weatherstone looked at his wife, raising his eyebrows. Mrs. Weatherstone frowned over what had been imparted to her with such enthusiasm, and suddenly Belle realized that her aunt's expression was not one of approbation.

"Oh, pray say that we may go, Aunt!" she exclaimed. "It will be a party of all my most particular friends."

Mrs. Weatherstone shook her head, a tiny frown between her brows. "Belle, I am somewhat hesitant to grant my permission for you to attend. It is not quite what I like."

"Vauxhall is not as select as it once was," remarked Mr. Weatherstone.

Belle had been sorting quickly through the invitations and had located the one that she had sought. "Only see, Aunt Margaret! The invitation came from Lady Moorehead. There surely cannot be any stigma attaching to it if her ladyship is involved," she said, holding out the gilt invitation for inspection.

With a sigh of resignation, Mrs. Weatherstone extended her hand for the invitation. "Very well, Belle. Let me see it."

Mr. Weatherstone suddenly chuckled as he saw the expression on his niece's face, while her anxious eyes were riveted upon her aunt. "You might as well give in, my dear. You will never hear the end of it otherwise."

"Well, perhaps I shall take it up with Lady Moorehead when I call on her later in the week," said Mrs. Weatherstone.

Belle threw her arms around her aunt. "Thank you, Aunt!"

"Belle, I haven't yet said that you might go," admonished Mrs. Weatherstone.

"Oh, I know, Aunt!" said Belle, with a quick smile at her aunt. "But you have promised to consider it, and that is enough for the moment."

Mr. Weatherstone coughed suddenly, and when his wife looked over at him, he turned his gaze to the ceiling as though he found something of considerable interest in the decorative trim there. "Perhaps a strategic retreat would be in order," he murmured.

"Yes," agreed Mrs. Weatherstone, with a smile of her own. "Belle, I am going to bed. We shall discuss this again tomorrow."

"Very well, Aunt."

Chapter 10

G ood as her word, Mrs. Weatherstone did broach the subject of the dinner party with Lady Moorehead, expressing her concerns delicately. "I am naturally quite comfortable
with any party that you may get up, my lady. But forgive me!
I must be honest with you and express my concerns that it is
to be at Vauxhall."

Lady Moorehead nodded. "I perfectly understand, Mrs.
Weatherstone. I, too, harbor a certain bias against entertainments at Vauxhall Gardens. It is not as select as it used to be,
nor as refined."

Mrs. Weatherstone smiled, a hint of relief on her face that
she had not given offense. "Indeed, a perfect example is this
masquerade that is being held there next week."

"Yes, and I so wished to go," sighed Clarice Moorehead.

"I have never been to a masquerade," said Belle speculatively.

"And you never shall," said Mrs. Weatherstone quickly, turning a stern glance on her niece.

Lady Moorehead laughed indulgently. "You mustn't be too
harsh with Belle, Mrs. Weatherstone. I suspect that all the
young ladies are struck by the allure of such a fast function.
Clarice begged and begged us to be allowed to attend the masquerade. She was quite astonished that we refused our permission. Well, you can certainly perceive why."

"Quite," Mrs. Weatherstone agreed. "It is just the sort of

amusement at which one does not wish one's charge to be seen."

"Do you mean that it is bad *ton*, Aunt Margaret?" asked Belle curiously. She did not understand why something that sounded so harmless as a company dressed in masks and costumes should be frowned on. It sounded rather amusing to her.

"Exactly so, Belle," said Mrs. Weatherstone. "All sorts of riffraff attend those public gatherings. It is not at all the sort of crowd to which I would wish you to be exposed."

"Oh," said Belle, disappointed but still curious. The thought that crossed her mind was that of all the functions she had been invited to, none had sounded quite so entertaining as the masquerade. She did not voice her opinion, however, well knowing that her aunt would be scandalized. She contented herself with a mild protest. "Such a pity, for I think that I should like to see something more of the city than I have."

"You sound very much like Clarice, who never tires of new entertainments," said Lady Moorehead, shaking her head. "Ah, youth! Believe me, my dears, you would not do well by your reputations if you were to attend a public masquerade and it was found out."

"I should leave before the unmasking," declared Clarice, tossing her head so that her curls bounced.

Belle smiled, catching her friend's lively gaze. "Yes, and so should I," she agreed. "If we never took off our masks, I quite fail to see how our reputations might suffer."

Clarice cocked her head, a thoughtful expression on her face. "That is quite true."

"We must think not only of your reputations but also of your safety," said Mrs. Weatherstone. Though she addressed herself to her niece, her glance encompassed Clarice as well. "I am anxious that you understand this, Belle. One simply does not know who might be attending a public masquerade. It is best not to place oneself in a position that could easily become rather uncomfortable."

"I couldn't agree with you more, Mrs. Weatherstone. However, knowing how disappointed Clarice was that she was not to be allowed to go to the masquerade at Vauxhall, and not wishing to see her so cast down, I came up with this alternative scheme," said Lady Moorehead. "It is not to be a party made up solely of young gentlemen, you know. I did not think that would be at all proper."

"Quite," said Mrs. Weatherstone, beginning to look more hopeful.

"Mama is inviting only our most particular friends," said Clarice.

"Indeed, it will be much more in the nature of a friendly gathering," said Lady Moorehead, nodding. "It will be Mr. and Mrs. Carruthers, with Miss Carruthers, Mr. Roland White, Lord Ashdon, and yourselves. Of course, Lord Moorehead and I shall host the gathering, and I have persuaded Angus that he is to come so that the numbers will be even. I thought that would be a large enough party to be entertaining, yet there would also be ample supervision of the young people."

"Well! You have quite persuaded me," said Mrs. Weatherstone with a smile. "I have no other concerns. A simple dinner at a box in Vauxhall Gardens will be eminently suitable."

"Oh, thank you, Aunt!" exclaimed Belle.

Lady Moorehead chuckled. "I perceive that you are as easily pleased as my own miss. Well, it will be a very good dinner party, I think."

"Lady Moorehead, I am curious on one point," said Mrs. Weatherstone. She glanced at her niece and Miss Moorehead, who had put their heads together and were talking animatedly. She lowered her voice. "How is it that you have invited Lord Ashdon to what is essentially a private party?"

Though Belle was exchanging confidences with Miss Moorehead, nevertheless her ears caught the viscount's name, and she instantly tuned in to her aunt's conversation as well.

"Does it seem odd to you, Mrs. Weatherstone? It is easily

explained. Roland White has been a particular friend of Angus's for ages, and since Lord Ashdon is Roland's cousin, I thought that I would include his lordship in the invitation. Lord Ashdon appears to get along so well with the younger gentlemen, and with our daughter and your niece," said Lady Moorehead.

"Quite true," said Mrs. Weatherstone with a nod. She casually moved on to another topic, and Belle lost interest in the conversation.

It was several minutes later that Mrs. Weatherstone and Belle took their leave of the Mooreheads. As they were driving back to the town house, Mrs. Weatherstone suddenly referred to the dinner invitation to Vauxhall Gardens. "I am glad that we have accepted the Mooreheads' invitation, Belle."

"Why, so am I, Aunt," said Belle. "I am always glad to spend time in Clarice's company."

Mrs. Weatherstone slid a speculative glance at her. "And Lord Ashdon's company, too?"

Belle was startled. She felt the slightest warmth mount into her cheeks, but she strove for a casual tone to cover her astonishment at the blunt question. "Of course, Aunt. I find his lordship's company very pleasing, as I am certain everyone does."

Mrs. Weatherstone gave a distinct sniff. "Just so, dear Belle! This easy explanation of the viscount's relationship to Mr. White and how agreeable his lordship makes himself! Really, I begin to suspect that Lady Moorehead has her eye on his lordship."

"What can you mean, Aunt?" asked Belle, quite taken aback.

"Why, it is certainly plain enough to anyone with wit. Lady Moorehead hopes to promote a match between her daughter and Lord Ashdon," said Mrs. Weatherstone roundly.

"Does she?" said Belle, a sinking feeling in her stomach. She suddenly recalled that Clarice had confided she had a new beau but had refused to reveal the gentleman's name. "I did not know."

Mrs. Weatherstone gave a small laugh. "No, how should you? You are too inexperienced to catch these little nuances. It would be quite unexceptional to include an unmarried gentleman who was related to one's family to a small, select dinner such as this, or a close family friend. Lord Ashdon is neither. His lordship's only entrée is his relationship to Mr. White, who is undisputedly a friend of the family. Therefore I am fairly confident that Lady Moorehead harbors hopes of promoting a match in that direction."

"I see." Belle managed to drum up a smile. "Well! I had no notion that such scheming was going on."

"Oh, it happens all the time. The Season is one big brew of plots and schemes and subterfuges to land the most eligible matches possible," said Mrs. Weatherstone.

"Aunt Margaret, are you plotting on my behalf?" asked Belle quietly.

Mrs. Weatherstone looked quickly, sharply, at her niece. The faintest tinge of color rose in her face. "Why, Belle, what a question! Of course I am not . . . *plotting!* I merely think it a very good thing that we are going to this dinner. And I wish you to wear that new gold gown to it, too; it will be perfect for the occasion, and you look so lovely in it." She reached out and patted her niece's clasped hands. "You will turn a few heads with it, I assure you."

"Then I shall certainly wear it, Aunt," said Belle promptly, as the smiling face of a certain gentleman came to her mind.

That afternoon Belle went riding with her friends. It was the party that Lord Ashdon had suggested. Belle was very aware of the viscount. If she was not speaking with him, she was listening to him and watching him. Most particularly, she was interested in the byplay between Lord Ashdon and her friend Clarice Moorehead. Once the notion had been put into her head, Belle could not shake it. She studied Clarice, wondering if her friend actually was smitten with Lord Ashdon, and if Lady Moorehead really was scheming to see her daugh-

ter a viscountess. Clarice was riding between Lord Ashdon and
Roland White, conversing animatedly with both, and her occasional laughter floated back to Belle.

Belle could not see that Clarice favored Lord Ashdon over
Roland White or, indeed, over her own brother. She glanced
sideways at the riders who kept her company. Of course, Angus
Moorehead had eyes only for Millicent Carruthers.

Belle looked again, blinking in astonishment. She was
stunned at the way that Angus and Millicent were staring into
one another's eyes as they exchanged pleasantries.

"Why, I never even noticed!" she exclaimed.

"What did you never notice, Miss Weatherstone?"

Belle turned sharply in her saddle. Lord Ashdon had come
up on his mount on her other side without its even registering
upon her. "What?"

A blush suddenly rose in her face as she realized that he
had overheard her. She could hardly explain what she had been
thinking that had led to her stunning revelation about Angus
and Millicent. "Oh! Wh-why, only see how bright the flowers
are today, my lord!" she stammered, gesturing with her whip
toward a long bed of late-spring blossoms nodding in the
breeze.

Lord Ashdon glanced in the direction she was pointing and
then looked back at her. There was a smile on his face, and
his blue eyes were warm in expression. "Yes, they are beautiful, as beautiful as those in Bath."

"In Bath?" said Belle, still a little off balance. She stole another glance sideways at the couple, whose horses were beginning to drift a little ways behind. "You are familiar with
Bath, then?"

Lord Ashdon laughed, a lift of surprise in his voice. "Of
course! I convalesced there for the better part of a year."

Belle recalled that her aunt had mentioned becoming acquainted with the viscount in Bath. His lordship had conversed
a few times with her sister, but Cassandra had not been so

struck by her passing acquaintance with Lord Ashdon that she had ever written a word about him. Looking at Lord Ashdon now, Belle could not imagine its being so. She flashed a smile. "Oh, yes! Of course. I had forgotten."

A small frown pulled Lord Ashdon's brows close over his well-formed nose. There was a puzzled expression in his eyes. "I see."

Belle felt that something more was expected of her. She wondered why the viscount was looking at her so oddly. "I suppose you have a wide acquaintance in Bath. Do you plan to journey there again?"

"I had thought to go down a few weeks ago, but then I—" Lord Ashdon shifted in his saddle, making the well-oiled leather creak. His gaze was focused entirely on her face. "I do not understand your meaning, Miss Weatherstone. Have I offended you in some fashion?"

"No, of course not!" said Belle quickly, completely taken aback. She was startled by the intensity and sharpness of his gaze.

Ahead of them, Roland White turned in his saddle, placing one hand on the broad rump of his mount. "Ashdon! I say, Ashdon, Miss Moorehead has expressed her desire to go to Gunther's. What say the rest of you?"

Lord Ashdon straightened and made an appropriate reply. His gaze necessarily left Belle's face, for which she was grateful. She had never felt the least bit uncomfortable in the viscount's presence before, but just for a moment she thought she had seen a flash of inexplicable anger pass over his countenance. It startled her, for she had never seen anything other than an amiable, smiling expression on his lordship's face. She did not know what to make of it or what to attribute it to. For the life of her, Belle could not imagine why the viscount had thought he had offended her. Nor how she had come to offend him to the point of anger.

Angus and Millicent rejoined the rest of the party, and the

equestrians set out for Gunther's. The famous sweet shop enjoyed a large patronage, and when the party arrived, they found others of their acquaintance already there.

While it was not patently obvious to everyone, it gradually dawned on Belle that she was not enjoying as much conversation with Lord Ashdon as she usually had. As she began to watch him, she became vaguely disturbed. If she had not known better, it would have seemed to her that he was deliberately avoiding her, by either word or glance. His attentions toward her were markedly absent.

She could not understand it. From the first, Lord Ashdon had been one of her most persistent suitors, and now he had withdrawn as though she had become some mere acquaintance. Surely it was her overactive imagination, she assured herself. It was simply that the viscount was too civil to ignore the claims that others had on his attention.

Despite all of her inner reassurances, however, Belle could not shake the odd feeling that she had somehow lost the viscount's regard. As the party left Gunther's and the ladies were accompanied by their escorts to their various domiciles, Belle felt that, for her, the ride had fallen sadly flat.

Chapter 11

Vauxhall Gardens instantly earned Belle's approval. She delighted in the long avenues of towering trees. There were fountains and cascades along the winding paths and Mr. Roubiliac's fine statue of Handel to admire before the company retired to one of the small supper boxes arranged in the leafy arbors.

The light supper was sumptuous, consisting of roasted game hens, fresh peas, Spanish onions, fruit and cheese, custards, syllabubs laced with wine, and arrack punch. Lady Moorehead confided to Mrs. Weatherstone and Mrs. Carruthers that she had had her own cook prepare the roasted game hens and then had brought them to Vauxhall in a basket. "None of that nasty powdered beef for my guests," she declared. Her ladyship was rewarded with praise from her guests, especially the gentlemen, for her thoughtfulness.

The orchestra played continuously in the pavilion, and there was dancing in the adjoining area that was bordered by the several wooden dinner boxes. The wind rustled the leaves in the tops of the trees overhead, while torchlight rivaled the gleam of stars in a darkening sky.

Belle thought the box that the Mooreheads had hired for the evening was very comfortable. The chairs were well upholstered, and the table furnishings were tastefully done. Of course, Lady Moorehead had left nothing to chance, and had in fact imported her own servants and tableware.

Belle felt that she had nothing to complain of either in her surroundings or in the company. Everyone appeared to be in the best of spirits. Indeed, she was amazed by how much at ease her uncle and aunt were in this particular company. Of course, Lord and Lady Moorehead were excellent hosts, making certain that no one was without refreshment or a partner for conversation.

When Belle observed the occupants in some of the other dinner boxes, she could well understand why her aunt might question the wisdom of a party at Vauxhall Gardens. Some appeared a trifle overbold in their loud conversation and indulged in raucous laughter. Probably an excessive flow of wine could be blamed, she thought.

She simply shrugged it off. She was not one who easily took offense or allowed something that had nothing to do with her to spoil her evening.

The only thing that really marred the enjoyment of the evening for her was Clarice's whispered confidence: "It is the strangest thing, Belle! Roland told me that Lord Ashdon had expressed a wish that he had not committed himself to our party."

Belle glanced quickly in Lord Ashdon's direction, to assure herself that he was still in conversation with Lord and Lady Moorehead and could not possibly overhear himself being talked about.

"Did-did Lord Ashdon tell Roland why?" asked Belle, her heart beginning to beat rather fast. Surely the viscount's about-face had nothing to do with her. He had not called at the town house that week, but that meant nothing, of course. Lord Ashdon naturally had many commitments. She couldn't expect him to continue to dance attendance on her as he had all of the Season so far.

Clarice frowned, tapping her chin with the point of her gilt-edged fan. "Roland was not certain, but he says he suspects it has something to do with Lady Ashdon."

"Lady Ashdon?" asked Belle, looking at her friend in perplexity. "Why, how could it?"

Clarice shrugged, then a dimpled smile appeared on her face. "Well, Roland hinted that Lady Ashdon considers each of us—you, me, and Millicent—eminently suitable as a match for Lord Ashdon. Roland thinks that his lordly cousin is wanting to put distance between himself and all of us. So he would have preferred not coming tonight, but naturally, since he had already committed himself to my mother, he couldn't very well not come!"

Belle felt a sense of relief flood through her. Was that it? Was that why Lord Ashdon had behaved so strangely the other day during the riding outing and had not been to call on her that week? He was distant this evening, too, she reflected, exchanging pleasantries but not actually joining in with their funning as he had done. She missed his smile, the one that began in his eyes before it came full-blown to his face. That was not to say that Lord Ashdon had not smiled all evening, but it was not accompanied by that same degree of warmth that Belle was used to seeing in his gaze.

Only once, when she had taken off her cloak and glanced up to meet Lord Ashdon's eyes as he looked at her, had she seen a flare of heat in his expression.

"You look lovely this evening," he had said, bowing over her gloved hand as he greeted her.

Belle's pulse had jumped in her throat. She knew that it was her gown, the shimmering gold gown she wore, that had elicited that scorching glance. She had murmured something, hoping that the viscount would remain beside her to talk. But he had not. After a short moment of exchanging pleasantries with her aunt and uncle, Lord Ashdon had excused himself to converse with others, and he had not really addressed a personal word to Belle since.

"I suppose that must explain it, then," she remarked.

"What?" asked Clarice.

Belle glanced at her friend, and then for no accountable reason felt herself blushing. "Oh, I was just thinking that Lord Ashdon does not seem quite his usual amiable self."

Clarice frowned slightly. "Why, yes, I quite take your meaning. He has hardly spoken to you or me or Millicent all evening. He has been talking forever to everyone else. How very rude of his lordship, to be sure! I shall see to it that we are no longer so ignominiously ignored."

"Clarice!" Belle hissed, but her friend was already walking away, with a backward glance full of mischief.

Whatever Clarice said to Lord Ashdon in her laughing way made the difference. Afterward, Belle was gratified when the viscount actually came over to address a few pleasantries to her. Of course, she couldn't very well believe that he had fallen back into his former easy way with her, when he excused himself after only a few minutes and moved away to speak with Millicent and Angus.

Her aunt, on the other hand, was eminently satisfied by his lordship's attentions. "I do believe that Lord Ashdon is quite taken with you, Belle," remarked Mrs. Weatherstone quietly.

"Oh, Aunt! I hardly think so. He is equally attentive to Clarice and Millicent," said Belle.

"Yes, well, his lordship is nothing if not civil," said Mrs. Weatherstone.

"Lord Ashdon is much like what I should wish for you, Belle," said Mr. Weatherstone in a low voice, his gaze having followed the viscount.

Belle's face flamed. "Really, Uncle, I don't think that—"

"Phineas, this is not the time nor the place," said Mrs. Weatherstone quickly.

"You are right, of course, my dear," said Mr. Weatherstone, with an apologetic cough.

Mr. and Mrs. Weatherstone decided to take a leisurely stroll through the gardens after their supper. Belle waved them off gaily, relieved to have them gone, since it had become obvious that they wished to discuss her possible matrimonial prospects. Besides, it was like a breath of fresh air to be able to relax and be more herself without her aunt's eagle eye always on her.

"Belle! You'll never guess the treat that is in store for us!" exclaimed Millicent, her brown eyes sparkling as she turned toward Belle. She was attired in a leaf-green gown that showed her glowing complexion to advantage, as Angus's admiring glances all evening had proved.

"Tell me, Millicent," urged Belle, smiling at her friend's infectious enthusiasm.

"There is to be a fireworks display!" exclaimed Millicent.

"By all that's famous! It is just what I like," said Roland with enthusiasm. "The bombs bursting in air and all that."

"I wonder how the fireworks are gotten up into the air and timed just right so that they explode overhead," said Angus, his expression thoughtful.

"All I know is that they are simply beautiful," said Clarice. "I don't care how they work."

"Well, I should like to know," said Angus. "I should like to make my own fireworks, wouldn't you, Roland?"

"Wouldn't I just!" exclaimed Roland, his eyes kindling with enthusiasm. "I imagine that they are something like artillery shells. What do you say, Ashdon?"

"If they are anything like artillery shells, Roland, then they are far more unpredictable than you might think," said Lord Ashdon with his easy smile. "It has been my experience that those don't always fly where you want them, but, on the contrary, turn back on the very ones who have set them in the air. And I've seen shells explode before they are ever safely away."

"I forbid any experiments, Angus," said Lord Moorehead, overhearing what to his lordship was the most important part of the conversation.

Angus grinned and shook his head. "Never fear, sir. I have too much respect for my inheritance to wish to blow it up!"

A general laugh was raised by Angus's sally. As the rest of the company continued to discuss the upcoming treat, Belle kept her smile pinned in place, but her heart sank. She had never been to a fireworks display, and if it weren't for that horrid description of Roland's she was certain that she could have looked forward to it with the same anticipation that all the others were. She hoped that he was wrong about the fireworks.

When the display began, Belle was at first thrilled with the brilliant colors and shapes. She was standing with her friends, watching in awe the glittering colors against the night sky. Before long, however, the loud, booming noises that went along with the bursts of color began to set her nerves on edge, and she discovered that she was digging her nails into her palms. She stepped back quietly, separating from the rest of the company, who were standing loosely toward the front of the box, and carefully lowered herself into an empty chair. She was breathing rather fast, and a light sheen of cold moisture had broken out over her body.

At the next explosion overhead, her fingers convulsed on the chair arms. She couldn't help herself. She couldn't control the violent start that she gave at each successive explosion nor her instinctive cringe against the upholstered back of the chair. No matter how often she reassured herself that everything was fine, it made little difference.

Belle was ashamed of her lack of fortitude. Everyone else in the party appeared to be having a marvelous time, laughing and pointing and clapping their approval. Even Lord Ashdon had gotten into the spirit of the evening, shouting "Bravo!" after particularly spectacular explosions.

Belle was positive that at some point her companions would notice her irrational tension, and that would be mortifying. She heartily wished that her aunt and uncle would return, for she wanted nothing more than to go home. She squeezed her eyes shut.

"Miss Weatherstone, are you quite all right?" The question

was spoken quietly, yet it made her jump just as surely as the fireworks did.

Her eyes flew open and she turned her head quickly to meet Lord Ashdon's keen eyes. Instantly a furious blush traveled up into her face. She managed a laugh and said, "Why, whatever can you mean, my lord?"

"You appeared very pale a moment ago. Are you perhaps feeling unwell?" asked Lord Ashdon, a note of concern in his voice.

"No—yes! I-I believe that I have a touch of the headache." Belle stumbled over the falsehood, for she was never ill. She could not admit to her fear of thunderstorms and like noises. It seemed so cowardly to be frightened by a mere fireworks spectacle when everyone around her, her friends and acquaintances, were gasping in delighted awe.

"Is there anything that I can do for you? Perhaps a cold draught of wine would help?" asked Lord Ashdon.

Belle curled her fingers around the chair arms as a particularly loud sequence burst above their heads. "That—that is kind of you, my lord," she managed to say.

As Lord Ashdon was starting to pour the wine, he looked beyond her. "Here are your aunt and uncle, Miss Weatherstone."

Belle closed her eyes again, intensely relieved. Lord Ashdon had risen and stepped over to intercept the Weatherstones. He spoke a few quiet words, which at once brought a hint of anxiety to Mrs. Weatherstone's face.

She hurried over to her niece. "Belle, are you feeling unwell?"

"I should like to go home, Aunt Margaret. Please!" said Belle in a low, urgent voice, not wanting to be overheard by the rest of the company.

Mr. Weatherstone came up in time to hear her desperate plea. "It is the fireworks, Margaret," he commented quietly.

"Of course. I should have guessed." Mrs. Weatherstone nodded. She rested her hand comfortingly on her niece's shoulder. "Yes, Belle, we shall take you home now. Phineas, pray make our excuses to Lord and Lady Moorehead."

Mr. Weatherstone stepped over to speak to their hosts, quietly drawing Lord and Lady Moorehead's attention away from the magnificent display, while Mrs. Weatherstone went to gather their wraps.

Lord Ashdon had stood back politely, allowing the Weatherstones private conversation with their niece. When he saw that they were preparing to leave, he approached again and held out his hand. "Allow me to help you, Miss Weatherstone."

Belle took his hand, grateful for his assistance in helping her to rise to her feet, but at the same time she wished him far elsewhere. She couldn't bear it if he should suspect the true cause of her indisposal. She, who was known for her intrepid riding and her spirited manner, which had done much to earn her the sobriquet the Belle of London!

"Thank you, Lord Ashdon. It is so silly of me, I know. But I shall be better in a trice once I am at home." Belle started at another boom and looked up at the exploding night sky, angry tears coming to her eyes. It was so incredibly beautiful and yet so terrifying.

Still holding her hand, Lord Ashdon felt her shudder. "I shall escort you to your carriage."

"No!" exclaimed Belle, pulling her fingers free. She was instantly sorry for her abrupt thoughtlessness when she saw the expression of surprise in the viscount's face and the way he stiffened beside her. She tried to amend her rudeness, her voice wobbling slightly. "Thank you, but I would prefer that you didn't, my lord."

Mrs. Weatherstone, approaching with their cloaks, froze at her niece's patent rejection of Lord Ashdon's services. She looked at her niece's ashen face, then turned to the viscount. "Thank you, Lord Ashdon. It will not be necessary for you to leave the party as well."

Lord Ashdon stepped back and made a short bow. His firm mouth had thinned, and there was a shuttered expression in his eyes as he glanced at Miss Weatherstone, who had averted her face while she tied the laces of her cloak. "Very well, ma'am. I shall make your excuses to the rest of the company. I trust that you will soon feel better, Miss Weatherstone."

"Thank you, my lord," said Belle, avoiding his eyes and anxious to be away.

As Belle and her aunt and uncle left Vauxhall and the sounds of the fireworks display faded behind them, the horrible tension seeped out of her. Belle's thoughts were somber on the return to the town house. She watched the pattern of the streetlamps as the carriage passed each one and moved on to the next. She had insulted Lord Ashdon, and she knew it. It was all because of her stupid fear of loud, continuous noises. More than anything, she wished that she could make things right with him. But how was she to convey her apology to his lordship when she couldn't bring herself to admit to such a childish weakness? She sighed and rested her head against the windowpane.

"Belle, are you quite all right?"

Mrs. Weatherstone had covered her niece's hand with her own, and Belle straightened, turning her head. With a small smile, she said, "Of course, Aunt. It is just a silly, idiotic thing, after all."

"It is not the least bit silly," said Mrs. Weatherstone, compassion in her voice.

"Of course not. It is not such an uncommon thing," said Mr. Weatherstone.

Belle gave a laugh and removed her hand from her aunt's warm clasp. "I know of no one else who suffers from such a nonsensical fear."

The Weatherstones said nothing more. When the carriage reached the town house and the trio entered it, Belle murmured her excuses to her aunt and uncle and went up to bed. She felt positively exhausted.

Chapter 12

A few days later, Belle was cantering her gelding in the park, as it had become her custom to exercise Rolly in the early mornings, when the dew was still heavy on the ground and the gossamer white mists strayed across the bridle paths.

Over the weeks of the Season, she had met Lord Ashdon a number of times along the bridle paths, and they had enjoyed several rides together. Of late, however, she had seen little of the viscount. Belle could not help but wonder at the reason for his lordship's giving up his habit of riding out in the morning. She felt that it had everything to do with her.

Whatever misunderstanding had arisen, it had all started during that equestrian outing, and the relationship between herself and Lord Ashdon had deteriorated further since the dinner party at Vauxhall Gardens. He did not exactly give her the cut direct when they chanced to meet at a social function, but it was certainly noticeable that he was no longer one of her most avid admirers. Indeed, Lord Ashdon seemed to have transferred his attentions more heavily in the direction of another young lady, Miss Abigail Fairchilde.

Belle had met the young miss, of course, and while she had originally liked Miss Fairchilde, she had privately thought the young lady was a bit colorless and without a spark of spirit.

Now she could scarcely bear to speak civilly to Miss Fairchilde when they chanced to encounter one another at the same functions. She had told her particular friends, Millicent

Carruthers and Clarice Moorehead, that she did not know what Lord Ashdon saw in Miss Fairchilde. She had pretended not to see the significant glances that her friends exchanged over that piece of unwonted criticism for she was afraid to run the risk of alienating them too.

With the damp wind in her face, whipping back her veil, Belle grimaced to herself. When she recalled how stupidly she had reacted to the fireworks and how she had practically bitten off the viscount's nose, she could readily see why he had made himself scarce. The Belle of London had become scarcely more than a shrewish baggage, especially in comparison with someone as perfect and proper as Miss Fairchilde.

Restless and depressed, Belle urged her gelding faster. Behind her, she caught the faint shout of her groom's alarm, but she did not heed his cry. At breakneck speed she raced through the park and back again, her mount's hooves tearing at the turf. When she reached the iron gates that gave onto the boulevard, her horse was blowing and she herself was breathing hard.

She had already started back to the town house before the groom caught up with her. He burst out, "Miss! Miss, what were ye thinking of?"

Belle did not reply. She did not know what to say. There were conflicting emotions fighting within her. She wanted to rage and cry. Such a horrible revelation had hit her. She was in love with Lord Ashdon, and he had turned to someone else, all because of her stupidity.

"Belle! I say, Belle!" Roland White sauntered his horse up to her. He tipped his hat, a smile on his face. "Fancy meeting you out so early in the morning."

"I think it stranger to meet you out, Roland," said Belle, managing to produce a teasing smile for her friend's benefit. "I had quite thought that you spent the better half of the morning hours with your valet."

"All too true," agreed Roland. He smoothed a wrinkle out

of his coat sleeve. "Actually, I have been up all night at my club. I returned to my quarters only a bit ago, but instead of being caught up in Morpheus's arms, as I fully expected, I was assailed by the most irresistible urge to throw a leg over my horse. And here I am." He thought for a moment, then shook his head. "I must be boskier than I thought."

Belle laughed. "Indeed, you must be!" She looked closely at his pale, weary face. "Roland, you look positively awful."

He looked alarmed. "What, is my cravat askew? Have I spilled brandy on my waistcoat? It leaves a terrible stain, my man tells me." He was hastily inspecting his front.

Belle shook her head, chuckling. "No, nothing of that sort. It is just that you don't look at all well."

He visibly relaxed. "Oh, is that all? That is nothing that a nap and a few kippers and eggs won't cure. For an instant you had me thoroughly panicked. I was in dread of being seen on the streets in clothes unworthy of my reputation."

"You must be drunk, Roland," decided Belle.

He considered it, then shook his head. "I don't think so. At least, not much. I'm talking sensibly, aren't I? And I am managing my horse all right."

Belle conceded that he was. Now that the novelty of seeing Roland out in the early-morning hours had worn off, she inevitably thought about his cousin. "How is Lord Ashdon?" she asked casually. "I have not had the honor of seeing as much of his lordship as I was used to."

Roland threw a comprehensive glance at her face. "Ashdon is very well. I suspect he is becoming a bit restless, however. I don't expect him to remain in London for the entire Season, not with my aunt forever gibing at him to wed."

Belle studied her horse's twitching ears. "Perhaps Lord Ashdon will oblige her ladyship."

Roland made a noncommittal noise in his throat. There was a moment of silence, which he broke by breathing in deep.

"Ah, the morning air is bracing, is it not? Well, Belle, I must be go—"

"No, stay!" Belle threw up her hand to stop him, then turned in her saddle to address her groom. "Drop back, Edwards!"

The servant stared at her, but obediently reined in until she and Roland had gained some distance.

Belle at once turned to her friend, who was regarding her with a measure of curiosity. She said urgently, "Roland, have you ever felt that you were so hemmed in, so set about, that if you did not do something about it, you would go stark raving mad?"

Mr. White appeared taken aback. "Why, I don't know if I—"

"Roland! Have you never felt an irresistible urge to do something outrageous or—or dangerous? Just to feel alive and free?" asked Belle, trying to express something of the staggering emotions that were bottled up inside her. She thought if she didn't do *something* she was going to explode.

Comprehension dawned on Roland's face. He slid an earnest glance at her. "Now, Belle, just because Angus and I have been tossing around the notion of finding out how fireworks are made doesn't mean that we are actually going to build some! How did you find out, anyway?"

Belle shook her head impatiently. "I don't care about any silly fireworks! In fact, I detest them!"

"You do?" He regarded her in amazement. "Why, everyone likes fireworks!"

Belle was recalling that humiliating night at Vauxhall Gardens. Suddenly an idea came to her. She could return to Vauxhall, the scene of that terrible terror she had felt, and regain her self-respect by doing something that others of her social class would not dare. She rounded on her companion. "Roland, I want to go to the public masquerade at Vauxhall Gardens."

"Well, of course you do. So does Clarice, and so do Angus

and I," said Roland with a shrug. "But that doesn't mean that you can go."

"I *am* going," declared Belle.

His jaw dropped slightly and he shook his head. "You can't possibly. Your aunt will never allow it."

Belle turned back to the view of the boulevard ahead of her. "I shan't tell her, of course. I mean to sneak away, Roland."

"You can't!" he exclaimed with horror. At Belle's sideways glance and curling smile, he amended hastily, "What I mean to say is, you shouldn't! What if you were caught, alone and unescorted? It might ruin you, Belle."

"I don't care for such paltry stuff!" said Belle, the memory of a certain gentleman's warm smile in her mind's eye, while her heart felt as though it was being squeezed. "I'm going!"

Roland reached out and took hold of her bridle, pulling her mount to a stop. Belle looked at him in surprise, for never before had he taken such a liberty. She was equally astonished by the set look of his mouth.

Resolutely, he said, "If you're set on it, Belle, I'll go with you. I won't let you risk yourself alone."

"Thank you, Roland! You are the best of friends!" exclaimed Belle, catching up her reins again.

"No, I am not!" retorted Roland irritably. "I am drunk!"

Belle surveyed the crowd through the slits of her mask. A smile trembled on her lips. The masquerade was just as exciting as she had thought it would be. A thousand lamps had been lit in the gardens, making the grounds a mysterious fairyland. Entrance was costlier than a dinner would have been, Roland had informed her, grumbling. She had not heeded her reluctant escort but merely drew him onward. She had been hesitant at first, but when no one seemed to recognize her or Roland through their disguising silk dominoes, Belle had felt nothing but anticipation for the evening.

Music was a mere backdrop to the din of laughter, the buzz

of conversation, and the glittering pageantry of costumes and
obscuring dominoes. The supper boxes were filled with various parties, many obviously of a lower social class than Belle
was used to. She noticed how her escort eyed those around
them with a distinct air of disapproval, but she thought he was
being priggish.

She turned to watch masked couples whirling about in lively
dance. "Oh, how marvelous!" she exclaimed. "How I would
like to join them!"

"Will you dance, ma'am?" asked Roland, reluctant but game.

"Yes, let's!" As her partner squired her into the midst of
the milling couples, Belle said, "Oh, Roland, I am so glad that
we came!"

Her escort hissed in warning and looked around quickly to
see if her words had garnered any interest. He was relieved
that no one seemed to be paying attention to them. "No names,
ma'am! We don't wish to be recognized!"

Belle laughed as he twirled her into the intricate step. "I
am sorry! I forgot for a moment in all of the excitement."

"Well, no harm done," he said comfortably. He grinned suddenly. "It is rather amusing, isn't it?"

Suddenly a large hand came down on his shoulder, making
him jump and glance hastily around. He and Miss Weatherstone stopped in the midst of the swirling couples to stare at
the unknown gentleman swathed in a domino. "Yes?" inquired
Roland haughtily.

"Greetings, cousin."

He looked closely at the masked gentleman who had accosted them. "Adam! By all that's wonderful, what are you
doing here?"

"I could ask you the same. This is not the sort of entertainment I thought would appeal to you," said Lord Ashdon.
He spared a glance at his cousin's partner, and his tone became biting. "Nor would I ever have believed you so lost to
propriety."

A flush mounted to Roland's cheeks, merging with the bottom of his satin mask. He stood his ground, however, and stepped to the side so that he partially shielded his partner from the viscount's wrathful gaze. "You are right, of course. It was poor judgment on my part."

Belle was angered by the viscount's manner. "It wasn't Rol—your cousin's fault, my lord. I made him escort me here tonight. I haven't been to a masquerade before."

"And has it measured up to your expectations, Miss—ma'am?" asked Lord Ashdon.

Belle tossed her head. "Up until this moment, it has indeed!"

"Then you are a sad romp, ma'am!"

As Belle gasped indignantly, Roland leaped into the breach. "We shall leave at once, of course."

"*I* am not leaving! Not just yet!" exclaimed Belle wrathfully. She could scarcely believe the viscount's arrogance. He had practically ignored her for a fortnight and now suddenly he appeared, like some avenging guardian, and had the audacity to quite ruin her evening.

"You will no doubt agree with me, cousin, that I can better handle a recalcitrant trooper than yourself," said Lord Ashdon.

"Well, of course! There can be no doubt of that," stammered Roland, somewhat confused.

"Then you will understand why I shall escort the lady home," said Lord Ashdon shortly.

"I don't wish to go anywhere with you!" exclaimed Belle furiously.

Roland met his cousin's hard glance, then turned an apologetic look to Belle. "I am sorry. It's best this way, I think. Good night, ma'am." He lifted her fingers to his lips in a polite salute.

Belle clung to his hand and whispered urgently, "You can't leave me like this!" She couldn't believe it when he merely smiled again and shrugged, before walking away to be swallowed up by the crowd.

She felt the viscount's hand close on her elbow and she turned on him, shaking free. "How dare you, sir!"

"Are you in need of help, my lady?" A rather heavyset gentleman appeared, eyeing the couple through his mask.

"Yes!" exclaimed Belle recklessly. "I don't wish to go with this gentleman."

"Don't make things worse than they already are, Belle," murmured Lord Ashdon in her ear. He had taken her elbow again, and this time she could not pull free. "Look carefully at your knight, my dear."

"Unhand the pretty little thing, you," drawled the other gentleman.

Belle, startled by the viscount's words, looked quickly at the gentleman. He was attired in a black domino, which had fallen carelessly open to reveal a disordered shirtfront and an outrageously striped waistcoat. The gentleman was masked, but there was a cut on his upper lip and he was absently sucking on a bloodied knuckle. There was a boldness in his eyes, besides, that Belle disliked. He certainly did not engender confidence in her.

"Er—on second thought, I should like to go with you, my lord," Belle said to Ashdon, halting her efforts to pull away from the viscount.

"My lord, is it? Well, pretty one, lord or no, you've called on my services, and by Jove, you'll have 'em. And then we'll find somewhere to be cozy together. How does that sound?" said the gentleman, with a definite leer.

Belle stepped a little closer to Lord Ashdon. "No, thank you," she said politely. "I prefer my present escort."

The gentleman's face flushed abruptly. "Turning me away, pretty one? We'll see about that!" He reached out and grabbed at Belle's shoulder.

She cried out as she felt the weight of the stranger's clutching fingers. Then Lord Ashdon stepped past her, a blur flew from him, and the stranger staggered back, crying out in pain. His hands covered his nose. "You broke my nose, you bastard! You broke my nose!"

"Come along, Miss Weatherstone," said Lord Ashdon softly.

Belle did not need any urging. She hurried along beside him as he wove their way through the crowd. The angry cries followed in their wake for a few seconds, making Belle nervous that the stranger would catch up with them. She threw a couple of anxious glances over her shoulder, but she did not see the stranger and she was relieved when his voice receded.

As she and Lord Ashdon emerged from the gardens, she said earnestly, "Thank you, my lord. That was very well done."

"It would not have needed doing if you hadn't been so foolish," said Lord Ashdon.

Belle bit back the instant retort that came to her lips. After a moment, she said meekly, "Quite right, my lord. It was my fault entirely."

Lord Ashdon glanced down at her without expression. "My carriage is over here, ma'am." He helped her up into the carriage and told the driver the direction before settling onto the seat and closing the door.

Belle had been doing some thinking, and now she asked her most pressing question. "How did you know I was here, my lord?"

"Roland told me, of course," said Lord Ashdon.

"Roland!" Belle was confounded. "But I don't understand—"

"There can be little doubt of that, Miss Weatherstone," said Lord Ashdon with some bite. "My cousin is a gentleman of conscience. He was very bothered by the prospect of this night's entertainment, and he came to me to ask my advice. Naturally he named no names and, in fact, pretended that it was someone else who was contemplating this madcap escapade, but I was well able to read between the lines. I went by his place earlier, and when I did not find him home, as he had said that he would be, I suspected that I would find him here. What I did not expect was to find you here as well, Miss Weatherstone!"

Belle blinked back angry tears as she heard the amazed contempt in his voice. "Oh, my lord? And why was that?" she asked with a semblance of dignity.

Lord Ashdon was silent a moment. Then he sighed. "I had thought you to be quite otherwise, Miss Weatherstone. I had thought you were a well-bred, proper young lady, with whom I had enjoyed many hours of pleasant conversation. I thought that the enjoyment had been mutual. You may imagine my disillusionment when I learned differently! And now, to discover that you are a sad romp into the bargain!"

Belle did not reply. She turned her head and stared out the window, too upset to make sense of her tumbling thoughts and emotions. Her hands were clasped tightly in her lap.

When the carriage stopped, Lord Ashdon opened the door and got out. He held out his hand to help her down, but Belle gathered her skirt and stepped down without his help. She did not think that she could bear any gesture of civility from him, not when she knew what hypocrisy it really was. Lord Ashdon thought her beneath contempt. Very well, then, let him! She hurried up the steps and entered the town house.

Lord Ashdon did not leave immediately. After ushering her into the sitting room, he held a low-voiced conversation with the manservant who had opened the door. He came back into the sitting room and shut the door behind him. "I have sent word up to your aunt that you were indisposed and so I escorted you home from your party," he said.

Belle turned away from him. "I see. I am grateful that you have spared me embarrassment with the servants, my lord."

"Rather, I have spared your guardians," corrected Lord Ashdon.

Belle felt his clipped words cut to the heart. She said noth-

ing, but moved away to stare into the fireplace, her head bowed
as she looked into the flames.

It was not a minute or two before Mrs. Weatherstone swept
into the sitting room. She glanced at Lord Ashdon and then
toward her niece as she closed the door behind her. "I received
your message, my lord. I am profoundly grateful to you for
your discretion."

"I suspected that you were unaware of Miss Weatherstone's
absence from the house, but I did not want to say so to the
servant," said Lord Ashdon.

"My lord, what happened?"

Lord Ashdon gave a brief account of what had transpired,
leaving out the incident with the stranger who had challenged
him. Mrs. Weatherstone thanked him profusely, then the viscount took his leave. Belle said not a word the entire time and
only turned toward her aunt once the door had closed behind
Lord Ashdon.

"My word, Belle! What were you thinking?" exclaimed Mrs.
Weatherstone, staring at her niece in great dismay. "Your reputation! The whole Season has been jeopardized!"

"I know how wrong it was of me, Aunt. And indeed, I am
very sorry," said Belle, holding on to her temper and fighting
back tears. She was still smarting from Lord Ashdon's biting
stricture, and it was difficult to show her aunt a contrite attitude.

Mrs. Weatherstone paid scarce attention to her niece's apology. She paced back and forth, her face and movements agitated. "I am extremely grateful to Lord Ashdon. He acted just
as he should have. I don't know what we would have done
otherwise. I trust that his lordship will keep his promise and
that no word of this deplorable affair will be cast abroad."

"Lord Ashdon will not say anything," said Belle, fully confident of it. She instinctively knew that the viscount was a
man of his word. However much she had resented his high-
handedness while she was with him, she could now appreci-

ate that Lord Ashdon had had only her best interests at heart. She was grateful to him for that much, at least.

Mrs. Weatherstone rounded on her niece. Her blue eyes sparkled with worry and anger. "Let us hope that Lord Ashdon will be able to enforce silence upon his cousin, Mr. White, as well! Really, Belle, how could you have behaved so thoughtlessly, so reprehensibly? I don't know how I am to trust you again."

"I have learned my lesson, Aunt Margaret," said Belle in a tense voice, her hands tightly clasped.

"So I should hope! I don't know what your uncle will say when I inform him of this. We have never been faced with this sort of contretemps before," said Mrs. Weatherstone. She looked over at Belle as though she had never really seen her before. "Perhaps it was a mistake to bring you to London so soon. Perhaps we should have waited until you had spent more time with us, until we had grown to know one another better."

Belle felt that her already wounded heart could bear no more. She knew that her aunt was not only expressing regret for ever accepting responsibility for her but also comparing her to her sister, Cassandra. Belle's throat closed tight as she fought back tears. In a choked voice, she said, "I am sorry, Aunt. May I be excused now? I should like to go up to my room."

Mrs. Weatherstone gestured her helplessness. "Yes, we shall do better to discuss this matter in the morning," she said in a tired, resigned voice. She walked over to her niece and kissed her. Without looking at Belle's face, she turned away. "Sleep well, Belle."

Belle fled, the hot tears beginning to course down her face. Fear was a knot in her stomach. She didn't know what the final outcome of her folly would be. Her aunt seemed to have come to a place where she questioned the wisdom of continuing with the Season and actually seemed to be on the verge of washing her hands of her.

Belle's thoughts tumbled on as she gained the sanctuary of her bedroom. Perhaps her aunt and uncle would decide to send her packing back to the Hall and her grandfather. That would be humiliation indeed, for she had been determined to make a successful come-out. Now, through her own thoughtlessness and rebellion, her entire status had been placed in question.

Lord Ashdon would not miss her, thought Belle. His lordship had been noncommittal toward her once he had finished lecturing her. No doubt he would be relieved to hear that she had been sent home. The viscount detested her, and she had no one but herself to blame.

Belle threw herself across the bed, fully clothed, and wept miserably.

Chapter 13

⌒

Lord Ashdon was not surprised when his cousin came to call on him the following morning. Since he was an early riser and did not spend a great deal of time on his wardrobe, he was nearly fully attired, in a white shirt, waistcoat, and pantaloons, before Roland sent in his card. The viscount was in the process of pulling on his gleaming Hessians when his guest was shown in.

Lord Ashdon stood up, stamping his stockinged feet firmly into his boots, and looked unsmilingly at his cousin. "Well, Roland? You surprise me."

Roland blinked at the trim, well-muscled figure before him. "My word, Adam. You would display to advantage at Jackson's."

Lord Ashdon took the blue frock coat that his valet was holding out and shrugged into it. "No doubt. You have not stirred yourself at such an early hour to discuss pugilistics with me, though, have you?"

"No, I—" Roland was so appalled by his cousin's ability to get into his coat without assistance that his thoughts were entirely diverted from his purpose. "I say, Adam, you really should have your coats cut by Weston."

"Spare me, Roland. Your aunt has been telling me ever since I set foot in the house that I should stop using Schultz," said Lord Ashdon with a small smile. He gestured for the valet to leave them.

Roland showed a tinge of alarm. "I had hoped not to disturb my dear aunt with my visit," he said hastily, throwing a glance at the retreating valet.

"Rest easy, cousin. I am not sending word of your arrival to her ladyship. My mother is still abed and will be until noon," said Lord Ashdon. His smile grew a little wider. "Now that I think about it, Roland, you are very much like her."

Roland was momentarily bereft of speech. He cleared his throat. "I see what it is, Ashdon. You are punishing me a little with these barbs. Well, I deserve it, and probably worse."

Lord Ashdon leaned a shoulder against one of the massive bedposts and crossed his arms over his wide chest. He was no longer smiling as he looked steadily at his cousin. "I am delighted that you are aware of that fact," he said.

Under that unblinking, considering regard, Roland felt that his neckcloth was becoming too tight and put up one finger to loosen its folds. "You must be aware why I have come, Ashdon."

"Why don't you tell me?" invited Lord Ashdon without change of expression.

Roland felt a spurt of irritation. "I've come to apologize, as you very well know! I should never have taken Belle—Miss Weatherstone—to that blasted masquerade. I know that. I am heartily sorry for it!"

"You knew it was wrong yesterday, Roland." Lord Ashdon straightened and took a slow step forward, and another. "You even asked for my advice, which I freely gave."

Roland eyed his cousin's advance with unease. "Quite right." He threw back his shoulders. "All right, then! Hit me, Adam. Go on, get it over with! I know that I deserve it!"

Lord Ashdon stared at him in astonishment, then burst out laughing. "What?! I have no intention of hitting you, Roland."

"You don't?" Roland drew a breath. "Well, that's a relief, at least."

"Why would you think that I would take a swing at you?" asked Lord Ashdon, his smile still lingering about his mouth.

"Well, knowing how you feel about Miss Weatherstone, I just thought . . ." Roland trailed off as the viscount's smile disappeared and a shuttered expression entered his lordship's eyes. "I am sorry, Ashdon. I did not intend—"

Lord Ashdon forced a smile back onto his face. "I haven't taken offense, Roland. I was simply taken aback for an instant. So, you believe me to be smitten with Miss Weatherstone."

"I-I thought you were, but if you say you aren't, then of course I believe you," said Roland quickly.

Lord Ashdon chuckled. He stepped forward to clap a hand onto his cousin's shoulder and shook the younger man slightly back and forth. "No, you did not misread the signs, cousin. I was very much smitten by Miss Weatherstone. The Belle of London!" He dropped his hand and turned away, to stare abstractedly at the small fire on the hearth.

"Er, if you don't mind my asking, Ashdon, what happened to change things?" asked Roland with delicacy.

Lord Ashdon turned to look at his cousin. His firm mouth had thinned. A kaleidoscope of memories flooded his mind, of vivacious conversations and a lovely, laughing face. The time that he had spent with her in London made his recollection of their acquaintance in Bath pale by comparison. He had hoped she felt the same; yet when she had asked him about Bath, implying that she placed no significance on their previous acquaintance by announcing that she had forgotten everything about it, he had been surprised and wounded. "Why, nothing happened, Roland. I merely discovered that a pleasant memory was merely a figment of my imagination."

"I don't understand," said his cousin, frowning.

Lord Ashdon sighed and shook his head. He was in no mood to explain. "It is unimportant. Let us simply say I have decided that I and Miss Weatherstone would not suit."

Roland's mouth dropped open and he stared in open dismay. "Adam! I had no notion that the affair had gone so far with you! I *am* sorry! Did Miss Weatherstone refuse you?" Before Lord Ashdon could reply, his cousin's eyes narrowed. "No, for everyone would have known if you had offered for her. If Mrs. Weatherstone had not seen to it, my aunt certainly would have!"

"Roland—" Lord Ashdon threw up his hand. But Roland could not be stopped.

"You were about to offer for her, weren't you, Adam? But then something happened, something—" Roland sucked in his breath sharply. "Never say it was because of my taking Belle to the masquerade, Adam! You must know that I would never have let her reputation suffer for it, I assure you!"

"It has nothing to do with you, Roland. It is Miss Weatherstone. I . . . fear that I was greatly mistaken in her," said Lord Ashdon.

Roland flushed and his mouth set. "I'll not let you say anything against Belle, Ashdon. She is a dear friend, to me and to others. She may be spirited and hardheaded at times, but there's no harm in her."

"I am certain of that. Roland, I truly have nothing against Miss Weatherstone. I don't think her fast or disreputable, as you seem to have assumed." Lord Ashdon hesitated, choosing his words carefully, for he had no desire to expose Miss Weatherstone to any censure, nor to uncover the extent of his disillusionment. "I said that Miss Weatherstone and I would not suit because we are too different. I am a disciplined soldier. I do not tolerate shallowness or the frivolous very easily."

Roland stared almost in incomprehension. "You are saying that Belle is shallow and frivolous?"

"Perhaps not that so much as spoiled," amended Lord Ashdon. He was recalling again the unsubtle way she had hinted him away during the riding outing to Gunther's and also the curt manner in which she had rejected him at Vauxhall Gardens. Miss Weatherstone had made it abundantly clear that she felt he had become too possessive of her and that she did not welcome his attentions. "Yes, I suppose that is more what I am trying to say. She is used to having her way. And she is not anxious to form a closer connection."

"I see," said Roland slowly. "I don't know what to say, Adam."

Lord Ashdon looked at him with only a hint of his easy smile. It did not reach his eyes. "Why, I don't think there *is* anything to say, Roland."

Lady Ashdon was appalled when her son informed her that he had decided that he would not attend the Mooreheads' gala at their estate. "Not attend? Are you mad, Adam? It is touted to be one of the crowning affairs of the Season! Why, everyone who is anyone will be attending."

"I weary of the social rounds, Mother," said Lord Ashdon with a hint of his wide smile. "I am toying with the notion of going down to my estates for a few weeks."

"Leave London? But that is preposterous! You cannot remove yourself now, not when you are expected any day to make an offer for one of the young ladies you have been dancing attendance on!" exclaimed Lady Ashdon.

Lord Ashdon contemplated his mother for a long moment. "And just who is it that expects me to betroth myself, my lady?"

Lady Ashdon raised her eyebrows, not at all intimidated by the question. "Adam, you must realize that in your position you are the subject of generous gossip. Of course you are expected to offer for someone! It would be thought odd if you did not after the way you have made up to Miss Weatherstone, among others."

Lord Ashdon got up and took a turn around the black-and-gold sitting room. "I detest this decorating scheme," he remarked without heat.

Lady Ashdon's mouth dropped open. She closed it with a

snap. "Well! It is quite obvious to me that you are laboring under some strong emotion. It is equally obvious that your reluctance to go down to the Mooreheads' weekend party has everything to do with at least one of the young ladies who will be attending. I wish you will tell me the truth, Adam!"

Lord Ashdon swung around, a frown between his blond brows. "The truth, ma'am? Very well! I have discovered in myself a distaste for the matrimonial state. I don't wish to wed."

Lady Ashdon stared at her son. When she spoke, it was a curiously softened voice. "Which one is it, Adam? Who is it that has so tied you in knots that you are afraid to face her?"

"What nonsense! I, afraid!" Lord Ashdon laughed the very notion to scorn. "I have faced bayonets and cannon fire, my lady. There is nothing more to fear."

Lady Ashdon rose from her chair. Her expression was cool. "I am very glad to hear it, Adam. You will not deny me the pleasure of your escort, then, to the Moorehead estate, since there is nothing and no one there for you to fear." She swept out of the sitting room.

Lord Ashdon stood staring after his parent. By and by, a reluctant grin came to his face. "She carried this one, by Jove."

Mrs. Weatherstone had her own reservations about the wisdom of attending the Moorehead party. "After this—this *start* of hers, I am not at all certain that I wish to go, Phineas. What if someone saw her and has said something? What if she does something else outrageous? Oh, I could not bear it to have the Season end badly, not when everything seemed to be going so well!"

"You must compose yourself, my dear," said Mr. Weatherstone. "It has been a full day since the masquerade, and we haven't seen any ill effects thus far. Perhaps no one but Lord Ashdon found her out. His lordship is an honorable man. He will not betray our confidence in him. Nor will Mr. White, I hope. He comes from the same honorable stock, after all."

"Yes, but—"

"It will appear very odd if we do not attend, Margaret. The Mooreheads are among our closest acquaintances," said Mr. Weatherstone quietly. "Our absence would inevitably raise unwelcome questions and could very well offend Lord and Lady Moorehead."

Mrs. Weatherstone sighed. "You are right, of course. We have no choice but to go. And if Belle's reputation is made to suffer, I suppose I would rather see the results of it outside of London. There it will be easier to claim that Belle is taken ill and must be sent back home than if she was still in town, where everyone will know differently."

"I agree," said Mr. Moorehead somberly. "But, Margaret, she is to be sent home to the Hall only if her reputation is completely tarnished. My father must be given no good cause to blame us if things do not work out as they should."

Though Belle was not privy to her aunt and uncle's conversation, nevertheless she perceived that they had spoken about her between them. It seemed fairly well agreed that nothing else was to be said to her about the masquerade. Mr. Weatherstone did make it quite clear in a little lecture that he and Mrs. Weatherstone would not tolerate any other such clandestine activities in future. "And I believe that I must ask you to forswear Mr. White's sole company," he ended. "The young gentleman appears to be rather more rackity than I had thought."

"It wasn't Mr. White's fault, Uncle," said Belle in a low voice. "It was mine. He merely agreed to escort me because he did not wish me to be unprotected at the masquerade."

"Mr. White's care for you would have been better realized if he had come to us instead," said Mrs. Weatherstone in reproof.

"Yes, I see that now," said Belle quickly. "I assure you, Mr.

White will never have opportunity to be forced into such a position again."

"Nevertheless, Belle, I must have your promise," said Mr. Weatherstone sternly. "You will not seek out Mr. White's sole company."

"You have it, of course," said Belle shortly. She was angered by the unfairness of it all. She was solely to blame, yet her friendship with Mr. Roland White was to be curtailed because he had been a party to her stupidity. As she looked from her uncle to her aunt and back again, Belle thought that perhaps it had not been such a wonderful opportunity to come up to London with them, after all. She had not been able to meet their high expectations, nor indeed, her own. It was a bitter thing to realize that she had earned their distrust.

Chapter 14

~~~

It was a short drive to the Moorehead estates from town. The Weatherstones made an early arrival and were greeted with pleasure by Lord and Lady Moorehead.

Miss Clarice Moorehead in particular was delighted to see them. She hugged Belle and drew her swiftly aside, while the servants took the Weatherstones' wraps. "Oh, I cannot wait for you to see the ballroom tomorrow. It will be so grand, Belle!"

"I am anticipating it already," said Belle. "May I help Lady Moorehead with any of the arrangements?"

"Oh, no! Mama's staff is handling every detail," said Clarice airily. Dimples appeared in her cheeks as she smiled, and her green eyes sparkled. "Besides, it is to be a surprise."

Since Clarice was the youngest and the last daughter, her parents were universally known to be indulgent of her whims. Never was that more evident than in the decor of the grand ballroom for this affair.

The ballroom was completely mirrored so that it appeared fantastically large. The high ceilings and walls were draped in white gossamer fabric and massive garlands of sweet-smelling flowers. Countless expensive wax candles were lit, and their hot brilliance was reflected over and over again in the mirrors with marvelous effect. The result was overpowering.

The following evening when the Weatherstones were ushered into the ballroom, Mr. Weatherstone looked around with a stunned expression. "My word!"

"It quite takes one's breath away, does it not?" asked Lady Moorehead complacently. "The notion was one of Clarice's, and I must own that it turned out quite well."

"Very pretty," approved Mrs. Weatherstone, shooting a warning glance at her husband. "Clarice, you are to be congratulated for your creativity. I can foresee that you will be a prominent hostess one day."

Clarice blushed with pleasure. "It is most kind of you to say so, Mrs. Weatherstone."

"Why don't you take Belle over to the refreshment table? I am certain that she would like an ice, for it is already quite warm in here," said Lady Moorehead, plying her fan.

"Yes, Mama," said Clarice obediently. She slid her gloved fingers around Belle's arm and led her friend off, leaving the older generation behind to fall into their own deep conversation.

As soon as she was certain that she was out of earshot of her parents, Clarice said in a low tone, "Belle, I have something terrible to tell you, something utterly awful!"

Belle was startled by her friend's intensity. "Why, Clarice, what is it? Are you in trouble of some sort?"

"Oh, no! Of course I am not! It is nothing to do with me," replied Clarice. "It has everything to do with you, however!"

"Then tell me quickly!" said Belle.

"It—it is Lord Ashdon, Belle. He mentioned something about you to Roland, and Roland told Angus, and Angus told me," said Clarice in a tragic tone.

Belle set down the ice and took hold of her friend's agitated hands. "Clarice, tell me this minute or I shall shake it out of you!"

"Oh, dear! I don't think I can, now," said Clarice, looking stricken.

Belle let go of her friend's hands and took hold of her slim shoulders instead. "I am warning you, Clarice."

"Belle! You wouldn't dare do so right here in the ballroom!" exclaimed Clarice, her green eyes widening.

"Oh, wouldn't I just!" Belle gave her friend an experimental shake. "Now, pray do not tease me any longer! What did Lord Ashdon say about me?"

Clarice capitulated. "Roland said that he was just talking to his cousin, the viscount, you know, and your name came up. Lord Ashdon said that he thought you were spoiled and shallow and frivolous." She spoke in an increasingly hurried fashion, as though she had to get everything out at once or choke on it.

Belle released her friend and half turned, so that Clarice was not able to see her face. She feared that if her expression was any mirror of her emotions, then Clarice would certainly know how deeply she had been wounded.

Belle drew a shuddering breath and pinned a smile on her face as she glanced fleetingly at her friend. "I see! Well! That is something, to be sure!" She opened her fan and waved it to and fro, scarcely noticing the effect of the breeze on her heated face, so turbulent were her thoughts. So this was to be the outcome of her rebellious desire to attend the masquerade. She had forfeited the respect of the one gentleman who had come to mean something to her.

"I *am* sorry, Belle! You are upset. Oh, I *knew* it would upset you. I shouldn't have said anything," cried Clarice, genuinely dismayed.

Belle gave a light laugh, though she had rarely felt less like it in her life. "Why, I am glad that you did, Clarice. It is better to know how one stands with someone, don't you think? I shan't need to waste my time on the viscount anymore, which is a very good thing."

Clarice regarded her in some amazement. "Why, Belle, I thought that you liked Lord Ashdon. That is why I was so torn about telling you what Roland said, though I knew I should."

"Oh, I rather thought that I liked Lord Ashdon, too, for a

little while," said Belle blithely. She snapped her fan shut, tired of the silly toy. Her knuckles whitened on the fan's ribs as she attempted to maintain her nonchalant appearance. It was vitally important to her that no one, not even her good friend, should realize how her heart was shattering. "But truly, what is his lordship to me? He is only one of my several admirers."

Clarice heaved a sigh. "I am so very glad! I was afraid that you would be quite, quite cast down."

Belle forced another laugh. "Why should I be?"

Clarice squeezed her arm. "If it is any consolation, Belle, the Crockers and Miss Fairchilde will not be coming this weekend. Mama received a message. Miss Fairchilde has the spots, and so she is to be sent home before the Season is over."

Belle stretched her mouth once again in a semblance of her usual smile. With effort she turned her mind to the other young lady. "Poor Miss Fairchilde. I do feel for her."

"Well, and so do I, naturally. But let us be practical, Belle. At least Lord Ashdon will not be able to make up to her anymore," said Clarice.

Belle wished that her maddening friend would be quiet. "Do let us forget Lord Ashdon! We have the whole evening ahead of us, Clarice, and I, for one, intend to enjoy every moment of it."

Later that evening, Belle had occasion to put her brave boast into practice. Lord Ashdon arrived, escorting Lady Ashdon, and paused to survey the crowded ballroom.

Belle watched him surreptitiously, anxious to see whether he would acknowledge her. His eyes passed over her without stopping, and her heart dropped to her toes.

She had been hurt by Lord Ashdon's sudden coolness toward her. That he had been the one in all the world to catch her cavorting in an unacceptable place had been disastrous. She had looked for him without success in the early morning after the masquerade at the park, hoping to offer an apology to him; but he had not appeared. Nor had he any other morning that entire week.

Never one to allow setbacks or obstacles to throw her for long, Belle nevertheless was depressed by Lord Ashdon's desertion. She had come to look forward to seeing him as she exercised Rolly. Indeed, those hours had come to be her favorite times in the viscount's company. She had learned a great deal about him and his hopes for the future and even his odd insistence that Napoleon Bonaparte would once more appear on the world stage.

Now she wished that she had known more about Lord Ashdon's personal character. She was certainly aware that he had taken offense at what she had done. That had been transparently obvious from the way he had spoken to her that night. She had hoped that their friendship was such that she could apologize and assure him that she did not habitually divert herself with scandalous behavior. She had hoped that Lord Ashdon was not so high in the instep that he could not forgive a stupid lapse in propriety.

Now, however, she knew that he was indeed just so proud. He had been utterly scandalized. He had so taken her in disgust that his entire perception of her had undergone a complete reversal.

It was the single most devastating blow of her entire life.

Chapter 15

Belle woke with one thought in her head. She could not fathom how she was to bear the remainder of the weekend. The day stretched interminably before her, and she longed to be gone from the Moorehead estate, though she knew that was not possible. She and her aunt and uncle were situated for the entire period of Lord and Lady Moorehead's hospitality.

She quite decided that she detested house parties, for one was always meeting the personage that one least wished to see. It seemed that everywhere she looked and wherever she went, she was forever running into Lord Ashdon. And every time she saw him, she had the most lowering inclination to cry.

It was not her way to dissolve into a watering pot. Rather, she was more inclined to throw up her chin and meet adversity with a defiant gleam in her eyes and a laugh on her lips. So it was that by that evening she had become the life of the party. It was she who was ever eager to accede to whatever entertainment was proposed by the host and hostess. Never would anyone, watching her, have discerned that she was hiding a bruised heart.

By evening coffee, however, Mrs. Weatherstone observed her niece with some misgiving. "She is too lively, too exuberant, Phineas," she remarked to her spouse from behind her fan.

Mr. Weatherstone looked over at the loose group of young people, where his niece was the center of attention. He bent

forward a trifle to reply quietly, "Quite. Belle has eclipsed Miss
Carruthers and Miss Moorehead. I don't think there is a gentleman here worth the name who has not sought out her company."

"There is one," murmured Mrs. Weatherstone, her gaze
going thoughtfully to a small group of gentlemen standing in
front of the windows. Lord Ashdon had his broad back to the
room, and his head was bent courteously as he listened to the
conversation of his peers. The viscount's omission bothered
Mrs. Weatherstone more than she could say. His lordship
seemed all of a sudden to have become indifferent toward her
niece, and she misliked it.

Lady Moorehead suggested that the evening be wound up
with a musicale and called upon her daughter and her son to
begin the program. "Clarice has a very pretty voice, and Angus's
is quite tolerable," she said complacently.

"Who will play for us?" demanded Angus, in rather obvious hopes of not being held to the task. "I cannot hold a tune
without some music, ma'am, you know that I cannot."

"Oh, really, Angus!" exclaimed Clarice, tossing her head.

"I shall play," said Millicent Carruthers a little breathlessly,
rising from her chair. She blushed when she found herself the
object of all eyes. "I-I am a bit out of practice, but I think
that I can manage."

"Of course you can, my dear," said Mrs. Carruthers en-
couragingly.

Angus's frown disappeared like magic. "I am certain of it,
Miss Carruthers." He offered his hand to the young lady and
escorted her to the pianoforte, solicitously finding the sheet
music for her.

Lady Ashdon watched the byplay between Mr. Moorehead
and Miss Carruthers with a rather thin smile. "It is a pretty
match," she remarked, glancing up at her son, who had come
to stand beside her chair.

Lord Ashdon had regretted that the impromptu musicale demanded that his own group join the others. He would far rather have remained talking politics than to be obliged to listen to a musical performance. When he was standing beside the windows, engaged in conversation, he could put his back to the room and so not be treated to the sight of Miss Weatherstone enjoying herself so thoroughly.

At her ladyship's remark, he glanced down. He grinned suddenly, quite able to read the speculation in her gaze. "Yes, it is a very good match. I like both Mr. Moorehead and Miss Carruthers. They will deal handsomely together."

"And what of Miss Moorehead?" asked Lady Ashdon.

"Sh, my lady. They are beginning," murmured Lord Ashdon, determined to give nothing away that could possibly feed her ladyship's curiosity.

At the end of the number, the trio was handsomely applauded. "Well done! Well done!" exclaimed Lord Moorehead. "Who else have we with us tonight? Of course! Miss Weatherstone, will you not favor us with a piece as well?"

Lord Ashdon unconsciously stiffened, while he looked across at Miss Weatherstone's obviously shocked face.

"I-I am sorry, my lord. I do not play the pianoforte or sing," said Miss Weatherstone in a stammering fashion that was quite unlike her usual confidence.

"Belle plays the harp," announced Miss Moorehead. "And very beautifully, too!"

There was a perceptible groan from most of the gentlemen. The harp was almost universally disliked.

"Yes, yes, that is right. My niece is quite accomplished," said Mrs. Weatherstone quickly. She urged her niece with a flip of her fan. "Do go on, Belle."

In a lowered tone, Miss Weatherstone said, "Aunt, I don't think—"

"Pray do not be so bashful, Miss Weatherstone," said Lady Ashdon in her forthright manner. "We are all your friends here."

A murmur of agreement rose, and now others added their persuasions.

Lord Ashdon watched silently as Miss Weatherstone hesitantly rose and approached the instrument that Lady Moorehead had signaled a footman to bring to the forefront. The cover was taken off of it, revealing a splendid gilded harp with ribs curved like angel wings.

Miss Weatherstone stood and stared at it, awe on her face. "It is quite beautiful," she said.

"It was my mother's," said Lady Moorehead. "I am sure that I have not heard it played since she passed away a little over two years ago. I have had it kept in tune in memory of her."

"Play it for us, Belle," urged Miss Moorehead.

Belle sat down on the wooden stool that was positioned behind the harp and placed her fingers on the strings. She plucked experimentally and a perfect chord sounded. She smiled and looked across at Lady Moorehead. "I hope that I can do it justice, my lady."

"Yes, and so do I," muttered a gentleman at Lord Ashdon's elbow.

Lord Ashdon looked around quickly. It was Lord Darlington, who had been one of the gentlemen he had been in conversation with. Earlier, the marquis had told him in a private moment that he wanted to accept his offer to put him in the way of earning a post in Vienna, with an eye to getting onto Wellington's staff.

"One could almost wish one was a little deaf whenever one of those instruments of torture is brought out," murmured Lord Darlington.

Lord Ashdon did not say so, but he heartily agreed with his companion. He had never yet heard a harp played that did not wreak havoc on the eardrums. He began to turn away, unwilling to watch Miss Weatherstone's humiliating performance. The gathering would be civil, of course, and applaud her efforts with their faces frozen in polite expressions. For once, Miss Weatherstone must suffer a check in her popularity, and however much he was disillusioned in her, he still did not want to see her fall on her face.

However, when the first chords were struck, all murmuring died away and the gathering began to listen in earnest. Miss Weatherstone's supple fingers gracefully worked the harp's strings, drawing from the instrument a charming piece that was familiar to them all.

When it ended, the applause was instantaneous and sincere. "Bravo, Miss Weatherstone!" bellowed Lord Moorehead. "I have never heard better."

Lady Moorehead had the sheen of tears in her eyes. "Quite, quite true. For an instant, I thought that my dear mother was playing for us again, but I do think that your skill quite put hers in the shade, Miss Weatherstone."

Miss Weatherstone's face was aflame as she glanced about her. "Th-thank you. You are all very kind, indeed."

Her hazel eyes chanced to meet Lord Ashdon's and wavered.

He smiled at her, still applauding. He was glad that she had come off so well.

"Miss Weatherstone has a bit of talent, doesn't she, Adam?" inquired Lady Ashdon, looking up at him.

Lord Ashdon instantly conditioned his expression to one of only civil interest as he turned to his parent. "Yes, I suppose one could say that," he replied. When he glanced up again, Miss Weatherstone had turned away and gone to sit down again.

"One must stand in admiration of such dash," said Lord Darlington. He smoothed his sleeve, his eyes fixed on the young woman who was sitting across the room. "Yes, I really must become better acquainted with the Belle of London. I suspect that we may very well be of a kindred spirit."

As Lord Ashdon watched the young gentleman saunter off in Miss Weatherstone's direction, he experienced an unusual burning in his breast. He decided that the oysters he had eaten at dinner had not agreed with him.

"Lord Darlington seems quite taken with our Miss Weatherstone," said Lady Ashdon. She was looking at her son. "Why, Adam, are you feeling quite the thing? You looked quite sour for an instant."

"I am very well, ma'am. It was only the oysters at dinner," said Lord Ashdon, annoyed.

Chapter 16

O n the last day of the Mooreheads' house party, the weather was very fine. A light breeze was blowing, and the blue skies were mostly clear, with just wisps of cloud. When Lady Moorehead suggested a picnic, the younger set voted unanimously in favor.

"I should like to picnic at the ruins, Mama," said Clarice. "If that might be arranged?"

Lady Moorehead smiled and nodded. "Dining al fresco is always so amusing. I shall have some baskets made up for you to take with you."

"Oh, I say! What a splendid notion, Clarice," said Angus approvingly. He turned to Millicent Carruthers. "The ruins are the remains of an old Gothic church just a few miles from here. There is a pretty view to be had of the surrounding countryside. We would have to ride, of course."

"I think it sounds perfectly delightful," said Millicent, smiling shyly.

"I am all for a riding party," said Belle with quick interest. "It will be wonderful to be out-of-doors, especially on such a gorgeous day."

"When would you not wish to go riding, Belle?" teased Clarice gaily.

Belle laughed and shook her head. "I honestly cannot say, Clarice! When I was at home, I was forever in the saddle."

"I will be happy to make one of the company," said Roland White.

Lord Darlington smiled across at Belle. Lounging at his ease in his chair, he drawled, "I am very willing to offer my escort, as well, ladies."

"It is settled, then," said Clarice, in greatest satisfaction. She turned to the viscount. "Are you joining us, too, Lord Ashdon?"

Ashdon had been on the point of crying off from the pleasure ride, but he instantly changed his mind when he saw how Lord Darlington glanced at Belle. It occurred to him that the marquis was exhibiting greater interest in the young lady than before. In fact, ever since yesterday evening's musicale, the marquis had been making himself very agreeable to her. And she did not appear to be displeased by his lordship's attentions.

"It would be a pleasure, Miss Moorehead," said Lord Ashdon.

It was scarcely an hour later before the party was gathered outside and mounted on horses from Lord Moorehead's stable. Three full picnic baskets had been securely fastened to the ladies' saddles. Angus led the way down the drive and across the fields.

They passed through a quaint village with neat houses and cobblestone streets, over which the horses' hooves clopped with a loud noise. Belle liked the picturesque inn and the wild arbor adjoining it.

The only circumstance that marred her unalloyed pleasure in the outing was her mount. She really wished that she had her own gelding, Rolly. Though the mare she was on was not precisely a slug, she quickly discovered that it had no fire, for it would produce nothing faster than a gentle, ladylike canter.

Clarice had lost little time in apologizing to her for the mare. "She is a sweetheart but scarcely up to your usual style, I fear."

"It is no matter, for we are not racing," said Belle gra-

ciously. "Besides, if I were to go careening off with this very
nice basket, everyone would accuse me of stealing away part
of their luncheon!"

Belle noticed at once that Lord Darlington was well
mounted, and she found herself envying his lordship the spirited animal. The marquis ruled his horse with an iron will, she
noted approvingly, but, she thought with frowning curiosity,
that was quite uncharacteristic of his lordship's languid style.

Lord Ashdon, too, had managed to procure one of the better animals from Lord Moorehead's stables. He was a horseman par excellence, as Belle already knew, and he managed
the stallion's little show of defiance with a firm hand.

Belle thought their company very fair indeed. She and Millicent Carruthers had riding habits of almost an identical cut,
except that hers was russet corded with gold and her friend
was all in green. Clarice Moorehead was stunning in a royal
blue habit, her glossy copper locks topped with a blue hat that
sported a floating veil. Angus Moorehead looked every inch
the country squire, while Roland White proved an amiable
counterpoint with his exaggerated shoulders and splendid red
coat.

Lord Ashdon, of course, appeared most pleasing to her eyes.
Mounted on a big gray, he rode with shoulders well back and
perfect posture. There could never be any doubt that he had
been soldiering.

Belle's gaze turned to study the newest member of their
company. Lord Darlington was immaculate in his riding cos-
tume. The white uppers of his glossy black boots were almost
dazzling to the eye. There was never a fault to be found with
his appearance, his manners, or his dress. His lordship was in-
variably courteous, yet something else, something that Belle
could not quite put her finger on, sometimes flashed out.

She wasn't certain whether she liked Lord Darlington or
not. He was so different from the other gentlemen whom she
had met. A drawling dandy, certainly. On the surface, he was

a shade too finicky for her taste. Yet Belle sensed some undercurrent in his nature. There was almost a hint of danger attaching to the marquis that she found appealing, perhaps because
he was so self-controlled. She well knew what it was to rein
oneself in, for she had constantly experienced it since coming
up to London and placing herself under her aunt's guidance. It
was an unseen but nevertheless strong commonality between
them, she thought.

Lord Ashdon, even while listening politely to Millicent Carruthers, caught snatches of the conversation that sprang up between Belle Weatherstone and Lord Darlington. He grimly
observed what was seemingly a growing friendship between
the two. He thought that as soon as he returned to town, he
would do something on Lord Darlington's behalf. The gentleman was far too idle.

Belle was curious about the country through which they
rode. "I have hunted all of my life, and these fields and woods
certainly look as good as any fox country I have ever seen,"
she commented.

"Yes, we see awfully good sport," said Angus.

The conversation as a whole then turned to hunting, proving a lively topic even among the ladies, all of whom had
hunted.

The ruins proved to be farther than anticipated, and after
the long ride all agreed that they were ravenous. The three
wicker baskets were unlashed, and the luncheon was set out
on some conveniently flat stones, which proved to be parts of
a broken and fallen wall of the old church. Cold chicken and
meat tarts, cheeses and a variety of fruit were greeted with approbation. Lady Moorehead had thoughtfully supplied a bottle
of wine as well.

After picnicking, the party began to explore the ruins. Belle
climbed to the top of a pile of stones, shaded her eyes, and
looked out on the countryside, stretching far and green before
her. "How beautiful it is," she remarked aloud.

"Quite," said Lord Ashdon.

Belle turned in surprise. She had resigned herself that he seemed to prefer anyone's company to her own, and now here he was. She could see Millicent walking about with Angus and Lord Darlington, and she could hear Clarice's bright laughter, as well as Roland's exuberant shout. She could not help but wonder why Lord Ashdon had sought her out.

"I did not hear you come up, my lord," she said.

"I saw you climbing and realized that you might wish a hand on your descent. These stones appear to be rather slick in places," replied Lord Ashdon.

Belle smiled at him. "Thank you, my lord. That was thoughtful." She turned once more to admire the view. "How I long to gallop across those greens!"

"Do you? Do you yearn also to travel, Miss Weatherstone?" asked Lord Ashdon.

Belle glanced across at him quickly. "How ever did you know?"

Lord Ashdon smiled. It was the wide smile that began with a crinkling at the corners of his eyes, warming to encompass his face. "It is not difficult to guess, Miss Weatherstone. I can easily imagine you tramping through the Alps or boating your way down a broad river."

Belle chuckled and slanted a gleaming glance at him. "Perhaps. But I think that wherever I went, my heart would remain in England."

"As will mine, ma'am," said Lord Ashdon, his smile fading a little as he continued to look at her.

Belle was suddenly discomfited. Now there were not the shouts and calls that she had heard previously, and she could see no one else of their party. "Shall we go, my lord?"

"Of course," said Lord Ashdon, offering his hand to her as they descended over the rougher of the stones.

When they had returned to the main ruins, it was to discover that the others were discussing the advisability of starting back. Lord Ashdon concurred, and Belle also murmured her agreement. Lord Ashdon had again withdrawn from her, becoming as distant and civil as before. For an instant—just for an instant—at the top of that incredible view, she had seen the flash of his former friendliness. He had smiled at her with such warmth. A thousand pities that it had not lasted.

They had lingered longer at the ruins than they had meant to and that, coupled with the picnic and the leisurely pace of the riding party, put them late in returning.

The day was becoming overcast, and a brisker wind began to rise. Belle cast a thoughtful, and increasingly anxious, glance now and again at the darkening clouds. Finally she suggested that they all ride a little faster, for it looked as though it was going to rain. The others agreed to it and set a marginally faster pace, though not nearly as quick as she would have liked.

Soon the heavens began to rumble and the air developed a noticeable damp heaviness. Belle felt the oppressiveness of the impending weather. Droplets began to fall, at first lightly but increasingly heavier.

"I suspect that we are set to be soaked," remarked Lord Darlington with a curl of his mobile lips, surveying the angry clouds.

At this, Roland White cried merrily, "Tallyho! We're for the inn!"

The others laughed, all except Belle. She was merely thankful that at last they would begin to make some time.

Thunder rolled, followed by the distinct crack of lightning. Belle jumped and cast a wild glance upward. Her breathing quickened as her nervousness increased. She had unconsciously yanked on the reins, and her mare threw up its head, giving a surprised whicker.

"Is there aught wrong, Miss Weatherstone?" inquired Lord Darlington.

"No, no, of course not," said Belle, making a conscious effort to erase the trepidation from her expression. She glanced around, feeling someone's eyes upon her. It was Lord Ashdon, regarding her with a curious gaze. Belle managed to summon up a smile, then averted her gaze and urged her mare faster, but the accursed animal never changed pace.

The thunder became incessant and the rain fell heavier. The riding party was somewhat subdued now, as each of the riders became cognizant of their own increasing discomfort under the downpour. The sight of the village, and especially the inn, magically revived their spirits.

"There we are! We'll soon be cozy before a roaring fire," said Roland White cheerfully.

Belle cringed every time the frightening rumble rolled over her. Her fingers were clenched tightly on the reins. "Oh, let's not stop! I should like to press on to the manor," she said. It was the thought of being able to shut herself safely away in her bedroom that sustained her.

"Intrepid to the end, Belle!" said Roland White admiringly.

"Some of us are not so brave as yourself, Belle," said Angus Moorehead, gazing at Millicent Carruthers's determined but waning smile.

Belle bit her lip, barely restraining her desire to laugh. If her friends only knew the truth! It was not courage that compelled her to brave the elements, but cowardice.

"I also am for stopping," said Clarice. "I have no wish to be soaked completely through."

Lord Darlington was the only other voice to express the desire to press on. The notion was outvoted by the rest of the party, which elected to stop at the inn until the threat of rain had passed over.

Chapter 17

So it was that the party took shelter at the inn, merrily taking up residence in the deserted public room. The gentlemen had a tankard of ale and went to stand at the inn door to watch the rain course down, then walked back to the table to converse with the ladies. Clarice and Millicent ordered tea, but Belle refused it. She was afraid that the shaking in her hands would cause her to slop the contents of her cup. She clasped her hands tightly in her lap to hide their trembling. The atmosphere was cheerful, and those in the party chatted amiably, but it was an effort for Belle to participate.

Then Lord Ashdon was there, bending down slightly to address her. "Belle, you're starting at every roll of thunder. Would you like to find a private parlor where you can lie down for a few moments?"

Belle looked up, startled, to see a measure of concern in his eyes. She felt a rush of grateful tears. It was all she could do not to blurt out that she wanted nothing better than to be able to climb into bed and take refuge beneath the bedclothes. Belle looked up at him with an appeal in her eyes. "Oh, my lord! I would be so grateful," she said in a low, trembling voice. She scarcely noted the familiar way in which he had addressed her.

Lord Ashdon laid his hand momentarily on her shoulder, then straightened and went away. In a few moments, he was back with the inn's mistress. "I have procured a private parlor, Belle. I shall escort you upstairs," he said quietly.

"Thank you, my lord," said Belle.

"This way, miss," said the inn's mistress. Her presence caught the attention of some of the others.

"Why, wherever are you going, Belle?" asked Clarice curiously, as she noticed Lord Ashdon escorting her friend away.

"I-I have the headache, Clarice. Lord Ashdon has been kind enough to get a parlor where I may lie down," said Belle.

Lord Ashdon looked down at her fingers, which had clenched tight on his arm. It was as though he was her sole support. Not a flicker of emotion showed on his face. It would not do to draw attention to the way she was leaning her weight upon him.

"You! The headache! I am surprised at you, Belle! You are always so energetic," said Clarice, astonished.

"It is a common ailment. I suffer from the headache myself occasionally," said Roland.

"But yours come on generally after a full night of cards," remarked Angus, his gaze focusing on Belle's white face.

Looking pained, Roland coughed slightly.

Lord Darlington gave a quiet laugh. "Your sins have found you out, White."

"Quite," muttered Mr. White, throwing a glance at Clarice's interested expression.

"As I recall, Belle's sister used to suffer from the same ailment," said Millicent. She smiled compassionately at Belle. "I hope that you will feel better presently, Belle."

"I shall. Thank you, Millicent," said Belle. She involuntarily cringed again as a crack of thunder nearly shook the beams of the public room. "Pray, pray get me away, my lord!" she murmured desperately.

Lord Ashdon swiftly guided her toward the stairs, the inn's mistress preceding them. The woman opened a heavy door and stood aside for them to enter. "Here you are, m'lord. The poor miss will feel more the thing in a trice, I'll wager, once she's warmer."

"Thank you," said Lord Ashdon. He escorted Belle into the front parlor, where a fire had been laid in the hearth and a bottle of wine had been set out on the table.

"I'll be returning to my duties now, m'lord," said the inn's mistress.

Lord Ashdon turned quickly. "Wait!" The woman had already exited, however, and closed the door firmly behind her. He turned back toward Belle.

Belle had gone over at once to the crackling fire and held out her shaking hands toward the warmth. She was shivering as though she was chilled, but that was nonsense, of course. It was warm enough, and she had not gotten altogether soaked.

Lord Ashdon watched her, a frown on his face. He poured out a small measure of wine in one of the glasses. He approached her and held out the glass. "Here, this might help calm you."

Belle shook her head and gave a strained laugh. She was hugging herself with both arms and shivering uncontrollably. "I don't think so, my lord. You see, it is the thunder. I have always been terrified of thunder." Her wide-eyed gaze went to the lead-paned window, where rain was coursing down in streams.

Lord Ashdon set the wineglass aside on the mantel. "Yes, so I gather. The fireworks at Vauxhall?"

Her gaze swinging back to him, Belle managed another laugh. "The same, though not quite so bad."

Lord Ashdon recalled what he had thought of her behavior that night. He had thought her spoiled and rude. Now he realized that she had rejected his overtures not out of shallowness but out of fear. Better than anyone, he knew how strangely fear could make one act. He had seen it too many times on the battlefield and had tasted it himself. He was not proud of his erroneous perception of her.

"Why don't you sit down, Miss Weatherstone? It will be more comfortable," he suggested, indicating the wingback chair behind her.

Belle glanced behind her, then quickly sat down on the very edge of the chair. It was patently obvious that she was too keyed up to be able to relax.

Lord Ashdon was quite cognizant of the inadvisability of his remaining upstairs alone with a young, unmarried lady while the rest of the party was belowstairs. It would not do his or Miss Weatherstone's reputation a bit of good. He wished that he had been able to stop the inn's mistress from leaving and had been able to leave Miss Weatherstone in her care.

Reluctantly, he stepped forward to take one of her trembling hands into his in a reassuring gesture. "Miss Weatherstone, I must go."

Belle's eyes flew to meet his. Her fingers tightened on his for the briefest moment, then abruptly relaxed. "Of course. I completely understand."

"I shall send one of the other ladies up to you," said Lord Ashdon, in an attempt to comfort her.

"Thank you. You have been very good to me," said Belle in a low voice.

A resounding crack of thunder boomed overhead. With a cry of distress, Belle flew out of the chair and flung herself into Lord Ashdon's arms. She was shaking like a leaf. Her face was pressed tightly against his shoulder, and her hands gripped the front of his coat. "Don't leave me! Pray, don't leave me!"

Lord Ashdon tightened his arms, which he had automatically drawn around her. "No, no, I shan't leave you," he murmured, yet wondering what would come of this inadvertent tête-à-tête. At least part of his duty was clear. He couldn't very well leave her to suffer through her terror alone. He drew her closer, and she gave a muffled sob against his shoulder.

The door to the parlor door opened, a step sounded, and the door shut. Lord Ashdon looked around quickly to meet

Angus's somber, challenging gaze. He stiffened, but he did not
thrust Belle away out of his embrace. He was formulating what
he had to say to excuse the picture that he and Miss Weatherstone must present. "Moorehead, you must give me a moment to explain before you pass judgment."

"Belle is afraid of the thunder, isn't she?" asked Angus,
crossing the room.

Lord Ashdon was relieved. Obviously the younger man's
perception was such that no explanation was required. "Exactly. I tried to prevent that woman from leaving, but I was
unable to do so. I was about to go ask one of the other ladies
to sit with Miss Weatherstone."

Belle, hearing their conversation and realizing its import,
was hideously embarrassed. She raised her head and released
her hold on Lord Ashdon's coat to dash one hand across her
wet face. Stepping back from the viscount, she said in a mor-
tified voice, "I-I am so sorry! I am such a baby!"

"It is quite all right, Miss Weatherstone," said Lord Ashdon politely. He dropped his arms from about her and took a
backward step himself.

Belle looked from the viscount to Angus. Her hands were
clasped tightly together against her skirts. "I suppose that it all
reflects very badly on our reputations."

"Precisely." Angus allowed a small grin to play over his
face. "I shan't tell tales if you don't, Belle."

Belle gave a shaky laugh. "Very gentlemanly of you,
Angus." She noticed a water pitcher and bowl sitting on the
sideboard and said, "If you gentlemen will excuse me, I shall
splash my face."

Lord Ashdon stepped across the room to the window. "The
worst of the storm seems to be over," he remarked, looking
back over his shoulder at her.

Belle smiled at the viscount and went over to the wash-
bowl.

Lord Ashdon gestured to Angus, and when the other man

had joined him, said in a low voice, "I would be very appreciative if you would say nothing about what you saw when you came into the parlor a few moments ago, Moorehead."

"As though I would," retorted Angus. "Belle Weatherstone is a good friend of mine. I'd have no part in tarnishing her reputation."

Lord Ashdon smiled and nodded. He clapped the younger man on the shoulder. "Good man."

Angus eyed the viscount speculatively. "I saw the way that you held her, my lord, and the expression on your face. It was not altogether altruism that I perceived. What are your intentions toward Belle, my lord?"

Lord Ashdon's well-marked blond brows rose at the frank question. "Why, you are very bold, are you not, Mr. Moorehead?"

"I repeat, my lord, Miss Weatherstone is a good friend of mine," said Angus.

"As I am also, Mr. Moorehead," said Lord Ashdon quietly.

The two gentlemen exchanged glances, Lord Ashdon meeting his companion's eyes squarely.

"I suppose that I must be satisfied with that," said Angus reluctantly.

"Quite," said Lord Ashdon. "Pray do not look so grim, Mr. Moorehead. It is a pleasure jaunt that we are on, interrupted for only a moment by the storm. But the worst is passing and we shall soon be on our way again."

Lord Ashdon was correct. The thunderstorm swiftly played itself out, and the damp riding party was able to return without further incident to the Moorehead manor.

The weekend party broke up the next morning, and all the participants returned to London.

Chapter 18

B elle and Mr. and Mrs. Weatherstone were still at breakfast when the butler came in to announce that visitors had
arrived. Mr. Weatherstone raised a brow as he looked at his
spouse. "This is rather an unseasonable hour for callers, is it
not, my dear?"

Before Mrs. Weatherstone could form a reply, a lady and a
gentleman came through the opened door, past the waiting butler, into the breakfast room.

Mrs. Weatherstone half rose, an expression of astonishment
on her face, her linen napkin slipping to the carpet. A glad expression lit her light blue eyes. "Cassandra! Oh, my dear!"

Laughing, Miss Cassandra Weatherstone rushed across the
space between them and enfolded Mrs. Weatherstone in an exuberant embrace. The egret feathers in her bonnet dipped and
swayed with the enthusiasm of her greeting. "Oh, Aunt! You
have no notion how wonderful it is to see you!" she exclaimed,
standing back but still entangled within her aunt's arms. She
turned her head to smile at Mr. Weatherstone. "Nor you, dear
uncle!"

"We are exceedingly pleased to see you, Cassandra. And
Philip, too, of course!" said Mr. Weatherstone, a wide smile
on his face, shaking the gentleman's hand.

Mr. Raven flashed a grin. "We have taken you completely
unawares. I am sorry for it, sir!"

"Nonsense! Think nothing of it," said Mr. Weatherstone

forcefully, clapping the younger man on the arm. "We are delighted that you have arrived earlier than expected."

"Indeed we are," said Mrs. Weatherstone, releasing her niece and advancing toward Mr. Raven with her hand held out in a friendly manner. "Welcome, Philip!"

Cassandra turned to Belle. Her shining eyes and laughing expression told the tale of happiness in her life. "Dearest Belle!" The sisters hugged one another with obvious affection.

"Oh, Cassandra!" exclaimed Belle, happiness lighting her on the inside. "How I have longed for you to come up to London to be with me. Are you staying long?" Then a thought hit her and she drew back. Catching her sister's hands in her own, she said in alarm, "Grandfather—is he all right?"

"Yes, yes! He is as irascible as ever. He penned a letter to you. One moment—I shall give it to you," said Cassandra, pulling her hands free to open her knotted reticule. She took out the sealed and folded sheet. "Here you are! He charged me with many messages to you, Belle, chief among them the command not to forget him."

"As though I could," retorted Belle, taking the letter. Half turning away and ignoring the rest of the chatting company, she broke the seal and opened the sheet, which was covered with her grandfather's familiar scrawl. A smile touched her face as she read his admonishments to behave herself and to mind her manners, then his grumbling that she was away for so long. It was so like her grandfather to scold and in the same breath let her know how much she meant to him. Belle refolded the sheet as a wave of homesickness swept over her. Tears pricked her eyes.

"Is Sir Marcus well?" asked Mrs. Weatherstone.

Belle turned to her aunt and put on a smile. "Yes, ma'am. Grandfather sounds quite his old self. Am I right, Cassandra?"

"Oh, yes, he is in fine form these days. He has completely recovered from that insidious fever. I left him terrorizing the household. Of course, Biddy and Weems and Steeves pay small heed to his cantankerous tantrums. Bye the bye, Biddy sends her love."

Again, Belle felt tears sting her eyes. "I do miss Biddy and all of them. It is wonderful being here in London, of course, but I still miss them. Especially Grandfather."

"But you haven't yet told us why you and Philip have come up to London. I quite thought you were settled at the Hall for the spring," said Mrs. Weatherstone, losing interest in Sir Marcus's communication.

Cassandra turned to her aunt. "It is the most exciting thing imaginable, Aunt Margaret. But I must let Philip tell you, for it is his to tell."

All eyes turned toward Cassandra's beau. He smiled and made a small bow. "Yes, it is rather good news. At least, I found it so, and I trust that you will feel the same. I have been accepted to a diplomatic post in Vienna."

"But this is marvelous, my boy," exclaimed Mr. Weatherstone, shaking Philip's hand again and clapping his arm.

Philip laughed. "Thank you, sir. Of course I need not tell you just what this means to me."

"No, indeed! It is a first-rate opportunity. Congratulations!" reiterated Mr. Weatherstone.

"Yes, it is the best news," agreed Mrs. Weatherstone. She turned to Cassandra. "But what of your wedding plans, my dear? Have you given any consideration to what you will wish to do?"

"That is why we have come up to London. Philip's appointment is effective almost immediately. We have had to abandon our original plans in favor of a smaller wedding by special license," said Cassandra. She took hold of her aunt's hands as Mrs. Weatherstone's expression turned to one of dismay. "Oh, I know it is not what you had wished for me, Aunt. But you must be happy for me and Philip."

"Of course I am!" said Mrs. Weatherstone, recovering her

poise. "It-it simply took me aback to hear that you would be leaving so soon."

"Will you be wed here in London, then?" asked Belle.

Cassandra turned to her sister. Her hazel eyes were gleaming with gladness. "Oh, yes! And the best part, Belle, is that Grandfather and Biddy are coming up to town in a very short time so that they may be a part of it."

"What! Sir Marcus and Miss Bidwell coming up?" exclaimed Mrs. Weatherstone. "Oh, Cassandra! Why didn't you say so at once? Why, I must see to their rooms at once. There will be so much to arrange. A scaled-down guest list, of course, and perhaps a few modifications in refreshments would be in order as well. Phineas, what do you think?"

"I leave all such arrangements to you, dear wife," said Mr. Weatherstone hastily. He turned his glance on Mr. Raven and his niece. "The only question I have for you is where you intend to be wed."

Mrs. Weatherstone looked questioningly at Mr. Raven. Rising to the occasion and displaying admirable qualities of diplomacy, he said, "Cassandra and I have not yet decided what will be best. Perhaps you may advise us, Mrs. Weatherstone?"

"I shall be glad to, Philip," said Mrs. Weatherstone, a smile coming to her face. Her expression was all anticipation. "Come! We shall go into the morning room, where we can be more comfortable while we discuss matters. Oh, it is all so prodigiously exciting, is it not, Phineas?"

Belle had stood back on the periphery, listening with interest to all of the changes that were taking place in her sister's life but feeling a little detached from it all too. She was at once happy and unsettled. When she looked at Cassandra's happy glow and Philip's smiling face, she was glad for them, but she was puzzled by the accompanying feelings of sadness. Her sister was embarking on a relationship that she dearly prized, while Philip was entering a new and wonderful phase of his career. Belle did not understand why she could not feel unalloyed joy for them, for she loved them both, but she felt almost envious of them and their good fortune.

"I shall be glad to accompany you, ma'am," said Philip.

Mrs. Weatherstone tucked her hand into his elbow and drew him out of the breakfast room, already voicing plans. Philip courteously inclined his head toward the lady. Chuckling, Mr. Weatherstone started to follow them, then paused at the door to glance at his nieces. "Are you coming, Cassandra? Belle?"

"In a moment, dear uncle," said Cassandra with a smile.

Mr. Weatherstone looked from one to the other and smiled before exiting.

Cassandra faced her twin sister, her smile fading. She quietly studied Belle's face. "Belle, are you quite all right? You have been so quiet since we arrived," she said softly.

"Have I?" Belle summoned up a smile. "I just have so many thoughts running riot through my mind, Cassandra. I had wished you to come up to London so that we could be together again, even if it was to be for only a short time before your wedding. And now you have, but you and Philip are leaving England almost at once, and I don't know when I shall see you again!"

Cassandra reached out and caught her sister's hand. Squeezing Belle's slender fingers, she said sympathetically, "I know just what you mean. Even though I am so very happy, I cannot help but think of all the dear ones that I shall be leaving behind—you, and Uncle Phineas and Aunt Margaret, plus Grandfather and Biddy and all the rest at the Hall. Sometimes I can't bear it."

"You mustn't say that!" exclaimed Belle, dismayed by the tears suddenly glistening in her sister's eyes. "I am sorry, Cassandra! I never meant to hurt you. You mustn't feel that way. Why, only recall what you once told me—that you would wait for Philip forever because you couldn't possibly live without him."

"You are right, of course," said Cassandra with a small

laugh, though there were still shadows of melancholy in her eyes. "Oh, dear! Why does it all have to hurt so much?"

"I think love and commitment demand it of us," said Belle seriously. "I have been giving a great deal of thought to that recently. Cassandra, I have been such a selfish little prig."

Cassandra's expression mirrored her amazement. "Belle! Why, what a thing to say about yourself! And completely untrue besides," she exclaimed.

Belle shook her head, a smile just touching her lips. "No, it is quite true. I have behaved selfishly all of my life. Why, it was I who talked you into that shameless masquerade so that I could go to that house party."

"But I wanted to be with Grandfather," retorted Cassandra. "So I was just as selfish in my motives as you were, Belle."

"And I wished to come up to London, simply to indulge myself with parties and entertainments and lovely clothes," said Belle.

"While I chose to blight Aunt Margaret's dreams for me of a magnificent come-out and a brilliant marriage," countered Cassandra.

"But you fell in love with Philip," objected Belle. "That doesn't count as selfishness."

"Oh, doesn't it, dear sister?" retorted Cassandra. "In the back of my mind was always the comforting thought that you were here to take my place, so that Aunt Margaret could at least have the satisfaction of making her ambitions come true through you."

Belle stared at her sister, then a small smile curled her lips. She said teasingly, "Why, Cassandra, that is quite utterly beyond the pale."

A flush rose in Cassandra's cheeks. "Yes, well. That is what comes of revealing one's deepest reflections to anyone, even one's twin. One comes off looking very much the shallow, selfish individual that one really is."

Belle threw her arms around her sister. "No, you aren't!

You are the very best of sisters and my best friend besides! I would be dying of boredom this very moment at the Hall and you wouldn't be marrying Philip and neither Grandfather nor our aunt and uncle would ever have known what a wonderful pair we are if we had done anything differently! So there!"

Cassandra burst out laughing. "Precisely! Now, are you through with your burst of self-pity? Which, by the way, is totally unlike you."

"Yes, I feel ever so much better," said Belle, with a laugh and a nod. "Now you must tell me all about your trousseau and your dress and all of your plans."

"I will do so, very willingly. But first, dear Belle, I will hear what you have to say for yourself," said Cassandra, growing suddenly serious.

"Why, whatever do you mean?" asked Belle, opening her eyes wide. She had a sneaking suspicion that her sister had gathered more about her state of mind than she would ever have wished to reveal to her.

"Belle, what has happened to you since I saw you last?" asked Cassandra quietly. "And don't shrug me off with a laughing glance and a frivolous statement. You know perfectly well what I am referring to. I perceived it immediately when I arrived. Are you in some sort of difficulty?"

"Of course not! What possible trouble could I have fallen into?" asked Belle with a quick smile. "Why, Aunt Margaret watches me like a dragon. She makes very certain that I make no misstep, for which I am very grateful. She and Uncle Phineas have taken me to their hearts and show me the greatest favor and affection. I have nothing of which to complain."

Cassandra regarded her for a long moment. She said finally, "Do you know, Belle, I do believe that this is the first time that you have ever lied to me. I wish you wouldn't." She turned and walked out of the breakfast room, leaving the door wide open in her haste.

Belle stared after her sister, feeling abandoned and ready to burst into tears. Disgusted with herself, she dashed the back of her hand across her eyes. "Oh, what is the matter with me?" she exclaimed aloud. "I have done nothing wrong. I am just a bit under the weather, that is all. I shall simply tell Cassandra the truth. I have been going the pace too much and—and I am tired."

Cassandra's head poked around the corner. "You are never tired, Belle."

Belle started violently. "Cassandra! You made me almost jump out of my skin!"

Cassandra came back into the breakfast room. There was an expression of compassion in her eyes. "Belle, you are hiding something from yourself."

Belle laughed shakily, not quite able to meet her sister's knowing eyes. "I have never done such a thing in my life, Cassandra. I am not at all self-deceiving."

"No, you are not. And that is what worries me so," said Cassandra. She hooked her arm through her sister's. With a gentle smile, she said, "I shan't tease you anymore, Belle. Come along—Aunt Margaret will wish to see my trousseau and you must be there as well. I don't wish to brag twice about what nice things I have, for that would make me appear very conceited."

Belle laughed, at once relieved that her sister was not going to pursue the cause behind her oppression. She knew the answer, of course, but it was one that she did not wish to face. After all, Lord Ashdon seemed to have become almost indifferent toward her.

Oh, he had been kind enough when he had perceived her weakness, Belle thought dismally. But that was to be expected of any gentleman worthy of the name. What mattered more to her was the fact that he had not called once since they had all returned to London from the Mooreheads' weekend party.

Chapter 19

—⁓—

"Lord Ashdon!"
Lord Ashdon was returning from his bootmaker's when he heard a feminine voice hailing his name. He turned, surprised to see Miss Weatherstone walking toward him, accompanied by her maid. He bowed, wondering what was behind this show of friendliness. Miss Weatherstone had recently taken to treating him with a certain reserve, quite unlike her manner with her admirers, especially Lord Darlington. At the thought of the young marquis, Lord Ashdon almost ground his teeth. It appeared to him that Miss Weatherstone favored that gentleman a little more than she should.

Miss Weatherstone held out her hand toward him, and out of civility he took it, letting go as soon as he could without giving offense. He would not allow himself to betray more than a friendly interest in her, as he had during the riding excursion. "Miss Weatherstone."

She was smiling up at him with the greatest friendliness. "I am glad to have met you, my lord. We enjoyed so many good conversations together in Bath. I hope that you recall such times with as much pleasure as I do."

Lord Ashdon stared at her. "Bath? Forgive me, Miss Weatherstone, you have taken me by surprise." He felt himself to be stiff in his manners, but he did not understand how Miss Weatherstone could suddenly be so cordial.

Miss Weatherstone did not seem to perceive his coldness.

"I am not astonished, for I am certain that you did not expect to see me again here. I have come up to London to order a few more things for my trousseau, you see, and—"

"Your trousseau!" exclaimed Lord Ashdon, completely taken aback.

Miss Weatherstone looked at him, her mild surprise at his startled reaction evident. "Why, yes. Oh, I thought perhaps you knew. I am marrying Mr. Philip Raven. The announcement of our betrothal was placed in the *Gazette* some months ago." She regarded his odd expression for a moment. "But I suppose that you were not yet in town then, and so did not see it?"

Lord Ashdon shook his head, feeling thoroughly confused. "Forgive me, Miss Weatherstone. I can't seem to take it in. Did you say that you are betrothed? And to Philip Raven?"

"Why, yes. Do you know him?" asked Miss Weatherstone, surprise on her face.

Lord Ashdon felt his way carefully. "Quite. We were fellow officers." He unconsciously touched the scar above his brow. "In fact, it was Philip who carried me out of harm's way when I received this."

Miss Weatherstone's face lit up. "How very extraordinary! Why, I never knew this. You alluded to someone helping you to safety when you were wounded, but I never dreamed that it was Philip! Of course, his name would have meant nothing to me then. But certainly I would have recalled it upon meeting him." A rueful expression crossed her face, and she shook her head. "It is better that I did not know! Knowledge of that sort most assuredly would have been my undoing then!"

"You have lost me, Miss Weatherstone," said Lord Ashdon, his fascinated gaze on her animated face.

She laughed. Her hazel eyes gleamed. "I am not at all surprised, my lord. And it is just as well, believe me. Shall I send you an invitation to the wedding? I do not think that my aunt and uncle will mind, for you are known to them."

"Miss Weatherstone, you and your maid have several packages. Will you allow me to help you carry them? Do you go to your carriage?" asked Lord Ashdon. He was determined to get to the bottom of what was proving to be a mystery. Miss Weatherstone was acting as though they had not met since Bath, when he had been paying court to her all Season.

"That is very kind of you, my lord," said Miss Weatherstone, relinquishing two or three parcels to him, the brown paper crackling as he took them. "There is my aunt's carriage. It is but a short walk, as you see."

Lord Ashdon murmured his agreement, then returned to the main question in his mind. "Miss Weatherstone, I feel that I must be blunt. Do you actually recall our previous acquaintance in Bath?"

Miss Weatherstone turned an astonished expression on him. "My lord! Why do you ask such an odd question? Of course I recall you! Why would I not?"

"I thought perhaps that you were pretending to do so now since I alluded to Bath in weeks past," said Lord Ashdon grimly.

Miss Weatherstone stopped short and turned toward him. Her expression was more startled than before. "You have alluded to—? But, sir, we have not spoken together since Bath."

Lord Ashdon raised his eyebrow and stared down at her with a frown. "Really, Miss Weatherstone! It seems to me that your memory is wonderfully original, since we danced together not two nights past!"

All of a sudden Miss Weatherstone's expression changed, and she began to chuckle. "Oh, I see! We—you and I!—danced together. And I suppose that we have also exchanged pleasantries any number of times over these past weeks."

"You seek to make jest of me, ma'am," said Lord Ashdon stiffly. Anger swept through him. He had never been made the brunt of such a stupid joke in his life. He had thought Miss Weatherstone was merely shallow and indifferent. Now he realized that she was also one of those ill-assorted personages who delighted in humiliating their fellow creatures.

At once sobering, Miss Weatherstone laid a gentle hand on his arm. "Forgive me! I do not make merry with you, my lord. It was not I who danced with you, but my sister. I am Cassandra Weatherstone. You have obviously made the acquaintance of my twin sister, Anabelle."

Lord Ashdon stood rooted to the spot. The full scope of his mistake was suddenly open to his horrified scrutiny. The maid murmured a request that he give the packages to her, and he relinquished them without even glancing at the woman. "Your twin sister? Belle Weatherstone? The Belle of London! What a fool I have been!"

Miss Weatherstone nodded sympathetically. "Why don't you ride back to the town house with me, my lord? I left Belle at home. I think that it would be very good for you to see us together in the same room."

"Yes," agreed Lord Ashdon. He felt as though he had been poleaxed. He was still not quite able to grasp it. Cassandra, Belle—his memory had not been at fault at all, then. He had not forgotten her name, but he had taken her sister to be her. He had made himself known to her that first incredible morning on the basis of an acquaintance that had never existed, and he had measured her every word, her every action, against a memory that she had never been a part of.

Lord Ashdon handed Miss Weatherstone up into the carriage and absentmindedly gave a polite hand to the maid as well. The woman flushed, but he did not notice. His mind was wholly occupied with what he had just been told.

As he settled back against the velvet squabs, he shook his head. "I cannot believe it! I cannot believe that I could make such a dreadful mistake."

Miss Weatherstone laughed again. "It is not an uncommon experience, my lord. My sister and I embarked on a masquerade only a few months past. Not our grandfather, nor our aunt and uncle, nor any of the household suspected that we were not who we were thought to be." She glanced at her maid. "At least, there was not more than one or two who suspected. Am I not right, Morse?"

"Quite, miss," said the maid with the smallest of smiles.

Lord Ashdon looked fixedly at the maid, then turned his head to study Miss Weatherstone's face. She looked precisely as she always had. Her thickly lashed hazel eyes held brown flecks, her nose was small and straight, her mouth was generous, though now in repose rather than in its usual laughing state.

Miss Weatherstone met his hard stare unwaveringly. There was only the slightest blush in her cheeks to reveal that she felt any discomfort. Could there really be two young women who bore such an uncanny resemblance to each other? he wondered. He shook his head. "I cannot grasp it yet."

"You shall, Lord Ashdon," promised Miss Weatherstone, a smile touching her face. "Ah, here we are. Pray let us go in at once. Morse, I will have the porter help you bring those in."

"Very good, miss."

Lord Ashdon escorted Miss Weatherstone up the steps of the town house, keenly anticipating what was about to happen. He felt that he was on the verge of a discovery that would make a tremendous difference in his life. Either Miss Weatherstone was completely delusional or she was the greatest jokester imaginable, or there was indeed a second, identical Miss Weatherstone to whom he had lost his heart.

Miss Weatherstone led him to the drawing room. A splash of harp music wafted out of the room as she opened the door. "Belle is practicing," said Miss Weatherstone in a hushed tone. "Pray go in, my lord."

"Come with me, Miss Weatherstone," said Lord Ashdon quickly.

Laughter lit her eyes. "Afraid, my lord?" She preceded him

and then moved slightly to one side, holding the door open for him.

Lord Ashdon stepped past her and then stood in stunned disbelief.

There was Miss Weatherstone, seated at a golden harp. Her eyes were closed and her cheek rested against the body of the instrument. Her mouth drooped a little in an attitude of melancholy. Her slender, strong fingers strummed and plucked a sad, shimmering melody that floated on the air. A shaft of sunlight coming through the window sparked fiery highlights in her chestnut hair and limned the folds of her white daydress.

The viscount felt something tighten in his chest. Never had he beheld or heard anything quite so beautiful. He drew in his breath sharply.

From out of the corner of his eye, he caught movement. Realizing at once that Miss Weatherstone was walking past him toward her sister, he instinctively shot out his hand, catching her wrist.

Miss Weatherstone stopped, looking up at him in surprise. He shook his head, murmuring as softly as he could, "No, pray do not disturb her just yet."

Puzzlement flickered in Miss Weatherstone's eyes, but she acquiesced. Lord Ashdon turned back to the lovely vision at the harp and lost himself once more, entangled in her beauty and the haunting music that she wrought.

When she struck the last lingering note, Lord Ashdon applauded softly. Miss Weatherstone looked up from her instrument, her expression startled, and when she saw who had come in, color surged into her face. "Oh! Lord Ashdon!"

Her sister, still wearing her straw bonnet, went forward to kiss her twin. "Belle, that was utterly superb. I am certain that Lord Ashdon must agree."

"Quite so," said Lord Ashdon. Words were inadequate to express what he felt at that moment. He had never heard such a haunting melody in his life.

As Miss Weatherstone drew her hesitant sister forward, Lord Ashdon looked from one face to the other. He was utterly amazed at how closely they resembled each other. He had heard it was so with twins, of course, but he felt that in this particular case it must be exceptionally so. "My word!"

"I met Lord Ashdon while I was shopping. He thought that I should have remembered our original acquaintance in Bath long before today!"

"Oh!" said Belle. A mischievous gleam came into her eyes. "How forgetful of me, to be sure!"

Lord Ashdon felt himself flush. He advanced until he could take Belle's hand and raised it to his lips. "Forgive me, Miss Weatherstone," he said contritely. "I made an assumption that I fear has cost me dearly. I have been cold to you. Can you forgive me?"

"Of course I can," exclaimed Belle, her color high. She looked at him with sparkling eyes. She pressed his fingers. "Thank you, my lord. Your friendship means more to me than you can possibly know."

"May I call you Belle?" he asked diffidently, looking again from one to the other. A rueful grin spread slowly across his face. "I fear that I might make the same error again if I do not have some way to identify the person to whom I am speaking."

The ladies laughed, and it sounded as though an echo was resounding in the room, so closely did even their voices match.

"Yes, pray do so," said Belle warmly.

"And I shall remain Miss Cassandra Weatherstone, my lord," said Cassandra, still chuckling. "Now I shall leave you. My packages have undoubtedly all been deposited upstairs. I shall send refreshments in directly."

"No, pray do not on my account," said Lord Ashdon, sparing the lady a glance even as his eyes quickly returned to Belle's face. "I shall be taking my leave shortly, for I have an appointment elsewhere."

"Very good, my lord," said Miss Weatherstone. She held out her gloved hand. "Good-bye."

Lord Ashdon took her hand and gave her fingers the lightest squeeze. He said quietly, with a wide smile, "Thank you, ma'am. You have cleared up a terrible misunderstanding."

"I am glad to have done so," said Miss Weatherstone. She glanced at her sister and smiled. "I shall let you visit with his lordship, Belle." She slipped out of the drawing room and closed the door behind her.

Belle looked after her sister in surprise. She would never have thought that Cassandra would do anything so unconventional as to leave her unchaperoned with a gentleman. She looked around quickly. The viscount was staring at her with the oddest smile on his face. "My lord?"

He shook his head. "I was only thinking what a fool I have made of myself. I trust that you will not only forgive, but forget, for I wish only to be on the best footing with you."

Belle moved to the harp and traced the strong curve of its wooden frame with her fingers. "I am honored to count you as my friend, my lord."

Lord Ashdon came close. He covered her hand with his, where it rested on the wood. Quietly, he said, "I wish to become more than your friend, Belle."

Belle did not dare to look up at his face. His breath had been warm on her cheek, so that she knew that if she turned her head it would be much in the order of an invitation for him to kiss her. Her heart was thumping, for she very much wanted to issue that invitation yet was afraid to do so.

"Belle."

His hand left hers, only to gently cup her shoulder and turn her round. She raised her eyes, feeling somewhat shy to be standing so close to him. She was disappointed when he took a step backward.

"You shouldn't look at me like that, Belle." There was a hoarseness in his voice.

"Why?" whispered Belle.

The viscount gave a laugh. "Because I have dreamed of seeing that look in your eyes. It is what sustained me through battle after battle."

Belle was startled. "What?"

Lord Ashdon smiled at her. "My dear Belle, it was that lovely face of yours that I thought about. When I returned to England, it was with the hope that I would find that face, that somehow I could make Miss Weatherstone mine. When I saw you that morning in the park, I thought that my dream had begun to take on reality at last."

"You've been in love with Cassandra all along?" asked Belle, a strange sensation sweeping through her. She had never felt such coldness as now was enveloping her heart.

Lord Ashdon shook his head and said emphatically, "No! Not with Cassandra! I was in love with who I thought she was."

"I don't understand you, my lord," said Belle in a faltering voice.

"When we raced in the park, I was struck with how pale my memories were in comparison to you, Belle. You were more vibrant, more beautiful, more fascinating than I ever would have believed," said Lord Ashdon. He gave a small laugh. "Indeed, I thought that you had changed beyond all recognition, except for your face. I think now that at some deep level, I instinctively knew that I had met someone entirely different from the young lady whom I had first met in Bath."

Belle slid a glance at him from beneath her lashes. "I am very glad that you have discovered who I really am, sir."

"As am I, Belle," said Lord Ashdon. His heated gaze was fixed on her face, bringing a delicate color into her lovely face. He cleared his throat of a sudden obstruction. "Miss Weatherstone, I—"

The door opened and Mrs. Weatherstone swept into the

room. She glanced quickly from her niece's blushing countenance to Lord Ashdon. With a civil smile, she said, "My lord,
I apologize that I was not immediately informed of your arrival. I just this minute learned of your visit to us."

Mrs. Weatherstone had come forward with her hand outstretched, and Lord Ashdon, who had swiftly stepped away
from Belle upon her aunt's entrance, bowed over her fingers.

"That is quite all right, Mrs. Weatherstone. Miss Weatherstone was able to entertain me very well. I knew that she played
well, but I had no notion that she was such an accomplished
harpist," said Lord Ashdon smoothly.

Mrs. Weatherstone shot a surprised look at Belle. "Indeed!
Why, I have never known Belle to give a private performance
before. Thank you for your compliment, my lord. I am certain
that Belle is quite appreciative of it."

"Indeed," said Belle demurely. She felt a happy glow, for
she had read a flicker of regret in his lordship's eyes when
her aunt had entered the room.

Lord Ashdon smiled at the two ladies. "Well! I must be
going. I had not intended to call, as you must know, Miss
Weatherstone. However, your sister's persuasions were difficult to resist."

"Cassandra?" asked Mrs. Weatherstone, her surprise obvious. "Why, how do you mean, my lord?"

"I chanced to encounter Miss Cassandra while she was out
shopping, and she requested that I escort her home," said Lord
Ashdon.

"I see," said Mrs. Weatherstone, her tone thoughtful.

Belle wished very much that her aunt had not come in when
she had. Her heart was still thumping at the memory of the
expression in the viscount's eyes. She was filled with disappointment that she would not now be able to hear what it was
he had meant to say to her.

Lord Ashdon made his good-byes, hesitating for the barest
second over Belle's hand, pressing her fingers between his with

unusual strength. His eyes lingered on her face. "Until we meet again, Miss Weatherstone," he murmured.

When the viscount was gone, Mrs. Weatherstone turned to her niece angrily. "Well, Belle, I believe that there is some explanation due me for your outrageous behavior. It is not seemly for a young lady to receive a gentleman alone, as you know."

Belle was startled by her aunt's attack. "I was not alone. At least, not at first. Cassandra brought Lord Ashdon in with her, and she only recently left his lordship with me."

Mrs. Weatherstone stared. "I cannot believe that Cassandra would ever do anything so thoughtless and unconventional!"

"I do not fib, Aunt," said Belle tightly. All the pleasure of Lord Ashdon's unexpected appearance was somehow tinged by the accusing air of her aunt.

"I am sorry for it, Belle, but I shall have to report to your uncle this latest scandalous behavior," said Mrs. Weatherstone, shaking her head. Her glance was almost pitying. "I fear that I cannot trust you, after what has already gone before."

Belle tossed her head, her temper suddenly flaring. "No, you wouldn't, of course! For Cassandra would never do anything wrong, would she? Not like me, whom you constantly compare to my wonderful, perfect sister!" She rushed out of the drawing room, almost blinded by tears.

Mrs. Weatherstone was horrified. "Belle!"

Chapter 20

❦

As the music played, Lord Ashdon surveyed the company. Most particularly, his eyes sought and followed a certain young damsel. Miss Belle Weatherstone had not had a single opening left on her dance card that evening. His own signature was on two of the lines, and he had already enjoyed the first dance with her. Their second, and last, dance of the evening was a waltz. He had made certain of that, for he wanted to hold Miss Weatherstone in his arms and not share her with all the other gentlemen, as was inevitable in a country set.

His waltz was some minutes away, however, so Lord Ashdon filled the time by making leisurely conversation with others at the ball. Even as he smiled and conversed on a number of polite topics, his eyes strayed often to the dance floor. He found that the sight of Miss Belle Weatherstone dancing with her other admirers grated on him. He was not a man of hasty temper, but there were some things, he had discovered, that did have the capacity to annoy him.

Lord Ashdon reflected that he had very nearly scuttled his own chances with Miss Belle Weatherstone because of his mistaking her identity. As he watched her, he reflected that he might still lose her to any one of a score of admirers.

If only Mrs. Weatherstone had not come into the drawing room just when she had, he thought with regret. He had been on the point of revealing the depth of his interest to Miss Weatherstone. If he had been able to do so, he would not now be wondering just exactly where he stood in her affections. He felt she cared something for him, and he harbored hopes that she would favor his suit.

Lord Ashdon smiled as he thought how circumstances had conspired to bring him to the point of declaring himself to be in love with the wrong woman. How disastrous it would have been to have actually become betrothed to the one sister and, later, to meet the other.

He had liked Miss Cassandra Weatherstone and had been drawn by her undeniable beauty as well as her empathy toward him while he was recovering from his wound. However, he had fallen in love with Miss Belle Weatherstone. He could not truly say why, for in appearance the two young ladies were identical. All that he could say for certain was that Miss Belle Weatherstone had somehow stolen his heart.

Lord Ashdon thought that if he was to make a lasting impression on the Belle of London, he had to make an effort to become her foremost and favorite suitor.

Lady Ashdon came up to the viscount, holding out her hand to him. "Adam, you do not dance."

He bowed over his mother's bejeweled fingers. "I have reserved a later dance, ma'am."

"I noticed that you danced earlier with Miss Weatherstone," remarked Lady Ashdon. "A very good family, I believe. I have remembered that my father knew the girl's grandfather, Sir Marcus Weatherstone. He dabbled in scholarly pursuits, as I recall. I do not believe that Miss Weatherstone has followed in her grandfather's footsteps."

"No, perhaps not," said Lord Ashdon noncommittally, though he felt quite sure of it. He could not imagine anyone being less of a bluestocking than Miss Belle Weatherstone. He was glad of it, for though his own education had been the best, and certainly he knew the value of a good education, he was not himself the least bit bookish or retiring in nature.

Lady Ashdon regarded her son for a long moment. "I quite thought that you meant to go to Bath long before now, Adam."

"I have changed my mind. I believe that I shall remain in London for the rest of the Season," said Lord Ashdon, his gaze straying once more to the dance floor.

Lady Ashdon noticed the direction of her son's eyes, and a little smile crossed her face when she saw that he was watching Miss Weatherstone. "Ah, I am so glad. Such a short visit as we have had could not possibly make up for the time that you were away from England. Perhaps you will at last be able to take your rightful place in Society this Season."

Lord Ashdon turned his head and looked squarely at his mother, his brows drawing together in a frown. "I trust that you do not still harbor hopes of making me into a court-card, ma'am."

"It would do your reputation good if you were to spruce up your wardrobe a bit. Look at your cousin Roland. Or better yet, Sylvan Darlington. I have never liked our new marquis, but one cannot help but admire his social acumen," said Lady Ashdon, gesturing with her fan in the direction of the gentleman.

"My ambitions run in different roads, my lady," said Lord Ashdon with a sigh. "If you recall, I intend to take my seat in Parliament one day."

"Yes, so you have told me. Your father was vastly interested in politics, of course. We scarcely agreed on anything of any importance," said Lady Ashdon in a bored voice.

Lord Ashdon felt the disappointment that he always did when it was brought home to him that his surviving parent had no interest in who he really was or what ambitions he held close. Lady Ashdon's world revolved around the *ton.* As he had known for many, many years, her sole ambition for him had been that he make of himself a social icon. In her ladyship's estimation, that would be the epitome of power and prestige.

The viscount knew that he had always been a grave disappointment to his mother. Not for the first time, he felt the loss of his father more keenly than perhaps he should after the years gone by.

Though he had been brought up mainly by tutors, Lord Ashdon felt that he had enjoyed an unusually close relationship with his father. His sire had taught him independence and had expected him to make a mark in the world. When he had declared himself mad for the army, his father had bought for him, over his mother's strong and vigorous objections, his first pair of colors.

Though the viscount hoped he was as fond of his mother as any son might be, he had long ago felt the need to distance himself emotionally from her. At a young age he had recognized that her ladyship could be overbearing. Lady Ashdon had never wanted him to become a soldier, and that was why he had not disclosed to her that he was not permanently settled in England. It was difficult enough to bear her questions and suggestions about whom he should choose for his bride. He knew that he would have had no peace at all if her ladyship had known that he had not left the army but, on the contrary, fully intended to return to active duty as soon as possible. The timing depended largely on what Napoleon Bonaparte might do. Otherwise, it would be dictated by his wedding date.

His original intention, of course, had been to wed and then leave his new bride at home in England while he went off to war again. Since coming to know Miss Belle Weatherstone, however, he increasingly had visions of taking her, as his wife, along with him.

Lord Ashdon was confident that Belle Weatherstone would not have the least difficulty in following in the tail of the army. He felt that she was up to anything that might be asked of her.

A smile touched his face. Indeed, he rather thought that she would revel in the experience.

"Adam, where have you gone? I am speaking to you."

Lord Ashdon started. He glanced apologetically at his mother. "I am sorry, Mother. I was wool-gathering. What were you saying?"

"I was commenting on the insipid entertainment this evening," said Lady Ashdon in an annoyed tone, waving her gilded fan slowly to and fro.

"I fear that I cannot agree with you, ma'am. I have enjoyed myself," said Lord Ashdon briefly. He had heard the familiar strains of the waltz strike up. "Pray excuse me, Mother. I have solicited this dance." With a bow and a smile, he escaped from his mother and made his way toward Miss Belle Weatherstone.

As always since the clearing up of the misunderstanding that had come between them, Miss Weatherstone greeted him with a brilliant smile and an outstretched hand. "Lord Ashdon! I have been waiting this age for the waltz."

Lord Ashdon laughed, at once feeling a lightening of his own heart in her enthusiasm. "Then let us not delay, Miss Weatherstone." He bowed to Mrs. Weatherstone, who smiled her approval at him, and held out his hand to his partner.

Belle placed her gloved hand in his and looked up at him, her eyes roguish in expression. "I warn you, my lord, I have been practicing. You will not find me wanting, I think."

"Practicing, Miss Weatherstone?" Lord Ashdon felt a spurt of jealousy. He glanced down at her as he escorted her onto the floor. "With whom, if I may make so bold to ask?"

"Oh, with Philip Raven, my sister's betrothed. Cassandra has been so good as to play for me while Philip spins me about the room," said Belle. She chuckled. "Poor Philip! I fear that I have been very demanding of his time, when he would far rather spend all of his hours with Cassandra. But he has always been excessively good-natured. As a boy, he endured my most bullying tactics."

"Then you have known Philip Raven since you were a child?" asked Lord Ashdon, leading her off with his arm laid snugly around her slim waist and holding her hand lightly in his.

"Oh, yes! He is my grandfather's godson and lived with us at the Hall until he went up to school. I missed him, of course, for he was my only playmate," said Belle.

"Ah, yes! I vaguely recall something he said once about his godfather," said Lord Ashdon.

"Then you are well acquainted with Philip?" asked Belle.

"I know Philip Raven from the war in Spain. It was he who carried me out of harm's way when I was wounded," said Lord Ashdon.

"Then I am very, very grateful to him, indeed," said Belle softly, glancing up at the viscount's scarred brow through her lashes.

"I do not see Raven or your sister this evening," commented Lord Ashdon. "Indeed, now that you have put me in mind of it, I have seen nothing of them. Do they not intend to go out in Society while they are in London?"

Belle shook her head. "Cassandra is refusing to go out into Society because she does not wish to get caught up in a round of entertainments when she is so busy preparing for the wedding and the trip abroad. Cassandra and Philip are dining with my uncle this evening." She smiled, a little wistfully, and shook her head again. "I am very happy for them, of course. I do wish, however, that they could remain in England a while longer. It will be difficult to let them go off to Vienna."

"The Congress of Vienna?" asked Lord Ashdon quickly.

"Why, yes. Philip has accepted a diplomatic post," said Belle, pleased by his lordship's quick understanding. "I envy Cassandra and Philip. It will no doubt be very exciting to be involved in such heady stuff as deciding the terms of the peace now that we don't have to worry about Napoleon Bonaparte any longer."

"Quite! However, I do not believe that everything will be decided over a table," said Lord Ashdon with a sudden frown.

"Why, what can you mean?" asked Belle, curious. She had assumed that with the forming of the international congress all threat of war breaking out must be gone. It had relieved her to think so, for she had not liked the thought of Lord Ashdon returning to the army.

He laughed and shrugged. "You must forgive me, Miss Weatherstone. I was but thinking aloud. It is still my unfortunate opinion that we have not seen the last of Bonaparte."

"Do you mean . . . despite the Congress, there will be war again?" asked Belle, surprised and dismayed.

Lord Ashdon hesitated, then nodded. Very seriously, he said, "Quite possibly, Belle. It is not a popular opinion, believe me, but it is what I suspect will happen."

"But . . . what will you or Philip or the rest do if there is war again?" asked Belle, a sinking feeling somewhere in the vicinity of her stomach.

"Why, we shall be off to earn another day of glory for England," said Lord Ashdon flippantly.

Belle shook her head. "My lord, pray do not shrug off my question. The answer is of vital concern to me."

Lord Ashdon looked down into her face as he turned her again and again in the graceful steps of the waltz. Slowly he said, "Very well, Belle. I shall speak openly to you. I myself am returning to duty in a few short months. I have been on extended leave this spring. You will naturally not tout that around, for I have not yet informed my mother of my plans."

"Lady Ashdon does not know that you are still with the army?" asked Belle quickly. "My dear sir, you must tell her!"

"I intend to, Miss Weatherstone, when the time is right," said Lord Ashdon.

Belle was silent for several seconds, turning over in her mind what he had confided to her. She looked up into his face, her eyes steady and frank in expression. "Lord Ashdon, I pray that you are wrong about Napoleon Bonaparte. I-I would not like to lose your friendship."

"You shall not, Miss Weatherstone, whatever the outcome," promised Lord Ashdon. More than ever, he regretted her aunt's unfortunate timing that afternoon. His hand tightened about her fingers, almost painfully. In a lowered voice, he said, "I shall not leave without first coming to you."

Belle felt her heart thumping at the intensity in his gaze and in his voice. She did not know quite what he meant by what he had said, but she hoped that she did. "Will—will you visit my uncle?" she asked breathlessly, then blushed fiercely at her boldness. She knew without hearing it from her aunt that she had been unforgivably forward. Quickly she said, "Forgive me, my lord! You need not answer that. It was a thoughtless question."

"However, I shall answer it, Belle, if you answer me this," said Lord Ashdon. His expression was somber, not at all that of a polite dance partner. "Do you wish me to wait upon your uncle?"

Belle felt her cheeks grow even warmer, if that was possible. She did not look directly into his face as she replied. Through uncharacteristic shyness, she stammered, "I-I would not be at all adverse to it, my lord."

"You have made me a very happy man, Belle," said Lord Ashdon quietly.

As Belle hesitantly met his gaze, he smiled at her. She responded with a glad peal of laughter. "Oh, Adam! I rather think that I shall enjoy following in the wake of an army!"

"What of afterward, ma'am? Will you be as enthusiastic about playing hostess to a great man in politics?" asked Lord Ashdon, a smile playing about his mouth.

Belle's mouth dropped open. "Me? My lord! I-I have never given a thought to such a thing."

"I have ambitions of sitting in Parliament, Belle. My social obligations will no doubt be extraordinary. Does that frighten you?" asked Lord Ashdon.

Belle shook her head. "No! At least, not as much as I suspect it might if I knew precisely what would be expected."

Lord Ashdon laughed. As the beautiful strains of the waltz ended, he stopped and drew her arm through his. "You need not answer me right now, Belle. There is time and enough to discuss everything between us. For now, reflect only on what answer you might make if I were to wait upon your uncle."

They had walked back the short distance to Belle's chair. He handed her back into the care of her aunt, murmuring pleasantries to both ladies before he left them. Catching Belle's gaze, he lifted her hand to his lips. "Until next we meet," he said quietly.

"Yes," said Belle, feeling warmth stealing into her face again.

After the viscount stepped away, Mrs. Weatherstone observed, "Lord Ashdon is a delightful gentleman." She looked searchingly at her niece's face. "I trust that you had an interesting conversation while you were dancing, Belle?"

"Yes, oh, yes!" said Belle, smiling. She turned shining eyes to her aunt. "Aunt Margaret, his lordship means to call upon my uncle!"

"Belle! Are you certain?" asked Mrs. Weatherstone, her eyes widening.

"He hinted at it very strongly, ma'am," said Belle. Her smile faded slightly as she looked anxiously at her aunt. The quarrel that had sprung up between them, and that had been resolved just as swiftly, was nevertheless very prominent in her memory. "Will that be acceptable, Aunt Margaret?"

"My dearest niece! I have not the least objection, I assure you!"

Belle went about for the remainder of the evening in a haze of happiness. Her preoccupation with her suddenly radiant future was such that she almost forgot her social graces. When someone or other engaged her in conversation or posed a question to her, she was apt to reply in a disjointed fashion that was completely uncharacteristic. It was fortunate that Mrs. Weatherstone was engaged in her own conversations, or otherwise Belle would certainly have earned herself a scold. During a lull after dinner, to which she had been partnered by Lord Ashdon, she was recalled to herself rather abruptly by her friends.

Clarice Moorehead's voice broke in on Belle's pleasant reverie. "Belle has not moved nor uttered more than two coherent sentences since dining with Lord Ashdon."

"Perhaps the viscount has bewitched her."

"Let us see."

Fingers snapped directly in front of Belle's eyes. Belle fell back in her chair, turning her head in astonishment. "Clarice! Whatever are you doing?"

"I wished to see whether I could awaken the sleeping beauty," said Clarice reasonably. Millicent Carruthers, seated on her other side, hid a giggle behind her pretty painted fan.

"I am very much awake," said Belle.

"I thought only the kiss of her very own prince could awaken a sleeping beauty," said Millicent teasingly, even as she gestured with her fan toward Lord Ashdon's approaching figure.

Belle felt her face flame, while her friends giggled at her expense. When the viscount came up to the trio, she lifted a fierily blushing countenance to his gaze. She pressed one hand against a hot cheek, scarcely able to greet him with equanimity.

Lord Ashdon gravely greeted each of the young ladies and conversed lightly for a few minutes. Belle was just beginning to regain her composure when he suddenly held out his hand to her. With the attractive smile that never failed to make her pulse flutter, Lord Ashdon said, "I believe this is my dance, Miss Weatherstone."

Clarice and Millicent bore twin expressions of astonishment and exchanged a quick wide-eyed glance, as Belle laid her hand in the viscount's and allowed him to draw her to her feet.

As Lord Ashdon led her toward the dance floor, Belle suddenly realized the import of her friends' obvious amazement. She faltered, a frisson of alarm running up her spine. She had already stood up twice that evening with Lord Ashdon. She knew, thanks to her aunt's stringent training, that to do so for a third time would be to court gossip.

"My lord!" she stammered, pulling back. "We must not!"

Lord Ashdon's grip tightened. "I know, but I care little for it!" There was a light in his lake-blue eyes as he gazed back at her, a hint of recklessness about his mouth, that she had never seen before.

Belle glanced swiftly around, hoping that none had yet noticed them approach the dance floor. "My lord, I implore you," she said in a low, urgent voice. "My aunt would never forgive me if I were to make a spectacle of myself."

The light died out of his eyes, and a rueful expression stole over his face. "Forgive me! For a moment, I felt able to defy the very gates of hell itself to waltz with you again this night."

Belle studied him closely. "Lord Ashdon, are-are you inebriated?" she asked cautiously. She had never seen the viscount in anything resembling that state, but then, she admitted to herself, she knew little about such things.

"Inebriated, no. Mad, very possibly," muttered Lord Ashdon. He sighed and changed directions, easing Belle's hand under his elbow as though they had not actually been headed toward the dance floor at all but were engaged in a slow promenade around the periphery of the ballroom. "Shall I escort you to the refreshment room, Belle? It is not far."

"An ice would not come amiss, my lord." Belle threw an upward glance at his lordship's extremely pleasing profile. She was at once troubled and thrilled by the viscount's odd behavior. "Lord Ashdon—would you really have danced with me again?"

He looked down at her, his smile crooked. "I wish that I was just so bold, Belle. But alas, I am not so self-centered or arrogant as to forget what is owed to you. I could not place your reputation in jeopardy or make you the object of insufferable gossip."

Belle shook her head, feeling mild confusion. "But just for a moment, I thought—"

"Just for a moment, I pretended that I could do as I pleased," he said almost roughly.

Belle thought it over, and a small smile came to her lips. She glanced up at his lordship. "I am glad—that you pretended, I mean. I should have liked to dance with you again, you see." She gave a laugh. "I fear that I am less conventional than I should be!"

"Miss Weatherstone, has anyone yet told you that your eyes smile like stars in the heavens, or that your laughter makes a man's pulse leap?" asked Lord Ashdon in a low but intense voice.

Belle felt a blush spreading over her face. She looked up quickly at him, wide-eyed. "My lord, are-are you making love to me?"

"Not as I should like, believe me," said Lord Ashdon. He spied an alcove, half hidden behind a wide column and deserted, and swiftly guided her into it, sweeping the curtain shut behind them. He grasped her about the waist, eliciting a small gasp of surprise, and pulled her into his embrace. He then kissed her thoroughly, before setting her away from him with a controlled movement. He lifted his hand and caressed her full half-parted lips with his thumb. "Would that I were making love to you, Belle," he said on a ragged breath.

Belle was pale and red by turns. She was speechless, her gaze locked with his. She had an intent expression in her eyes, as though she sought to read his very thoughts.

"We shall not long remain undiscovered," said Lord Ashdon in a more normal voice. He tucked her hand into his elbow and proceeded with her out of the curtained alcove. "I believe that you mentioned an ice, Miss Weatherstone."

"Yes, yes, I did," said Belle somewhat breathlessly.

Chapter 21

⁓

Belle was informed by her aunt on the following morning at breakfast that Lady Ashdon had sent round her card and an invitation for them to wait upon her that afternoon.

"Why, isn't that rather unusual, Aunt?" asked Belle, looking curiously at the card and the short penned message on it. She knew enough now about London social mores that her question was almost rhetorical. Lady Ashdon's request was definitely out of the common.

"Let me see it, too, Belle." Her sister held out her hand, and Belle relinquished the calling card to Cassandra.

"Yes, indeed. Her ladyship is very high in the instep. It could, however, very well have to do with what you related to me last evening," said Mrs. Weatherstone with a twinkle in her eye.

Belle looked round quickly and, meeting her aunt's gaze, felt warmth steal into her cheeks. "Oh! You mean about Lord Ashdon."

Mrs. Weatherstone nodded and smiled. "Precisely. I suspect that Lady Ashdon is in his lordship's confidence and has decided that she should get to know you a bit better than a social setting has allowed."

Belle felt a twinge of dismay. "Oh, dear! I suppose this means that I must win Lady Ashdon's approval." She worried her lip with her teeth. "I do hope that I may impress her ladyship favorably."

Cassandra had been listening with interest, her teacup held between her slender hands. She chuckled a little. "Now is your chance, Belle, to prove you are pluck to the backbone as ever! I know if I had received such a summons as that I would be quaking in my shoes at this instant."

"Nonsense, Cassandra! Belle has nothing whatsoever to fear," said Mrs. Weatherstone calmly. "Lady Ashdon has bestowed a very gracious invitation upon us, which we shall naturally be pleased to accept. I daresay that it will be a very nice tea."

Belle exchanged a speaking glance with her twin sister, who merely chuckled again and shook her head.

"I am glad not to be in your shoes, Belle," said Cassandra. She gave an exaggerated shiver. "What you and our aunt have said about Lady Ashdon has given me a decided impression about that fearsome lady."

"That will be quite enough, my dear," said Mrs. Weatherstone with a reproving frown. "Pray do have some consideration for Belle's natural trepidation. There is much at stake concerning her future happiness."

"Oh, isn't that a comfortable thought," said Belle with exaggerated cordiality.

Cassandra laughed, and even Mrs. Weatherstone chuckled.

Later that afternoon Belle and her aunt were driven to Lady Ashdon's address in a fashionable part of town. They were let into the town house by a supercilious servant and ushered into the drawing room, where they were met by their hostess.

Belle had a fleeting impression of imposing black-and-gold decor before she turned her attention to her ladyship.

Lady Ashdon came forward to shake hands with Mrs. Weatherstone and then with Belle. Her wintry gaze encompassed them, taking note of their fashionable ensembles with apparent approval. "Ah, Mrs. Weatherstone! And Miss Weatherstone. I am so pleased that you were able to call on me today."

"It is our great pleasure to do so, my lady," said Mrs. Weatherstone with polite civility, removing her gloves. Belle also removed hers, knowing full well from her aunt's reaction that she had decided to stay for several minutes.

Lady Ashdon nodded, as though she had expected nothing less. "Pray do be seated. We shall have tea momentarily. Meanwhile, let us be cozy together, shall we?"

Belle thought that nothing could be more ludicrous than Lady Ashdon's admonishment to "be cozy." Her ladyship was as starched up as always, looking down her long nose at whomever she was addressing and always with the slightest condescending smile upon her lips. She was turned out in an elegant gown that had obviously cost a fortune, diamonds winking from her ears and from around her neck, while bracelets adorned her wrists. There was nothing either about her ladyship or in the fantastically furnished drawing room that was the least bit cozy.

Belle merely smiled politely and waited for her cues from her aunt. She did not wish to do or say anything that might offend the grand lady. Of course, she wouldn't have cared a snap of her fingers for the outcome of this grand audience except that she did not wish to let Lord Ashdon down.

While Lady Ashdon and Mrs. Weatherstone were exchanging pleasantries, the tea was brought in. Lady Ashdon broke off to instruct the servants where to place the cakes and biscuits. "Belle, would you be so good as to pour tea?" she asked, turning her cool, imperious gaze on the younger woman.

"Of course, my lady," said Belle with a smile. At her aunt's long look, she smiled again. She well knew that the proper pouring of tea was the first test of gentility, but she was confident that she could perform the social graces without embarrassing herself or her aunt. Her governess had at least been successful in instilling that much into her.

Lady Ashdon continued to converse with Mrs. Weatherstone while Belle poured the tea. Her ladyship nodded her approval of the younger woman's performance. "Very well done, Miss

Weatherstone. You are not made nervous in my presence, or
if you are, you hide it very well."

"Thank you, Lady Ashdon," said Belle, feeling laughter bubbling up inside her at the lady's condescending attitude. Nevertheless, she managed to keep a solemn face. It would not do
at all to laugh at her ladyship.

Lady Ashdon sipped delicately at her tea, only tasting it before setting down the cup. "Miss Weatherstone, you have undoubtedly wondered why I asked that you and your aunt visit
me. I have asked you here because my son, Lord Ashdon, has
shown signs of favoring you over some of the other young
ladies. In light of this, I wished to get to know you a little
better than we might have done at some insipid function."

"You flatter me by your attention, my lady," said Belle
briefly, inclining her head in a civil gesture.

Mrs. Weatherstone nodded, her eyes expressing approval for
her niece's polite disclaimer. "Indeed, you flatter us both by
this kind invitation, my lady."

Lady Ashdon waved aside their thanks as though it was her
due. "I know nothing detrimental about your family, my dear
ladies, which naturally is all to your credit. In fact, I do believe that I have heard that one of the Weatherstones was quite
a scholar in his day. I happen to recall Sir Marcus very well.
He was a contemporary of my father's you know."

"Sir Marcus is my father-in-law. He is Belle's guardian and
raised her at his estate, providing a very good governess for
her," said Mrs. Weatherstone. "It was with his permission that
Mr. Weatherstone and I brought our niece to London for the
Season."

Lady Ashdon nodded with a thoughtful air. "Very proper, I
am sure." She turned to Belle. "How is Sir Marcus, Miss Weatherstone? I apprehend that you are close to him."

"He is well, my lady. I had a letter from my grandfather
not so long past," said Belle, wondering at her ladyship's expression of interest. She rather thought Lady Ashdon was sim-

ply indulging in civilities, for she could not imagine that her ladyship could actually be interested in a recluse such as her grandfather. Lady Ashdon's world revolved around the *ton,* and Sir Marcus had been gone from London for a number of years.

"I am glad to hear it. Mrs. Weatherstone, you have done admirably well by your duty. I distinctly recall reading a betrothal notice for Miss Weatherstone's sister not long since," said Lady Ashdon. "Is the other Miss Weatherstone marrying well?"

"Cassandra is betrothed to Mr. Philip Raven, who is my father-in-law's godson. He has recently accepted a diplomatic post to Vienna, and they will be leaving England shortly after the wedding," said Mrs. Weatherstone proudly.

"Quite respectable," approved Lady Ashdon.

"Yes, quite," said Belle, a little irritated that her ladyship seemed to feel that her personal blessing was required for the happy couple.

Lady Ashdon turned to stare at her rather haughtily, while Mrs. Weatherstone briefly closed her eyes. Belle met her ladyship's gaze steadily. The tick of the mantel clock was loud in the stretching silence.

Lady Ashdon finally allowed a small smile to touch her thin lips. There was even a gleam of amusement in her cold eyes. "It is my considered opinion that you are a trifle high-spirited yet from youth, Miss Weatherstone—though that is not a great fault. You will undoubtedly grow beyond it."

Mrs. Weatherstone smiled and agreed, only sending a begging glance in her niece's direction. Belle acknowledged her aunt's concern and decided to mind her manners. She therefore smiled demurely at Lady Ashdon, saying, "I am more flattered than I can say, my lady, by your kind words."

Lady Ashdon inclined her head. She subsequently brought the tea to an end, bestowing her gracious good-byes and two fingers to each of her guests. "Regis shall see you out. I trust that we shall see one another frequently as the Season progresses, Mrs. Weatherstone, Miss Weatherstone."

"Of course," agreed Mrs. Weatherstone.

Belle murmured something polite and followed her aunt out of the drawing room. They were shown out of the town house and handed up by a black-liveried footman into their carriage, which was waiting at the curb.

As the carriage pulled away into the traffic, Belle turned to her aunt. "Well! Her ladyship wasted no time on us, did she? It was fifteen minutes to the dot, and our carriage was at the door. What a very strange interview, Aunt Margaret!"

Mrs. Weatherstone laughed. "Oh, it was not so very strange, Belle. It is as I told you. Lady Ashdon merely wished to take your measure because her son has expressed an interest in you."

Belle blushed at her aunt's cool observation, but she felt some indignation. "I do resent, just a trifle, being inspected like some prime filly on the block."

"If it makes you feel any better, Belle, I believe that you acquitted yourself well. Though I do admit that I was put in a bit of a quake when you made it ever so obvious that her ladyship's approval of Cassandra and Philip's union was superfluous," said Mrs. Weatherstone.

"Which indeed it was," retorted Belle. "However, I do apologize for my quick temper, ma'am. I realized almost at once that I had made a mistake, but there was really no fixing it once I had spoken."

"I am just thankful that Lady Ashdon decided not to take offense," said Mrs. Weatherstone with a sigh. There was a hopeful smile on her face and a far-off look in her eyes. "Oh, Belle, if you were to receive an offer from Lord Ashdon it would be quite wonderful."

"I am beginning to think so, too, ma'am," said Belle quietly.

As the carriage neared the town house, she began daydreaming again about the viscount. He was really quite handsome, and he never bored her when he spoke with her. He was always interested in what she had to say, besides. Belle thought that they were compatible in their tastes and interests as well. They both liked to ride and hunt and had agreed that the country had certain advantages over town. Lord Ashdon would naturally wish to spend each Season in London if he was to step into politics, which would suit her very well since she did like to go to parties and other entertainments.

Belle sat up a little straighter. A disturbing thought had occurred to her. If she were to marry Lord Ashdon, then naturally she would be obligated to play hostess during the Season, and she had not the least notion how to be a good political hostess.

"Aunt Margaret, I think it would be a very good thing if I learned a little bit about how to go about entertaining," said Belle decisively. At her aunt's surprised glance and raised eyebrows, she felt a blush coming to her face. "Miss Bidwell did try to teach me the rudiments, but I fear that I have forgotten most of what she tried to impart to me. Will you take me in hand, Aunt?"

"Of course I shall, Belle. I will be delighted to do so, in fact," said Mrs. Weatherstone quickly. She reached out to squeeze her niece's hand. "My dearest Belle, you continue to amaze me. I am very proud of you and of what you are becoming."

"Thank you, Aunt," said Belle, truly grateful for her aunt's support. She was determined to learn as much and as quickly as she could, for she did not wish to be a disgrace or a detriment to Lord Ashdon.

A pang of anxiety struck her. That is, if he did indeed talk to her uncle and offer for her hand.

Belle hoped very much that he would. She remembered that Lord Ashdon had remarked that he would be returning to duty in a short time. She hoped not only that she would have an offer from him before he left but that they could be wed so that she could accompany him overseas. It bothered her not a whit that there could not possibly be time for a fine wedding before that embarkation. It would probably be a scrambling affair, but what of it if she were able to achieve her new ambition? Lady Ashdon. How fine that sounded!

Chapter 22

Belle and her sister had spent a companionable afternoon shopping and had returned laughing and laden with packages. As they looked over their purchases upstairs in Cassandra's bedroom, a knock sounded on the door. At being bidden to enter, a maid came in, bearing the look of one with important news. "Beggin' yer pardon, Miss Belle." She looked uncertainly from one of the ladies to the other.

Understanding the woman's dilemma, Belle chuckled. "That is me."

The maid appeared relieved. "Yes, miss, o' course it is. I was sent by the missus to tell you that his lordship is below-stairs."

Belle started up at once, losing all interest in what she was to wear that evening. "Oh, am I to come down? I shall be there directly."

"No, indeed, miss!" The maid looked appalled. "I was sent to tell you that his lordship is closeted with the mister in his study."

"Belle!" Cassandra caught her sister up in a quick hug before looking at her face. She went into a peal of laughter. "My dear, you look positively dazed."

"Cassandra, he has come to offer for me," whispered Belle, raising her hands to press them against her blushing cheeks.

"Well, of course he has, ninny! It is obvious that Lord Ashdon is in love with you," said Cassandra. She looked around at the maid, who was standing in the doorway and listening with patent interest. "Pray go down and tell my aunt that Miss Belle shall be here in her room awaiting my uncle's summons."

"Yes, miss!" The maid whisked herself off.

"Do you wish me to wait with you?" asked Cassandra.

"Yes-no . . . oh, Cassandra, I am all shaking inside," exclaimed Belle, throwing out her hands in an appeal for her sister's understanding.

Cassandra smiled, just a little. "I understand perfectly, my dear. You've got a few minutes to compose yourself, I should think, and you will do it better if I leave you alone. I know how self-reliant you are!" She kissed her sister on the cheek and let herself out of the bedroom.

Belle at once rushed over to the cheval glass and anxiously began to take stock of her appearance.

Lord Ashdon's arrival a few minutes earlier had not created much of a stir in the household at first, for it was well known that he was an admirer of Miss Weatherstone's. However, his lordship had asked not for Miss Weatherstone but for Mr. Weatherstone. Instantly, the purpose of his visit was embued with all the import of a royal visit. The news flew from mouth to mouth, eventually resulting in Mrs. Weatherstone's hurried message to her niece.

Lord Ashdon knew nothing of the excitement that spread swiftly through the house. His perceptions were harnessed to a single purpose. Feeling that a sufficient understanding had developed between himself and Miss Belle Weatherstone, he had requested an interview with her uncle.

Mr. Weatherstone received him in a friendly way in his study and urged the viscount to make himself comfortable, coming round his mahogany desk to usher his guest toward the striped wingbacks situated before the warm fireplace.

Lord Ashdon smiled as he sat down opposite the older gentleman. He felt a twinge of nervousness, much as he might have experienced before the dawn of a day's battle. "You may imagine my errand, sir."

Mr. Weatherstone nodded. His eyes were keen with intelligence. "I am unsurprised, my lord. I thought that I could shortly expect a visit from you."

Lord Ashdon nodded, relieved that his announcement had been received with complete civility. He leaned forward and said earnestly, "Mr. Weatherstone, I respect and love your niece, Miss Belle Weatherstone. I have come to ask your permission to solicit her hand in marriage."

Mr. Weatherstone smiled in a kindly fashion. "My dear sir, my permission is granted. Though I am not Belle's guardian, my father, who is, entrusted her to my care. I can assure you already that the pressing of your suit would be acceptable to Sir Marcus."

Lord Ashdon flushed. "That is gratifying, sir. May I request a short audience with Miss Weatherstone so that I may relate what I hope to be good news?"

"Of course, my lord." Mr. Weatherstone stood up, and upon the viscount's standing also, he shook hands with the younger man. "I will show you to the drawing room, where you may wait while I go in search of Belle. Perhaps you would like a glass of brandy."

Lord Ashdon agreed and allowed himself to be ushered into the drawing room, where the impassive butler thoughtfully provided a full decanter and a pair of glasses, before removing himself quietly from the room and leaving the viscount to his own reflections.

Lord Ashdon poured himself a small measure of wine, but before he had done more than swirl the brandy in the glass, his gaze fell on Belle's harp. He set down the wineglass and walked over to the harp, to touch a few of the strings. The discordant sound made him smile, for he was remembering how Miss Weatherstone had made the instrument sing. He trusted that in years to come she would play often for him alone.

The door opened behind him and he swiftly turned. Miss Weatherstone had stepped into the room and was now regarding him with an inquiring and somewhat startled expression. "My lord!"

Lord Ashdon grinned and strode up to her. He took both her unresisting hands. "Miss Weatherstone! I am the most fortunate of men. I have been granted permission to press my suit with you, which I intend to do because you are the loveliest creature that I have ever beheld. Will you consent to become my wife?"

Miss Weatherstone had colored up. "Pray let go of my hands, Lord Ashdon! I have no intention of wedding you, my lord!"

Lord Ashdon was taken aback. Her announcement took him completely by surprise. His fingers tightened on hers. "You do not wish to wed me?"

"Oh, no!" exclaimed Miss Weatherstone, shaking her head quickly but with a smile trembling upon her lips. "I couldn't possibly."

The door opened again. Another Miss Weatherstone entered the room. Lord Ashdon took one look and closed his eyes in acute embarrassment.

When Belle saw her sister's hands in Lord Ashdon's clasp, she gave a peal of laughter. "Lord Ashdon, I hope that you do not mean to declare yourself to Cassandra. You will be vastly disappointed in her answer, for she must perforce confess that she is already betrothed. But I would be delighted to wed you, if it is really I that you want!"

Lord Ashdon dropped Cassandra's hands, heat flushing his face. "My pardon! I am sorry, Miss Weatherstone! I did not realize—"

Cassandra chuckled. "Yes, so I am aware. I thought you were with my uncle in his study, otherwise I would have waited to come in for my embroidery. I shall just retrieve it and remove myself, and so any lingering confusion. Good-bye, my lord!"

The door closed behind her. Belle waited only to be certain of their privacy before she advanced toward the viscount, a roguish smile on her face. "You were saying, my lord?"

Lord Ashdon loosened his starched white cravat with one finger. "Ah! Yes, I almost forgot in my mortification." With sincere regret on his face, he said contritely, "Forgive me, Belle! I did not realize that she wasn't you. I hope that Raven doesn't call me out for this."

Belle laughed at him. "Really, Ashdon! You are such a nonsensical creature on occasion."

Lord Ashdon swooped down on her and caught her up in his arms. He smiled down into her suddenly very wide eyes. "Am I, indeed! And you, my dearest girl, are a sore trial and temptation!" He lowered his head and kissed her thoroughly.

When he set her back onto her feet, Belle staggered slightly. She held on to his lapel with one hand and his coat sleeve with the other. "My goodness! I am so glad that I came in when I did. Cassandra would have been covered with confusion if you had kissed her."

"I think it is just as well that your sister and Raven are going to Vienna. It would be quite disconcerting to keep mistaking your twin sister for you," said Lord Ashdon.

"Yes, if you made a practice of kissing her, Philip *would* have to call you out," said Belle.

Lord Ashdon laughed and agreed, then kissed her again. Afterward they sat together for several minutes, their hands entwined, and quietly discussed the future. When he was preparing to take his leave, he told Belle that he had persuaded Mr. Weatherstone to put the announcement of their betrothal into the *Gazette* at once. "For I don't wish to take the chance that someone else will turn your head."

"It couldn't be done," whispered Belle, looking up into his face.

Instead of raising her hand to his lips in the conventional manner, as he had intended, he kissed her again.

Belle exited the drawing room in a happy haze, accompanied by her betrothed. Lord Ashdon left the town house with the congratulations of Mr. and Mrs. Weatherstone and of Miss Cassandra Weatherstone and Mr. Philip Raven, who had arrived to take his lady for a drive in the park.

After the viscount and the others were gone, Belle turned to her aunt. "I hope that you will help me, Aunt, in making the wedding plans and getting together a trousseau."

"Oh, you need not fret, Belle. There will be ample time to do so," said Mrs. Weatherstone comfortably. "The date has not yet been set, but I anticipate that it will be sometime in June."

Belle shook her head. "I am sorry, Aunt, but the wedding must take place much sooner."

"Why, whatever for, Belle?" asked Mrs. Weatherstone in surprise.

"Belle, is there something that you wish to tell us?" asked Mr. Weatherstone quietly.

Belle smiled at her uncle. "Yes, sir. Lord Ashdon told me in confidence that he is still with the army. I am going with him when he returns to duty."

"Still with the army! But how can this be?" exclaimed Mrs. Weatherstone in dismay. She looked from her spouse's suddenly thoughtful expression back to her niece. "I have heard nothing of this before. You must be mistaken, Belle."

Mr. Weatherstone held up his hand. "Peace, Margaret. Belle, are you certain of this?"

"Quite certain, sir. Lord Ashdon has not informed Lady Ashdon of his plans, which is why it is not generally known," said Belle.

Mr. Weatherstone regarded her for a long moment. "It has to do with Bonaparte, does it not?"

Belle was surprised. "Why, yes. Lord Ashdon told me that he is expecting there to be war again."

"War! What nonsense!" exclaimed Mrs. Weatherstone sharply.

"It is not so nonsensical as one might think," said Mr. Weatherstone with a deep frown on his face.

Mrs. Weatherstone stared at her husband, then turned swiftly to her niece. "You will not go, Belle! I'll not have you anywhere near danger."

"It is not our decision, Margaret," said Mr. Weatherstone.

"But Phineas, if there is to be war—! Why can she not remain here safely in England with us?"

"She will abide by her husband's wishes, Margaret. If Bonaparte does indeed break the peace, I trust that Lord Ashdon will choose to send Belle home," said Mr. Weatherstone heavily.

"So I should hope!" said Mrs. Weatherstone, agitatedly searching for her handkerchief.

Belle hugged her aunt. "Pray do not be so concerned, Aunt. You know that I am just like a cat. I always land on my feet."

Mrs. Weatherstone gave a watery chuckle. "Thank you! You have put things quite in perspective, Belle! Like a cat, indeed!" She gave a sniff and put her handkerchief away. "Well! It seems that we shall have two weddings before the Season is out. There is much to be done. Belle, I think that perhaps we shall go to the modiste tomorrow and begin making some decisions on your wedding gown and trousseau."

"Thank you, Aunt," said Belle gratefully, flashing a swift smile. "Now if you will excuse me, I must pen a letter to my grandfather to inform him that I am wedding a soldier!"

"You might mention that he is also a viscount," suggested Mrs. Weatherstone. "I don't wish Sir Marcus to think that I have been behind in my duty toward you and allowed you to contract a colorless marriage!"

"Yes, we would undoubtedly hear the eruption from here," murmured Mr. Weatherstone.

"Oh, but I think that I shall tease Grandfather for a few

pages," said Belle mischievously. "Then, at the very last, I shall make a note of Lord Ashdon's title. He will feel very sheepish over his outburst when he realizes that you have done well by me after all."

Mr. Weatherstone threw back his head and laughed.

"You are a minx, Belle," said Mrs. Weatherstone severely, but with a smile in her eyes.

Chapter 23

~

The next week Belle went around in a haze of happiness. The viscount had put an announcement of their betrothal into the *Gazette,* and everywhere she went she received the congratulations of the *ton.* Lord Ashdon was solicitous in his escort. Belle never set foot into another ballroom without the viscount beside her. It was a wonderful, fabulous time.

Belle's particular friends expressed their happiness for her and also a little envy. "For you have managed to snap up one of the most eligible *partis* in London this Season," said Clarice Moorehead with a small pout.

Millicent Carruthers agreed. "Indeed! However, we all knew that Belle was nutty on Lord Ashdon, so it works out very well."

"I have heard that we are shortly to hear an interesting announcement about you, too, Millicent," said Belle with a teasing smile.

Her friend blushed and shyly admitted to it. "Yes—that is, I am hopeful that Papa will consent."

"Why should he not? Angus is a very good catch," said Clarice instantly.

"You must say that, since he is your brother," said Belle.

A dimple peeped out at the corner of Miss Moorehead's smiling mouth, "Quite true, Belle."

"Oh, no, no! You mustn't put it just that way, Belle, even

in fun. Angus and Clarice are very fond of each other," said Millicent, a little distressed.

"Of course we are," agreed Clarice. "I own, however, that I am surprised that Angus has shown such good sense. I never expected him to offer for anyone whom I should like. Actually, I did not think that there was a lady alive who could put up with his crotchets and his teasing."

"I do not think that Angus is the least crotchety," said Millicent.

"Wait until you have lived with him for a while," advised Clarice.

Millicent blushed furiously and was so consumed by confusion that she was rendered momentarily speechless.

Belle laughed. "For my part, I believe that you must love him very much, Millicent, since you actually like his abominable poetry!"

Recovering her composure somewhat, Millicent smiled and shook her head. "Angus composes some very nice verse."

"Of course he does," said Belle. She threw a laughing glance toward Clarice, who rolled her eyes eloquently. Though she teased Millicent, she knew exactly what her friend was feeling. She was herself still dazed by her own good fortune.

She had already written her grandfather and had received his letter by return post. Sir Marcus had bestowed his blessing upon her choice and expressed his amazement and contentment that she had done so well for herself.

"I know of the Ashdons. They are an old and honorable family. I could not have wished better for you, Belle," he had written.

Surrounded by goodwill and approval, Belle felt that everything was right in her world. She seemed to have entered a new dimension where everyone she met and everything she did was pleasant.

*   *   *

A few days later, Lady Ashdon was driving down a main thoroughfare, wrapped in pleasant thoughts of her son's soon-to-be marriage. Though Miss Weatherstone was not her first choice for the viscount, the young lady would do quite well. Lady Ashdon had been satisfied with the outcome of her little tea with Miss Weatherstone and her aunt. Quite a respectable family, and from what she had been given to understand through discreet questionings of her friends and acquaintances, Miss Weatherstone had a very decent portion.

Lady Ashdon was well pleased. The viscount would soon be safely settled into married life, and his unfathomable thirst for adventure would be quenched forever. An increasing nursery had a tendency to do that to a man.

When the viscount had returned to England, Lady Ashdon had detected that same familiar restlessness in her son. It seemed that nothing had changed except that he had finally agreed with her that it was time to take a wife. She had been thoroughly invigorated by that reluctant admission and had redoubled her persuasions that he remain in London for the Season. When the viscount had given up his announced intention to go to Bath—for what reason he wished to go there had never been made perfectly clear to her—and announced that he was staying in town, she had been made hopeful that some young miss had indeed caught his eye. And so it had proven, she thought with satisfaction. Naturally she had not discussed the matter with her son. The viscount was peculiarly jealous of the conduct of his affairs, as Lady Ashdon well knew. She did not wish to set up the viscount's back and possibly set a stumbling block in the way of his impending betrothal.

Lady Ashdon chanced to glance out of her paned window and caught sight of Miss Weatherstone entering a prominent bookstore, with her maid following behind. On impulse, Lady Ashdon called out to her coachman to stop. The carriage drew over to the curb and the groom let down the iron step.

Her ladyship descended, crossed the walk, and entered the

bookstore, intending to inquire of Miss Weatherstone if she could give her a place in her carriage. It would be a good way to converse a little further with her future daughter-in-law, she thought.

Lady Ashdon looked around. There were others in the aisles, and she did not immediately perceive her quarry. When her ladyship's gaze finally fell on Miss Weatherstone, she stood rooted to the spot. Disbelieving, Lady Ashdon watched as Miss Weatherstone received a wrapped package of what was obviously books from a gentleman who was completely unknown to her ladyship. Before her ladyship's affronted eyes, Miss Weatherstone blushed prettily. The gentleman raised Miss Weatherstone's fingertips to his lips and gazed ardently into her eyes. The maid, who discreetly stood some feet away, covered her smile with one hand.

Lady Ashdon had seen enough. She sailed forward, utterly outraged. "Well, miss! Explain this if you can!" she said challengingly in an imperious tone.

Miss Weatherstone and the gentleman looked around at her ladyship with startled expressions. "Pardon me?" asked Miss Weatherstone.

Lady Ashdon snorted. She skewered Miss Weatherstone and the tall gentleman with a contemptuous look. "Such a wanton display is beyond pardon!" She turned on her heel and swept out of the bookstore, straight back to her carriage, where she curtly commanded her coachman to take her home. As she settled back against the velvet squabs, Lady Ashdon ground her teeth over what she had just discovered. Miss Weatherstone was meeting some unknown on the sly, with the full knowledge and cooperation of her maid. What affronted her ladyship most was that neither Miss Weatherstone nor the gentleman had looked the least bit guilty at being caught in their clandestine rendezvous.

"Well! I shall know what to do about it! Adam shall not wed that—that brazen, wicked deceiver!" exclaimed Lady Ashdon, already determined in her heart that she would do everything in her power to rescue the viscount from the clutches of such a shameless hussy.

Cassandra showed Belle the present that her betrothed had given to her. "I know that you will not quite appreciate it, Belle, but I am so very happy with it," said Cassandra with a smile. She held out two books with tooled-leather covers. "They are journals! One for me and one for Philip. We will be able to record all of our thoughts and observations during our diplomatic tours. Isn't that a marvelous notion? Philip thought of it, of course."

Belle took the journals and opened one, flipping through the gilt-edged blank pages. She wondered that her sister could be so enthusiastic over something so mundane. She knew it wouldn't do to say so, however. "Oh! There is so much white space! How shall you ever fill it up, Cassandra?" she asked with a flashing grin.

Cassandra laughed. "I shall have not the least difficulty, I assure you. And I shall write to you, too."

"So I should hope!" retorted Belle. She returned the journals to her sister and then gave her a tight hug. "I *shall* miss you, Cassandra!"

"And I, you! But I am not gone yet, so let us not grow maudlin," said Cassandra. "See, I am already fighting tears." She pulled out her handkerchief.

"Oh, no! We mustn't weep. We have another week, do we not?" asked Belle, dashing her hand across her own eyes.

"Yes, and then Philip and I shall be wed," said Cassandra, her eyes suddenly shining like brilliant stars.

"You do realize that the fashionable do not go about with their spouses," said Belle teasingly. "The ladies all acquire gallants to escort them to the theater or an entertainment and leave their husbands to their own devices."

Cassandra shook her head quickly. "Philip is the only gallant that I shall ever need! That does remind me of an odd thing that happened this afternoon, though. Philip and I were at the bookstore when an old dragon accosted us. I gathered the impression she was affronted that Philip kissed my hand in such an informal setting. She was quite rude to us and then huffed off. I've never been so astonished in my life."

"Do you know who it was?" asked Belle curiously.

Cassandra shook her head. "I haven't the least notion. I had never seen her before in my life."

Belle shrugged, her mild curiosity passing. "I shouldn't worry overmuch, Cassandra. It is not as though you were doing anything scandalous, after all."

"No," agreed Cassandra. "Now, Belle, which gown are you wearing this evening? I favor the pink, for I think it looks utterly dashing on you."

"Do you? It is one of my favorites as well," said Belle, adding teasingly, "and are you wearing Philip's favorite tonight?"

A slight blush rose to Cassandra's face. "Of course! Now I must hurry or I shall be late, so do go away, Belle!"

Laughing, Belle left her sister to her toilette and went away to attend to her own. She was eagerly looking forward to the evening, which was a select ball. It could hardly be anything but perfect, for her betrothed, Lord Ashdon, was to make one of the Weatherstone party.

When Belle entered the ballroom, one of the first personages she saw was Lady Ashdon. She urged Lord Ashdon to take her over to her ladyship as quickly as possible so that she could make her greetings.

"Lady Ashdon! I am so glad to see you," she said, holding out her gloved hand.

Belle was a good deal shocked and dismayed when she was treated to a chilly reception by that lady.

"Miss Weatherstone. How nice to see you again." Lady Ashdon extended two fingers to Belle. Her ladyship's expression was cold, her eyes were filled with antagonism.

Belle was surprised and confused by the turnaround in Lady Ashdon's attitude. She was glad of the viscount's presence beside her. The warmth of his hand on her elbow was very welcome. "I am glad to see you again, my lady," she said politely. "It has been too long since we last visited."

Light flashed in Lady Ashdon's eyes. "Has it, Miss Weatherstone? I quite thought we met just recently. Do you actually like to read, Miss Weatherstone, or is shopping for books simply an artful dodge?"

Lord Ashdon's blond brows had snapped together. "Ma'am, be warned. I shall not allow any uncivility toward my betrothed," he said quietly but with authority.

Lady Ashdon turned her wrathful gaze from Belle's astounded face to her son. "Adam, you cannot marry this woman! You know nothing about her true character, as I do."

"My lady, that is quite enough! I will not tolerate either your insulting implications nor your interference," snapped Lord Ashdon.

There was beginning to be some interest in their low, heated exchange and conversation around them quieted as others started to pay attention and listen to what was being said.

Belle had been struck by something that Lady Ashdon had said. "My lady, are you referring to a meeting in a bookstore earlier this day?"

Lady Ashdon's lip curled. "How clever of you to admit to it, my dear! I suppose you intend to explain away your reprehensible actions?"

"What reprehensible actions?" exclaimed Lord Ashdon, a pronounced frown on his face and anger in his eyes.

Belle laughed. She could not help it. She felt such relief to have discovered the cause of Lady Ashdon's antagonism. Laughing was, however, the wrong thing to have done, which she immediately realized.

Lady Ashdon swelled up. "I shall not stand here to be ridiculed!"

"My lady! Pray allow me to explain!" exclaimed Belle, trying to put her hand on the elder woman's arm in an appeal for her ladyship to pause.

Lady Ashdon's eyes shot fire. She removed Belle's hand. "You dare, Miss Weatherstone!" She swept aside and made her way through the crowd of interested bystanders.

Belle stood, her face ablaze as she realized how many people had overheard at least part of the confrontation. She drew a deep breath of dismay. "Oh, dear!"

"What did my mother mean? What were you going to explain to her?" asked Lord Ashdon.

"Oh, Ashdon! It is terrible. Cassandra came back from shopping this afternoon and told me she had met Philip at a bookshop, where he had presented her with a betrothal present of some journals. She remarked that she and Philip had been accosted by a dra-dragon," said Belle, faltering on the unflattering description.

Lord Ashdon had no difficulty in following her. "My mother," he said grimly.

"Yes, apparently so," conceded Belle. "Cassandra said that just as Philip kissed her hand, this lady sailed up and censored them for what she called their lewd behavior. Ashdon, I very much fear that it was your lady mother. And she thought I was Cassandra and that I was playing you false!"

Lord Ashdon regarded her with a deep frown for a very long moment. Then a twitch started near his mouth, and he began to laugh.

"Ashdon, it is not the least amusing!" exclaimed Belle.

"Just so! That is why you laughed a moment ago," said Viscount Ashdon, nodding, a grin still on his face.

Belle gave a reluctant laugh. "Yes, it is amusing. But not really! Oh, Ashdon, what are we going to do?"

"Do? Why, nothing! We shall allow Cassandra to explain

her reprehensible actions for herself," said Lord Ashdon. He lifted Belle's hand to his lips and smiled at her. "Do not be anxious, my heart. We shall overcome my mother's aversion to you quite easily."

"I do hope so," said Belle on a sigh. Rather wistfully, she confessed, "I had quite thought that Lady Ashdon liked me."

"She did. She does. It is Cassandra that she dislikes heartily," said Lord Ashdon with wry assurance.

"Yes, so it is!" exclaimed Belle, brightening.

Belle waited for Lord Ashdon to convince his mother that there had been a mistake and to allow Belle to explain. Lady Ashdon remained unmoved. She would not discuss anything with Miss Weatherstone.

Lord Ashdon apologized to Belle for his mother's hardness of heart. "I have never known her to be so adamant," he said, frowning.

"Never mind," said Belle, managing to smile at her betrothed. She was determined to put as good a face on the situation as possible. "I don't mind so very much."

Lord Ashdon caught up her hand and brought her fingers to his lips. "You are a terrible liar, Belle," he said tenderly.

Belle laughed, even as tears stung her eyes. "Well, perhaps," she conceded.

"And it matters to me," said Lord Ashdon somberly. "I do not wish my future wife to be subjected to any injustice or incivility. We will bring her around, Belle, I promise you."

"Yes, of course we shall," said Belle. She managed a smile for his sake, even though her heart was sinking. It was scarcely fortuitous to begin one's betrothal with the loathing of one's future mother-in-law. The most frightening thought was that Lady Ashdon would remain of her same opinion and that as a consequence there would come to be a permanent schism between her ladyship and her son, Lord Ashdon. Belle did not think that she would like to be the cause of such a terrible circumstance.

Chapter 24

~~~~~~~~~~

Belle's unhappy reflections were given some respite by the arrival of her grandfather, Sir Marcus Weatherstone, and her dear governess, Miss Bidwell. When she was apprised of their arrival, she flew down the carpeted stairs, her skirts billowing behind her.

The travelers were still being relieved of their wraps when Belle impetuously rushed into the entry hall. "Grandfather! My very dear sir!" she exclaimed, throwing her arms around the tall elderly gentleman.

She felt her grandfather's arms close around her and smelled the familiar scent of his coat, which she had known practically all of her life. She lifted her head. "Oh, Grandfather, you've come at last! I have been waiting this age for you."

"Well, well, my girl. It is easy to see that you have not changed much," said Sir Marcus gruffly, setting her aside, though a gleam had appeared in his rather hard eyes. "What say you, Miss Bidwell? Do you recognize our lady in all her finery?"

"Indeed I do, sir," said Miss Bidwell composedly, her spectacles glinting in the light as she moved forward to receive her former charge's fervent hug.

"Oh, Biddy, I have such things to tell you!" exclaimed Belle. "You will not believe the half of them, I am persuaded."

"Perhaps you may tell Miss Bidwell of all your doings over tea, Belle," said Mrs. Weatherstone with a smile, coming forward with her hand outstretched to her father-in-law. "It is good to have you with us, Sir Marcus. And you as well, Miss Bidwell!"

Sir Marcus shot a keen look at her face. "Thank you, my dear. That is very kind of you, I am sure. Where is my son, Phineas?"

"He is still at his club, but I expect his return shortly. He will be sorry to have missed your arrival," said Mrs. Weatherstone.

Sir Marcus snorted. "That's rich, by Jove! We don't get along by half."

Mrs. Weatherstone's composure was unruffled. "Pray come into the drawing room and we shall have tea. You must be famished after your long journey. I shall have your bags taken up to your rooms." She nodded to the butler as she took Sir Marcus's elbow and showed him the way, with Belle and Miss Bidwell coming up in the rear.

The visitors were ushered into the drawing room and made comfortable. A tea, which fortuitously included a heavy plum cake, a favorite of Sir Marcus's, did much to improve that gentleman's disposition. Belle had not stopped talking about everything that had happened to her during the Season.

"And what of the viscount? Am I to be honored by an introduction, puss?" asked Sir Marcus abruptly.

"Indeed, sir! I could not ask for anything better than that you should meet him," said Belle, sending a laughing glance in her grandfather's direction. She was blushing, but she hoped that no one would take notice of her heightened color.

"I shall send 'round a note to Lord Ashdon presently, requesting that he dine with us, if it is at all possible," said Mrs. Weatherstone. "We shall have Mr. Raven join us, too." She shook her head, smiling at her niece. "It is a happy day for me, Sir Marcus, when both of my beloved nieces have contracted themselves so well."

"You have done well, madam, you and Phineas between you. I congratulate you," said Sir Marcus.

Mrs. Weatherstone turned a surprised countenance in his direction. "Why, I am overwhelmed, Sir Marcus."

"You never thought to have a compliment from me, I daresay," said Sir Marcus, amusement lacing his voice.

Mrs. Weatherstone flushed, jolted out of her composure at last.

That evening, upon being introduced to Lord Ashdon, Sir Marcus fixed the viscount with his disconcerting fierce stare, obviously taking his lordship's measure. Lord Ashdon was not at all flustered, having been the subject of just such harsh scrutinies many times before while on active duty in the army. He was actually rather amused. "Do I pass muster, sir?" he asked respectfully.

Sir Marcus gave a nod and a sharp laugh. "You'll do, my lord."

It was not long, however, before Sir Marcus noticed the tension in the air and wondered if there was any trouble attending his granddaughter's betrothal to the viscount. He at once taxed Mr. and Mrs. Weatherstone for the truth of the matter. When his son and daughter-in-law admitted that Lady Ashdon had proven unexpectedly against the match, Belle groaned inwardly. She well knew her grandfather's temper. She would have given worlds if her well-meaning relations could somehow have softened their bald statements.

Of a choleric disposition, Sir Marcus at once fired up. Red-faced with anger, he bellowed, "What! Is Belle to be insulted? I'll not have it! I shall call on Lady Ashdon, and we shall see then what she has to say!"

"Calm yourself, sir," said Mrs. Weatherstone, laying a restraining hand on her father-in-law's arm.

Sir Marcus shook her off. "Nay, I'll not be calm, madam!" He pointed a long, bony finger at his granddaughter, who stood before the mantel staring at him. "That girl is all of my life. I'll not stand by and see her made unhappy."

Approaching Sir Marcus, unaccustomed tears swimming in her eyes, Belle gave a chuckle. She raised one of his clenched blue-veined hands and held it between her own. She looked up into his angry countenance. "My dear sir, how can I be unhappy when I have you to champion me?"

Sir Marcus awkwardly patted her shoulder, saying gruffly, "You've always been a good girl, Belle. I'll say that for you."

"Sir, may I suggest that it is more properly Lord Ashdon's place to reproach his parent?" asked Mr. Weatherstone calmly.

"Much good it would do you to reproach me, Phineas, if the shoe was on your foot," retorted Sir Marcus.

Mr. Weatherstone smiled a little and made an ironic bow to his sire. "Quite."

Despite Sir Marcus's biting words, however, his high color was fading. "Very well! I shall hold my peace for now."

"Thank you, Grandfather," said Belle in some relief, letting go of his hand. She had had visions of the irascible gentleman running Lady Ashdon to ground to demand an accounting.

"Are you capable of it, Ashdon? That is what I wish to know!" growled Sir Marcus, his bushy brows forming a solid bar over his long nose. Anger was still evident in his wintry gray eyes.

"I can assure you, Sir Marcus, that I am taking the greatest care to resolve this unhappy circumstance."

"You had better or you shall answer to me! Or better yet, your lady mother shall!" Sir Marcus audibly ground his teeth. "Ridiculous woman! I recall very well when she came out. They despaired of her, you know. Spots!"

"Lady Ashdon had spots?" asked Belle, fascinated by this piece of ancient history. Her imagination was boggled at the possibility of the elegant Lady Ashdon ever having suffered such an ignoble plight.

In the midst of everything, Lord Ashdon finally realized that there was only one possible way to completely lay to rest his mother's unreasonable bias against his betrothed. He hesitantly requested Cassandra's help, at the same time apologizing for his timing.

"Of course I shall do anything else that I may," said Cassandra at once. "I have already sent around a note to Lady Ashdon, as you requested, my lord, explaining that it was I and not Belle whom she saw that day in the bookstore. I am so sorry that it was not enough."

"My mother rejected what she termed an obvious ruse," said Lord Ashdon with a shake of his head. "She did not believe that she could mistake one Miss Weatherstone for another."

"But did not Cassandra write that we were twins?" asked Belle, looking anxiously from one to the other.

Cassandra nodded. "Of course I did." She looked at the viscount, raising her eyebrows in inquiry. "But her ladyship apparently did not believe me."

Lord Ashdon inclined his head. "Precisely. It was too pat an answer. Her ladyship had never heard that Miss Weatherstone had a sister that was her twin. Why had she not met the other Miss Weatherstone if there was nothing to hide, et cetera."

"Forgive me, Ashdon, but I begin to suspect that her ladyship is being deliberately obtuse," said Belle roundly.

"Belle!" Mrs. Weatherstone admonished, shocked.

Lord Ashdon laughed, not at all put out by the assessment. "Quite! I believe now that the only remedy is to confront her with both of you at one and the same time."

"Well, I am certainly willing to do my part," said Cassandra.

"Thank you! I realize that it is an untimely request for you when you and Raven are so busy with your wedding plans," said Lord Ashdon.

Cassandra stood up. "Pray think nothing of it, my lord. It is the least that I can do for my dear sister."

Belle embraced her sister. "Thank you, Cassandra! You do not know what this means to me," she whispered, her gaze sliding to the viscount's face.

Cassandra hugged her back. "Don't I, indeed?"

Chapter 25

⟋⟍

The following morning Lord Ashdon emerged from the carriage into the misting rain. He glanced up at the overcast sky in satisfaction. He had chosen his day well, it seemed. His mother disliked to go out in the wet and avoided it whenever possible.

He turned to the open carriage door and solicitously handed down from the carriage the two veiled ladies who had accompanied him. They were attired in fashionable pelisses that were very nearly identical in cut and color. He smiled, saying, "If any of the neighbors catch sight of our arrival, it will no doubt give rise to a great deal of talk as I escort inside such a mysterious pair."

One of the ladies chuckled. The other shook out her skirts, remarking, "Do you recall the last time we wore veils, Belle?"

"Very well, indeed! It was the day that we first met at the crofter's cottage and we embarked on our masquerade," said Belle fondly.

"I really must hear this tale in detail one day," said Lord Ashdon as he escorted his two companions up the wet stone steps of the Ashdon town house.

"It is not very edifying, I fear," said Belle, with a small laugh.

"No, it scarcely rebounds to the credit of either of us," agreed Cassandra. "We were both given a raking scold by our assorted relations."

"Nevertheless, I suspect that I would find it well worth listening to," said Lord Ashdon. Without ringing the bell he opened the front door and ushered the ladies inside.

"Oh, no doubt you would find it vastly amusing, Ashdon," said Belle, a thread of merriment in her voice. "If you did not think me a total baggage before, you would certainly do so after this tale was done!"

A footman immediately hurried forward to inquire of his lordship's needs, sparing a curious glance for the viscount's unknown companions.

"I wish nothing at the moment," said Lord Ashdon as he began stripping off his gloves.

"And the ladies, my lord?" asked the footman. "Shall I call for refreshment?"

"I don't think that we shall be staying long," said Lord Ashdon.

Belle glanced questioningly toward Lord Ashdon. "Are you doubting that we shall find Lady Ashdon available?"

Though he could not distinguish Belle's features very well through the concealing netting of the veil, Lord Ashdon thought he knew what concerned her. "It is early yet and the weather is inclement, so my mother will not have left to make her round of calls," he commented. "And perhaps her ladyship will not be in a mood to entertain us after we have seen her."

"Oh, dear," said Belle, somewhat inadequately. She felt an unaccustomed nervousness, which she disliked very much.

"Never mind," murmured Cassandra, reaching out to squeeze her fingers. "Everything will work out just fine. You'll see."

A paneled door set into the wall opened, and the butler came forward in a stately manner. "My lord! We were not expecting you to return so soon."

"Ah, Regis," said Lord Ashdon. He finished pulling off his supple kid gloves and handed them along with his damp beaver to the footman. His long coat swung as he turned with a gesture to his companions. "I have brought company for her lady-ship."

A comprehensive but impressive glance from the butler swept over the party, and he looked at the viscount. "If you will wait in the drawing room, my lord, I shall see if her lady-ship is at home to visitors."

"Never mind, Regis. I know that my mother takes her choco-late and toast in her rooms at this time of the day. I shall show myself up," said Lord Ashdon cheerfully. He was not about to be put off by the butler's ingrained training to protect her la-dyship from intrusion.

"The ladies, my lord—"

"Are coming with me," said Lord Ashdon firmly.

"But, my lord!" exclaimed the butler, aghast. "Her ladyship will not like it, my lord!"

Lord Ashdon did not acknowledge the butler's shocked state-ment but simply brushed past the obviously bewildered ser-vant. He started up the well-carpeted stairs at a good pace, forcing his fair companions to practically run to keep up with him.

Belle shot a glance at the viscount's determined profile and chuckled. "You are certainly very high-handed, my lord," she commented, her skirts clutched high in her gloved hand so that she did not trip over her hems while on the stairs.

"I learned in the army that a good rush almost always car-ries the enemy back," said Lord Ashdon amiably.

Belle and her sister both laughed.

"You have a very determined gentleman, Belle," remarked Cassandra.

"Indeed I do," Belle agreed, casting the viscount another fond and admiring glance.

On the landing Lord Ashdon escorted the sisters to his mother's apartments. At his hard knock, the door was opened. The dresser looked out and an expression of surprise crossed her face. In a lofty voice, she announced, "Her ladyship is not in to visitors, my lord."

"I think that she shall see me," said Lord Ashdon cheerfully. He carried the day by simply walking through the door as though it did not exist, the dresser giving way before him, but putting up an objection to the two ladies that followed in his wake. They paid no attention to the dresser's remonstrations, but pressed close behind Lord Ashdon.

"I shall take whatever blame her ladyship hurls at you for allowing me to invade her privacy," said Lord Ashdon over his shoulder.

When he strode into the elegantly fitted sitting room, Lady Ashdon was seated at a small table, where the remains of her meager breakfast could be seen. She was already looking toward the doorway and when she saw her son, she demanded, "What is the meaning of this, Adam?" She rose from her velvet chair, drawing her silk-embroidered dressing gown closer. She gestured imperiously. "Who are these ladies? I do not recall inviting you and your company to breakfast, sir!"

"Nonetheless, I have come," said Lord Ashdon. He turned and gave a hand to each of his companions to draw them forward. "I have brought Miss Weatherstone and her sister, the soon-to-be Mrs. Philip Raven, with me."

"I see!" Lady Ashdon's expression turned cold and her voice dripped ice. "You step beyond the bounds of what is pleasing, Adam. Well, I have nothing to say to any of you. I bid you good day!"

One of the ladies stepped forward, defying Lady Ashdon's rejection. Belle watched as her sister lifted her veil and spoke to her ladyship.

"My lady, you were angered when you saw me and my betrothed at the bookstore," began Cassandra.

Lady Ashdon's gray eyes widened, then narrowed. "Your betrothed! Well! You are more brazen than even I believed, Miss Weatherstone!" she exclaimed.

"You are under a misapprehension, ma'am," said Lord Ashdon in an even voice. "This is Miss Weatherstone's sister."

"Nonsense! It is Miss Weatherstone, who is playing a part. Adam, surely you must see that you cannot wed such a woman," said Lady Ashdon, gesturing with contempt at Belle's sister.

"I don't care to have my sister addressed in such tones, my lady," said Belle. Her voice was level, even though she felt her temper stirred by the lady's inexcusable rudeness.

Lady Ashdon had turned quickly when she spoke. Belle threw back her own veil and stepped forward, her face in full view of the elder woman. Lady Ashdon stared, her mouth dropping open. She looked from one lady to the other, and the strangest expression crossed her face.

Belle smiled. "Yes, Lady Ashdon, it is quite, quite true. My sister and I are identical twins. It was Cassandra and Philip Raven you saw that day at the bookstore."

Lady Ashdon opened and closed her mouth a time or two, but no words issued forth. Then she shook her head as a dull red color mounted into her powdered cheeks. "I very seldom admit when I make a mistake. I make so few, as you may imagine. In this instance, however, it is made shockingly plain to me that I have indeed made a grave error."

Her ladyship stepped forward and took Belle's hands between her own. "I am so sorry, my dear. I have been very wrong about you. I am horribly embarrassed by my mistake. Can you forgive me?"

Belle was astonished to hear sincere contrition in her ladyship's voice. "Of course I can," she said quickly. She gently pulled her hands free and hugged Lady Ashdon, which startled that haughty lady very much.

Lord Ashdon and Cassandra stood looking on, both with smiles on their faces.

"Well!" Lady Ashdon straightened her shoulders and turned a proud countenance to Belle's sister. She held out her hand.

"I owe you an apology, as well, Miss Weatherstone. I beg your pardon."

"I accept, my lady. I am only glad to have gotten things sorted out before Mr. Raven and I embark for the Continent," said Cassandra with a chuckle.

"So am I," said Belle in a heartfelt voice. She smiled tentatively at Lady Ashdon, who had turned her gaze on her again. "It would have distressed me to have you dislike me so amazingly, my lady."

Lady Ashdon bestowed a smile on them all. She spoke in her usual authoritative fashion. "Allow me to make amends, my dear. I shall make all right in society, for no doubt I have created some unpleasant gossip. Miss Cassandra Weatherstone, you will do me the honor of allowing me to give you and Mr. Raven a bon voyage rout on Thursday. I assure you, it will be a grand affair at which everyone who is anyone will see you and your sister together. I think that will put an end to any lingering doubts over Miss Weatherstone's suitability to become Lady Ashdon."

"Mr. Raven and I shall revel in your hospitality, my lady," said Cassandra graciously.

Lady Ashdon turned to her son and her future daughter-in-law. With a smile that was actually reflected in her eyes, she said, "I shall take the other Miss Weatherstone off with me now. I wish to discuss a guest list. We must be quick to put the cards into the post. Or, no, I think it best if I have them personally delivered, don't you? Come along, Miss Weatherstone. We have much to do."

"I am at your disposal, Lady Ashdon," said Cassandra with a smile as she followed her ladyship out of the sitting room.

Lady Ashdon spoke sharply to her dresser, who was standing as though rooted to the carpet. "Come along! I shall have no slackers in my service!"

"Yes, my lady!"

As the door shut and they were left alone, Lord Ashdon

turned to his betrothed. "Shall you be able to stand my mother's overbearing ways?" he asked with a smile.

"Oh, her ladyship is nothing in comparison to my grandfather," said Belle with a shake of her head and a chuckle. "I shall undoubtedly get along with her famously."

"And what of me?" asked Lord Ashdon, slipping his arms around her narrow waist.

Belle felt suddenly a little short of breath. "Why, no doubt I shall get along famously with you, as well, my lord."

Lord Ashdon laughed, just before he bent to kiss her. When he raised his head, he said with a searching look, "I am going back to the army, Belle. Will you mind it?"

"I am already packed, my lord," said Belle with a roguish smile.

Lord Ashdon caught her up more tightly than before. He looked down at her with an ardent light in his eyes. "I am very glad that I met you that foggy morning, Belle."

"And I am very glad that you raced me, my lord," murmured Belle. "For you have won my heart for your prize."